Critics Rave

THE LAD

"This is a quick-wit
run amok."

"Fabulously amusing."

—*The Midwest Book Review*

GIRL ON THE RUN

"Keeps you laughing at the pitfalls of young love."

—The Best Reviews

"A wonderfully humorous spin that will keep readers laughing [while they] devour this fun tale."

—*The Midwest Book Review*

"Refreshing, fun, and a real page-turner... If this story is any indication, we will be seeing some wonderful stories from [Jennie Klassel]."

—A Romance Review

"A fantastic read, filled with laughter, insecurity, vulnerability, revenge, and really hot love scenes."

—*Romance Reviews Today*

SHE WHO LAUGHS LAST

"Jennie Klassel has a large funny bone, but the audience has the first, middle, and last laughs at the antics of the cast."

—*The Midwest Book Review*

"Exciting [and] funny."

—The Romance Reader

UNDER THE RIGHT CIRCUMSTANCES

Blossom MacMorrough possesses that rare ability to winnow the wheat from the chaff; discover order where others see only chaos; zero in on the heart of the matter.

"Did you have an orgasm?"

I blinked. "Orgasm?"

"He used his tongue, right? That can do it under the right circumstances."

"Right circumstances? *Right circumstances?*" I stomped around the parlor waving my arms in the air. "For God's sake, Blossom, the man practically kidnaps my grandmother. Some maniac is stalking me from Montego Bay to Miami Beach to Key West to Key Largo. I've got federal agents standing in line waiting to serve me with warrants. I've been threatened with arrest for obstruction of justice. I've got a hotel I can't sell; I've got tenants I can't evict; I've got cats coming out of the woodwork. I'm standing in a McDonald's parking lot in ninety-five degree heat kissing a man who's trying to nail me—for smuggling, that is—with my Aunt Ginger's killer thirty feet away, and you want to know if I had an *orgasm?*"

"Well?"

"No," I muttered.

"Early days yet, sweetie, early days."

Other books by Jennie Klassel:

THE LADY DOTH PROTEST
GIRL ON THE RUN
SHE WHO LAUGHS LAST

IT HAPPENED IN SOUTH BEACH

JENNIE KLASSEL

LOVE SPELL

NEW YORK CITY

For Shari Boullion,
Tilly's Fairy Godmother.

LOVE SPELL®

October 2005

Published by

Dorchester Publishing Co., Inc.
200 Madison Avenue
New York, NY 10016

ISBN 0-505-52635-2

Printed in the United States of America.

Visit us on the web at www.dorchesterpub.com.

ACKNOWLEDGMENTS

Tilly would never have made Sex Detective if not for the kind and patient assistance of:

William Carey, Director of Design, Preservation and Neighborhood Planning in Miami Beach; Detective Lou Vince, Los Angeles Police Department; Deputy Sheriff Marc Ratner, L.A. County Sheriff's Department; Sgt. Howard Zeifman, Miami Beach Police Department; Michele Lang Palter, legal eagle; Genevieve Jones, my expert in all things canine; Robert Guillemin (Sidewalk Sam); Richard Hill of www.RentMotherNature.com; my sister Joan Pleune, who cruised the Keys with me; and David M. Ratner, who talked me through it.

"Who am I then? Tell me that first, and then, if I like being that person, I'll come up: if not, I'll stay down here till I'm somebody else."

—*Lewis Carroll,* Alice in Wonderland

One

It isn't easy being Tilly Snapp. Not anymore.

Not all that long ago it wasn't a problem. I'd wake up to each new day reasonably comfortable in my own skin. I'd look in the mirror and there I'd be: good old Tilly Snapp, twenty-six-year-old widow lady; a sensible, practical, professional individual living a safe, uncomplicated life.

For reasons known only to the fickle finger of fate, on an unseasonably hot day in early October, a day that dawned innocently enough, I answered the telephone and, much like Alice, tumbled into my very own rabbit hole. Alice stayed Alice, but I found myself on a bizarre journey toward becoming someone who was most assuredly *not* good old Tilly Snapp.

I am rarely at a loss for words. I make my living by them, after all, with my syndicated column, *Hold that Thought!*, and freelance commercial writing projects, but I couldn't find even one that begins to describe just how annoyed I was at this wholly unexpected development.

I am not what you would call the adventurous sort. "Because it's there" just doesn't cut it with me as a reason to risk life and limb climbing Mount Everest. The call of the wild is not music to my ears. Just why the bear went over the mountain to see what he could see has always been a mystery to me.

Be that as it may, there I was on Air Jamaica flight 222 en route from Montego Bay to Miami, on a trip that had, by my calculations, lasted about a week.

I huddled in mute misery in the center seat of five across, with the garish gilt urn containing the cremated mortal remains of my aunt Ginger braced between my ankles. I'd considered stowing the urn in the luggage compartment above my head, but an unbidden image of sudden turbulence and Aunt Ginger raining down on the heads of unsuspecting passengers made me think the better of it.

Two enormous Jamaican women occupied the seats to either side of me, their bulk overflowing their own allotted space into a good portion of mine. They chattered to one another across me nonstop in a bewildering patois of English and Jamaican slang. One smelled suspiciously of ganja and the other of coconut oil and jerk-goat rub—each aroma pleasing enough in its proper milieu, but not all that alluring when blended with the body odors of 243 passengers sharing the same stagnant air in a Boeing 757.

"What you got in dat pretty can, dearie, you holdin' on to it so tight?" one of the women inquired as I struggled to stretch the seatbelt snugly around the urn and myself in the event that this particular plane was slated by the Almighty to make an unscheduled landing in the Bermuda Triangle. The word "eccentric" barely does justice to my late Aunt Ginger, but I loved her dearly. We'd go down together.

"My aunt."

"You got ants in dere?"

"Just one."

The woman frowned. "Aren't you s'pose to put de animals in de cargo hold? We don't want no ants here."

Two days spent haggling with the funeral home director in Montego Bay, dodging the groping hands of the proprietor of the Happy Fields Crematorium, and facing down enough bureaucrats to populate every island in the Caribbean had left me in a decidedly surly frame of mind.

"They only put domestic pets, werewolves, and zombies in the cargo hold," I informed her. "Insects under the age of three fly free as long as they don't occupy a separate seat."

The woman made a hasty sign of the cross, muttered what sounded like a voodoo incantation, and left me to my own dark thoughts.

These were dark thoughts indeed.

I scrunched lower in my seat and started looking for someone to blame. It wouldn't be sporting to blame Aunt Ginger, she being dead and unable to speak to her own defense. The dry-as-dust lawyer, Mr. Wickerby, was my next candidate, but he had merely been the bearer of ill tidings. It really isn't fair to kill the messenger, although I hadn't dismissed the idea out of hand.

It was Halsey Wickerby, Esq., whose call that fateful autumn morning turned my safe, simple life upside down, inside out, and every which way but loose. He delivered the news of Aunt Ginger's tragic death in appropriately somber tones, although I could have sworn I heard a smothered chuckle now and then. A long silence ensued when he had said his piece.

I warned myself not to ask. I didn't want to know, really I didn't.

Of course I just had to ask.

"She had on a bathing suit, right? I mean, she wasn't . . . ?" I closed my eyes against the image of fifty-year-old Aunt Ginger sailing bare-assed through the Jamaican moonlight.

A snigger, barely suppressed, crackled through the ether, but Mr. Wickerby recovered nicely with, "Your aunt was registered at Sin and Sand. It is, I understand, a resort devoted to the uninhibited pursuit of, er, unusual pleasures. Night parasailing in the nude is not to be wondered at."

"That depends on who's doing the wondering," I shot back.

Not that I was all that surprised. Lorraine Louise Snapp—known as Ginger Snapp from the day she dyed her hair fire-engine red at age sixteen and stormed out of her parents' house for the last time—had departed this life as dramatically as she had chosen to live it. She had taken a nosedive stark naked into the warm waters off Negril Beach in Jamaica in the middle of the night when the eighty-foot tow line that connected her harness to the powerboat snapped. I suspect it was an exit Aunt Ginger would have approved of had she been given the choice.

"Positively orgasmic," Aunt Ginger seemed to whisper from the Great Beyond.

My personal experience with orgasms was so limited that I wasn't entirely sure an eighty-foot plunge would qualify as such. I resolutely pushed the image aside as Mr. Wickerby outlined what must be done to retrieve Aunt Ginger's remains from the Dovecote Mortuary in Montego Bay and return them to Miami for burial at sea. He had already arranged for cremation, as stipulated in Aunt Ginger's will. I should encounter no difficulty in bringing my loved one home to rest.

That wasn't quite true, I thought in a brief moment of panic as the plane banked sharply to the right over the Everglades and the snoring woman to my left toppled toward me, threatening to crush the life from my body. She oozed back into her own space as the plane leveled off, and I returned to my brooding.

It was a given that I would be the one to go to Jamaica. Tilly would arrange a memorial service; Tilly would sort through and dispose of her aunt's possessions. No one else was likely to step forward—certainly not my sister or brothers, all of whom regarded Aunt Ginger in much the same way they would a pterodactyl winging its way north amid a flock of robins. Certainly not my maternal grandmother Grammie Jones, who was spending the remainder of her allotted time span shuffling up and down the halls of the Hope of Resurrection Home in Key Largo waiting for Humphrey Bogart to call.

The fact that Aunt Ginger had designated me her sole heir, with all the privileges and benefits thereof and in possession of her home, business, and worldly goods, cemented the deal. I was Aunt Ginger's, and heaven help me, Aunt Ginger was mine.

So Tilly would do it; Tilly always did. Ever had it been since my parents set off to test their extreme-skiing skills against the notorious Tuckerman Ravine in the White Mountains of New Hampshire. The ravine had won—by a landslide. The old joke was bearable now, ten years after my siblings and I found ourselves in the custody of Grammie Jones. On hearing the news, that born-again Christian lady fell to her knees to thank Almighty God for delivering her grandchildren from the heathen, hippie life of her daughter and "that awful Snapp person" she had married.

No one had ever had the heart to tell Grammie Jones that the union had been performed without benefit of sanctioned clergy by the self-styled guru Shri Bhuyari Baba Baba, a.k.a. Hiram Bronstein from the darkest reaches of Brooklyn, who, shortly after the ceremony, was escorted away by a phalanx of federal agents on the one-size-fits-all charge of being a threat to the American way of life. By then, of course, my parents had partaken of enough LSD to believe that God himself had descended from on high and performed the ceremony in person.

Grammie had done her best, really she had. Alas, demon rum brought her low despite the best efforts of her resurrectionist brethren. I had stepped in to steer my younger sister and three brothers through the rocky shoals of adolescence and send them out into the world to live safe, sensible lives. Lives in no way like those of our hippie parents, our Bible-thumping grammie, or the irrepressible Aunt Ginger.

"She got ants in dat can," the woman to my right was complaining to a dismayingly perky flight attendant.

"We can't have ants in the plane, ma'am," the attendant admonished me. "I'm afraid you'll have to dispose of them in the lavatory."

"It's just one," I assured her. "And it's not ant, A-N-T. It's aunt, A-U-N-T. I have no intention of flushing my aunt down the toilet."

The attendant straightened up, a bright, satisfied smile creasing her heavy makeup. "Oh, that's all right then."

"No, it don't be all right," my jerk-rubbed neighbor persisted. "I don't want to be sittin' by no dead people."

"It's only one dead person," said I, my patience unraveling like the rope that sent Aunt Ginger into her orgasmic descent.

"Time to fasten your seat belts. We're about to land," the attendant interjected happily. I suspect she was profoundly relieved that the real contents of the urn had not been discovered sooner, thereby creating what was threatening to burgeon into an unpleasant fracas in a full plane with no empty seats available to separate the combatants.

Twenty minutes later, as the plane taxied up to the gate, I had settled on Grammie Jones as the author of my present dilemma. Grammie, who had hounded my mother into wild rebellion, thereby delivering her into the arms of Samuel "Starman" Snapp, elder brother to Ginger. And by extension, Grammie's grammie, and grammies back unto many generations until one came to a stumbling halt before the missing link, who must have had a grammie somewhere out there on the great savanna, although it would have been a chimpanzee, which probably doesn't count.

"You'll have to come with me, Ms. Snapp-Allenby."

I glanced up from where I squatted, rewrapping the urn containing Aunt Ginger's ashes in a beach towel graced with a picture of Bob Marley crowned with marijuana leaves. A sturdy, no-nonsense woman in the crisp khaki uniform of Immigration and Customs Enforcement was motioning me toward a row of interview rooms to the side of the arrival hall.

I took a deep breath. One wasn't enough. I took two. Pull yourself together, I counseled myself. It's probably just some minor misunderstanding. Ants, that's it. They think I'm smuggling ants into the country. That stupid, stupid woman.

I was less apprehensive than embarrassed as I trudged along beside the officer like an unruly pupil being led out of class to the principal's office; I hadn't done anything wrong and was just naïve enough at that moment to believe they'd mistaken me for some miscreant up to no good. Two Rambo clones clad in jungle camouflage took up positions on either side of the door, ready to blow me away should I seek to terrorize the hall and bring down the U.S. government with so much as a sneeze.

"Bags on the table. Passport," the woman ordered. "Have a seat. He'll be with you in a few minutes."

"He? He who?" I asked in alarm.

"Special Agent Maitland," she informed me.

"Look, there must be some mistake," I began, but she was already gone, closing the door firmly behind her.

I plopped into the battered metal chair as ordered and stared up at a picture of President Bush, who looked less like a commander-in-chief than a man on the way to his doctor's office for a colonoscopy. A few minutes turned into half an hour, which turned into eternity.

Grammie Jones was going to pay for this.

Finally, the woman returned. "He's running late."

She set about removing everything from my shoulder bag, right down to bits of fluff and crumbs from a prehistoric chocolate-chip cannoli. The carry-on suitcase was next, then my black leather laptop case, a bit of celebratory self-indulgence when my column was picked up for national syndication.

"I don't understand this," I protested. "What are you looking for? There are no drugs in there. I don't use drugs. I was only in Jamaica for three days. I didn't even leave Montego Bay. I bought one tote bag, one beach towel, and three T-shirts. I'm not a terrorist. Do I *look* like a terrorist?" I demanded.

Officer Velma C. Dixon—for so her badge proclaimed her—did not deign to reply.

Evidently, it was going to be up to me repack my bags, as she made no move to do it. Instead she pulled a chair away from the table and settled into it with arms folded across her chest. I'm not sure a small nuclear device would have budged her if I tried to make a run for it, assuming of course I had one to hand.

"Can I put my stuff away?"

"Go ahead."

I was too annoyed to pack the suitcase as carefully as I had at the Montego Bay Holiday Inn that morning. I crammed everything in and slammed the lid down hard to make known my displeasure at this invasion of my privacy, if my angry mutterings had not already alerted Officer Dixon to that fact. Then I replaced everything in my purse, collecting each bit of fluff, each cannoli crumb from the tabletop in an embarrassingly childish display of defiance.

Fortunately for her, Agent Dixon had made only a cursory search of my "Bad Girls Go to Jamaica" tote, which contained the cremation urn. She unwrapped the towel, lifted out the urn, shook it, then set it on the table. I swear, if she'd so much as dipped a finger into Aunt Ginger's ashes, I couldn't have been held responsible for my actions and the brothers Stallone could make Swiss cheese out of me for all I'd care.

Now that the ordeal appeared to be over, I thought it wise to make a stab at civility. If I played it right I might just get out of that room before menopause set in.

"Are we done now, ma'am?"

"No." A woman of few words.

"Rats, bats, and bellybeans," I groused, letting loose with the only oath Grammie Jones had permitted in her house. I folded my arms, dropped my head in defeat, and profoundly wished myself back in my comfy little condo across the street from Buck Riley's Pub in Boston. Oh, for the smell of stale Guinness and the cacophony of ballads brayed by soused sons of the old sod and the endearingly familiar *pop-pop-pop* of a Saturday-night special.

"Ms. Snapp-Allenby? I apologize for keeping you waiting."

I lifted my head off the table just far enough to stare across the expanse of scratched mauve laminate at a pair of black jeans that caressed firm thighs, slim hips, and what promised to be a very, very impressive package of masculine distinction.

Not that I had all that many packages to measure it by. To be honest, I had exactly one: that of my late husband, Alexander Markham Allenby, who had been considerably less well endowed than he, or I, might have wished. But I do have two perfectly good eyes in my head, and can appreciate a well-favored gentleman when one wanders into my line of sight.

I raised my eyes. If the bottom half looked promising, the top half quite simply blew me away.

Two

Thomas Jefferson had it all wrong. All men are not created equal, not by a long shot. There are men. And then there are *men.*

Adjectives swarmed around nouns as my brain set about cataloguing the face and form of the tall man who was settling gracefully into the chair opposite me; scrabbling through the huge stockpile of synonyms, similes, and metaphors that are the tools of my trade, I tested one and then another to take me far beyond the woeful inadequacy of "tall, dark, and handsome."

Hair: deepest, darkest, burnished mahogany; run-your-fingers-through-it thick and Harrison-Ford spiky, melt-a-woman's-heart little-boy cowlicky.

Eyes: fathomless pools of bittersweet chocolate, Irish coffee, aged brandy.

Mouth: yes, oh-god-yes.

Actually, "tall, dark, and handsome" just about says it all.

My nostrils quivered like a pointer's on the trail of a plump quail. Scent: limy, spicy, alpha male.

"Ms. Snapp-Allenby?"

"Huh?"

Men have no business looking like that, parading past the not-nearly-up-to-scratch women of the world, all splendid and studly and godly. Especially when they have the nerve to wear tight jeans; a wide black leather belt with a silver buckle; and a crisp white shirt with the two top buttons unbuttoned, beneath a well-weathered brown World War II bomber jacket.

Talk about your weapons of mass destruction.

"I'm Special Agent Will Maitland. I hope we haven't inconvenienced you. I have a few questions and then you'll be free to go."

"Aunt," I managed. "Not ant. And it's only one. Aunt."

Special Agent Maitland glanced up from examining my passport. "I beg your pardon?"

"Nobody smuggles ants, for goodness sake. Do I look like someone who would smuggle ants?" I babbled on. "Okay, maybe there are eco-pirates who might smuggle ants, although heaven knows we have enough of them and I can't imagine there's much of a market. But I do not," I declared, my voice skating into the upper registers of indignation, "smuggle insects of any phylum, age, ethnicity, religious persuasion, or sexual orientation."

Agent Maitland appeared to be unfazed by my outburst. His fathomless pools of bittersweet-chocolate, Irish-coffee, aged-brandy eyes regarded me with polite curiosity.

"And I do not smuggle aunts. I only have one. A-U-N-T. But if I had twenty A-U-N-T-S I would not smuggle a single one of them either."

Special Agent Will Maitland nodded encouragingly. "Is that so?"

"Yes, it is so. I've got all the proper papers. The American consul said I wouldn't have any trouble. I can't imagine what the problem is and why you stuck me in this stupid room. It's that stupid woman, isn't it? Why would you listen to a stupid woman who uses jerk-goat rub like talcum powder? It's a stupid misunderstanding. It's just . . . stupid," I finished lamely.

He waited patiently until I concluded my little harangue, pulled a small leather notebook from the inside pocket of his jacket, and made a notation. I'm surprised he didn't send for a straitjacket then and there.

"Perhaps we should start over." He examined my passport photo, raising those eyes to compare the image with the glowering reality sitting opposite.

I wish I could claim the photo does me a grave injustice, that I was just having a bad hair day, that poor lighting made my eyes look like purple bruises, that the photographer caught me in an off moment, which was why I looked like a cat swallowing a canary.

"I don't look like that," I assured him.

He closed the passport, sat back, tilted his head. "What do you look like?"

"For one thing, I don't look like Medusa. My hair is not a nest of writhing black snakes. I like to think of it as cascading in long inky spirals. My eyes are not purple. Only people who wear colored contacts have purple eyes. Elizabeth Taylor's are violet, of course, but then she's Elizabeth Taylor. Mine are blue, plain old blue. I don't eat canaries."

"Canaries?"

"And I might look like I'm 5'5", but I really am 5'6"."

"Of course."

"I take calcium," I explained. "So I won't shrink—"

"Perhaps," Agent Maitland managed to interrupt, "we should return to the purpose of this interview."

I lifted my chin, sniffed, and resumed my role as the offended party. "Let's."

"What was the purpose of your visit to Jamaica?"

"I went to get my aunt," I said, emphasizing each word to underscore the fact that I had just explained all that.

"That would be Ms. Ginger Snapp?"

"Yes, my *aunt* Ginger. She died."

"I'm sorry for your loss. I understand she met with an unfortunate accident while parasailing."

How had he known that? And why?

"Yes." I tapped the "Bad Girls Go to Jamaica" tote. "Her ashes are in here."

"Did you pack your own bags before you left Jamaica?"

"Yes, I did." I glared over at Agent Dixon. "Neatly."

"And they have been in your sole possession ever since?"

"They already asked me all this when I checked in." I only just caught myself before I rolled my eyes, a habit that my friend Blossom predicts will one day have grave consequences. They'll pop right out of the sockets, drop into a sewer drain, be swept out to sea, and eaten by sharks.

"Yes, my bags have been in my sole possession at all times. Oh, well, now that I think of it . . ."

"Yes?" he prompted.

"There was that snarky little man in the airport who tried to snatch my tote."

"Someone attempted to steal Ms. Snapp?"

"Well, he tried to grab the tote, but he let go when I kicked him in the shin. I doubt he'd have tried if he'd known she was in there." I smirked. "He probably thought it was filled with those ants everyone tries to smuggle out of Jamaica."

"Tell me," Agent Maitland continued, either oblivious to my rudeness or too polite to comment on it, "does the name Win Win Poo mean anything to you?"

"Of course. Everyone knows Pooh," I replied, wondering how we'd wandered off into a discussion of children's literature.

He sent me a sharp glance. "You do?"

Please understand. I'm as grateful as the next patriotic American for my government's efforts to keep evil from our shores, but the educational qualifications for its customs agents could be a tad more rigorous. "You know, Winnie the Pooh, bear of little brain? Lives in the Hundred-Acre Wood? Hunts Heffalumps?"

Agent Maitland leaned back in his chair, folded his arms across his chest, and favored me with the flat stare perfected by practitioners of law enforcement the world over.

"Do you know the penalty mandated by the Homeland Security Act for failure to cooperate with a federal agent in the performance of his duties?"

Oh-oh. That didn't sound good.

"I wasn't being uncooperative, sir," I said quickly. "You asked me if I knew who Winnie the Pooh was, and I answered to the best of my knowledge."

"Win Win Poo, not Winnie the Pooh."

"Er, no. Who is he?"

"She."

"Okay, she."

"What about pillow boxes?"

I didn't have a clue what he was talking about. I might have been at the Mad Hatter's tea party for all that.

"Did your aunt possess any pillow boxes?" he repeated in that same deep measured voice, although I detected just a whisper of impatience around the edges.

"I don't know, sir. What is a pillow box?"

For the first time Agent Maitland looked just a bit uncomfortable. "It is," he began carefully, "a small carved chest containing erotic paraphernalia used by courtesans in ancient China and Japan." He held his hands about two feet apart. "About so big."

"Oh." Nice hands I thought. Big hands.

"The pillow box of Win Win Poo is considered the most valuable in the world," he continued. "It dates from the late seventeenth century. It was stolen last May from a private collector in Singapore."

"Oh?" It dawned. "Oh! I see. Aunt Ginger."

He nodded. "Given the unusual nature of her business enterprise, we think she may have had some information about its disappearance when she met with her unfortunate accident."

I'd missed it when he'd used the term before. Unfortunate accident: police-speak for murder.

"You think . . . ?" I couldn't go on.

Agent Maitland returned his notebook to his jacket pocket. "It is possible Ms. Snapp was somehow involved in the theft of the pillow box of Win Win Poo. Possibly had it in her possession. We traced it as far as Jamaica, but we didn't find it in her room at Sin and Sand. You do not appear to have it in your possession either."

I gave up, rolled my eyes, and tried to wrap my mind around this bizarre scenario. "Nonsense. Aunt Ginger was as nutty as a fruitcake, but I can't imagine her involved in something like that."

Agent Maitland pushed back his chair and stood up. I kept my eyes carefully focused above his waist.

"Believe me, your aunt was very much involved and she was murdered because of it."

No one impugned the integrity of my aunt Ginger. I jumped up, planted my hands on the table, and glared at her accuser. "That's absurd and . . . and libelous!" I huffed. "She wasn't a thief, and she fell out of a parasailing harness. End of story."

"So she did," he replied mildly. "She fell because the rope was sliced halfway through. When the powerboat reached maximum speed, it snapped."

I dropped back into my chair. "Oh." Someone had *murdered* my aunt Ginger? Tears threatened.

"We believe the pillow box has drawn the attention of a number of international thieves who act on behalf of unprincipled private collectors. They will stop at nothing, not even murder, to get their hands on it. Your aunt was not the first victim in this affair. We discovered the body of a man with his throat slit who had only just arrived from Singapore to a brothel in Kingston. And if Ms. Snapp was attempting to smuggle the box into the United States, she will not be the last. I believe you stand to inherit her entire estate."

I didn't just fall off the turnip truck. "You think I have something to do with this?" I yelped. "Are you out of your mind?" I could feel my eyes bulging out a good inch.

He didn't look like he was out of his mind. He looked like he thought I just might be.

"I am a nice person! Can't you see I'm a nice person?" I protested. "I am not a criminal. I am not a homicidal maniac. And definitely not a *double* homicidal maniac. I can't even kill a cockroach, much less send my naked aunt plummeting eighty feet into the Caribbean. Nor do I skulk around whorehouses looking to carve up strange men *in flagrante delicto.* The only private collector I know is my mailman, who collects bottle caps. I didn't even know what a pillow box was, remember? Heck, it's been months since I replaced the batteries in my vi . . ."

Agent Maitland raised a brow. "Your what?"

"My flashlight," I snapped.

"Hmmm. Good idea to keep spare batteries in the house," he replied. "It must be frustrating to find dead batteries in your . . . flashlight when you need it most."

I looked daggers at him. "I believe in being prepared in case of emergency."

He nodded gravely. "Very sensible."

"I consider myself a very sensible person," I informed him.

"To return to the subject at hand, I must warn you that you will be placed under surveillance."

I was back on my feet in a flash. *"What?"*

"For your own protection."

"What?"

"You're free to go."

"What?"

Agent Maitland smiled for the first time. I nearly had a stroke. "You seem at a loss for words. I find that strange, considering you write a nationally syndicated column on the subject."

I managed to swallow the snarl that was forging its way up my throat. "What is so valuable about a box of sex toys?"

"Oh, did I forget to mention that some of Win Win Poo's 'toys' are made of solid gold? They're worth a fortune, quite apart from their historical value."

"Gold?"

"Gold, silver, ivory, pearls, precious stones." He stepped aside and held the door open for me. "Good afternoon. Thank you for your cooperation."

I grabbed my bags, slung Aunt Ginger over my shoulder, and swept past him into the arrival hall.

"Good day, Agent Maitland," I said, nose in the air. "I can see my tax dollars are well spent when it comes to the United States Immigration and Customs Enforcement Service."

"I'm not with ICE, ma'am."

Ma'am. Is there any sexier word in the English language when drawled by a gorgeous male of the species? Well, maybe "darlin'," but I doubted I'd ever hear it from the scrumptious lips of Special Agent Will Maitland, which really was a pity.

I stopped and turned around. I should have known he wasn't with the customs service. No uniform, no badge.

"The Miami police?"

"I'm afraid not."

Just a hint of an accent. England? No, the islands—Jamaica.

"You're with the Jamaican police? But you're not . . . not, er—"

"Not what?"

"Black," I blurted out.

"Oh, I see. You think all Jamaicans are black? Do we all wear dreads and prowl the beaches picking up horny American women?"

If the earth ever really opened up to swallow the terminally embarrassed, I would have plunged straight through to the molten core at that moment. I believe it would have been a short trip from the arrival hall of Miami International Airport.

"I'm sorry," I stammered. "I didn't mean to offend you."

"No offense taken. My parents own a resort in Ocho Rios. I was born and raised there."

"Oh. So if you're not customs and not the police, what are you?"

He pulled a wallet from the inside pocket of his leather jacket and flipped it open to show me an ID. "Interpol. Property Crime, Stolen Works of Art."

"Wow!" said I, abandoning all semblance of cool.

Special Agent Will Maitland, my very own James Bond, handed me his card, an enigmatic little smile on his god-yes mouth.

Anything's possible when you fall down the rabbit hole.

THREE

I could barely put two thoughts together as the taxi battled its way out of Miami International, crept south on I-95, then east across MacArthur Causeway to the heart of Miami's ultrafashionable South Beach.

Courtesans. Corpses. Ants. Sex. Bob Marley. Gold dildos. Nude parasailing. Sex. Special Agent Will Maitland. Sex, sex, sex.

Murder. My sweet, harmless, oddball Aunt Ginger murdered.

I thought I'd cried out the worst of my grief after Wickerby's call, but a tear slid down my cheek as the taxi cruised through the famous Art Deco District.

Anger was quickly replacing grief. No one, especially some perverted sex fiend or his minions, was going to get away with murdering my aunt Ginger. I might not be up there with the likes of Xena, Warrior Princess, or Lara Croft, Tomb Raider, but the murderer of Aunt Ginger was going to be toast when I got through with him.

The taxi turned left onto Fourteenth Street, leaving behind the bland, ubiquitous Gaps, Banana Republics, Guccis, and such, and swung to the curb before a three-story building of sandy pink stucco tucked away on a cul-de-sac. Faded lettering declared it to be the Hotel St. Claire, although the last guest to check out had probably checked in at the pearly gates decades ago. Some of the windows on the two upper floors were boarded up, and what had once been a shady arcade in the Mediterranean Revival style of the 1920s had been blocked in during alterations forty years earlier by some lunatic masquerading as an architect.

In startling juxtaposition to the forlorn, peeling facade, five enormous wood panels were attached to iron railings at ground-floor level. Each bore a reproduction of some masterwork—Whistler's mother, a scene from Michelangelo's Sistine Chapel ceiling, a Van Gogh self-portrait, Edvard Munch's *The Scream* and Klimt's *The Kiss.* A small shop occupied one remaining bay of the lost arcade.

Aunt Ginger had waxed ecstatic when she took me on a square-foot-by-square-foot tour of her new property when I'd passed through Miami two years earlier on my way to Key Largo to visit Grammie Jones. She'd just bought the hotel and had great plans for renovating it, perhaps turning it into an artists' cooperative. She hired a Cuban street artist to oversee the renovations. Alonzo took up residence on the top floor, knocked down walls and set up a huge studio and workroom.

The cabbie peered at the Van Gogh. "You sure this is where you want to go?"

"No," I sighed. "But I'm here anyway."

"What's wrong with the guy's ear in that picture? It's all bandaged up. He hurt himself?"

"You might say that. He cut it off."

He shook his head. "World's full of loonies," he opined as he popped the trunk and set my bags on the sidewalk.

I gazed up at the Hotel St. Claire, and sighed deeply.

I, Matilda Snapp, was now the proud owner of a derelict hotel and sole proprietor of Erratica, "The Emporium of Curiosities for the Discriminating Collector," which specialized in *les objets d'amour et le boudoir,* as Aunt Ginger was wont to say.

As I contemplated my newly bequeathed little empire on that sultry October evening, I might not have known the difference between a vintage tickle pickle and a kosher dill, but I was about to embark on a sex ed course that would have had my health and hygiene teacher, Mrs. Stickle, at Willard Middle School back in Berkeley spinning in her grave.

"Why me, Aunt Ginger?"

I could have sworn I heard a faint giggle from the Great Beyond.

Four

It's probably just as well that the seven or eight million visitors who swarm through Miami Beach each year aren't aware they're sleeping, eating, sunning, and shopping on barely seven square miles of land at an elevation of just four feet above sea level. Oh, the place looks solid enough, but it's really just a paved-over sandbar with a spectacular beach the width of two football fields that's "renourished" with white sand each year. It's not going to take all that much more in the way of global warming before everyone's walking around in thigh-high wading boots.

The charming mix of Art Deco and Mediterranean Revival hotels and shops on the ocean side weren't built wall-to-wall for aesthetic effect; the truth is there wasn't that much land to build on to start. The original owners of Aunt Ginger's Hotel St. Claire had somehow managed to hold on to a pocket of open space next to it, although it was a weedy wasteland when she bought it. Even if the arcade, ugly louvered windows, and facade had not yet benefited from

Alonzo's healing touch, the side yard certainly had, now transformed into a brick patio garden dominated by an enormous bush resplendent with dazzling yellow blossoms.

At the moment, a small group was gathered in front of one of the wood panels—Botticelli's *Birth of Venus*—which was leaning against the side of the building. No one noticed as I opened the elaborate ironwork gate, pulled my bags through, and joined them.

Aunt Ginger would have loved it. Immortalized, she rose from an azure sea on an enormous clamshell, the ethereal countenance of the goddess of love now transformed into the earthy features of Lorraine Louise Snapp.

"The hair's wrong," someone observed. "It's not red enough."

"Needs a touch of orange."

"Too long."

"Too curly."

"*Madre de Dios,* everybody got to be a critic," the man I remembered as Alonzo grumbled. Whipcord-thin, with long hair pulled back into a tight ponytail and hooded black eyes, he didn't look like someone you'd want to take on in a bar fight. He had somehow managed to pour his lower half into a pair of impossibly tight black jeans that displayed his wares, both fore and aft, to their very best advantage, and an orange muscle-shirt that bragged to the rest of the world that "Cubans Do It Better." He stood contemplating his work, hands on hips, head cocked to one side, with the handle of a paintbrush clamped between his teeth.

"Woman don't look right. What's wrong with her shoulder? She got arms like a chimpanzee."

Alonzo glared at a well-upholstered woman of perhaps sixty with skin the color of rich dark espresso beans and a full Afro straight out of the 1970s, all the more startling in that it was pure white. "I didn't paint her damn shoulder, Missy Mae, Botticelli did."

She thrust forth a pugnacious chin. "Well, why don't you call him and get him over here to fix it?"

"Because he's been dead for five hundred years," Alonzo snapped. "That's why."

Missy Mae folded her arms across an eye-popping bosom that severely tested the extendible capacity of a mustard yellow spandex tube top and considered this unhappy piece of news.

"Well, what I think is, you'd be doing him a favor to make it right. He don't want to be remembered as someone who couldn't paint a decent shoulder. 'Sides, you changed the face, so where's the difference?"

"She has a point," said a rail-thin, bleached-out blonde whose deep, leathery tan promised an ugly encounter with melanoma sooner or later. Her hot pink romper outfit did her no favors.

"I think it's perfect," I piped up from the back. "It's exactly the memorial she would have chosen for herself."

Eight curious faces turned in my direction.

I wiggled my fingers at them. "Hi, I'm Tilly."

Obviously the name meant nothing to them.

"Tilly Snapp," I clarified. "I've brought Aunt Ginger home."

"What you talking about, girl?" barked Missy Mae. "Ginger's gone."

"Well, yes, strictly speaking I suppose that's true," I said.

"Gone but not forgotten," intoned a man with a braided beard down to his waist.

"No," I said. "Of course not. Who could forget Ginger? But—"

Missy Mae gazed up at the sky. "Singin' with the angels, that's what she's doin' right now. Hallelujah!"

"Yes, I'm sure she is, but—"

"Let her talk," Alonzo ordered. "Wait. I remember. You're Ginger's niece. You came around a couple of years ago when she first bought the St. Claire."

"Yes," I replied, grateful for the acknowledgement and validation. "And I've just come from Jamaica."

I reached into the tote and brought forth the gaudy, heart-shaped urn.

"Here she is," I announced.

Perhaps it wasn't the most diplomatic way to put it.

A heavy silence settled over the garden. Someone sniffled; someone cleared his throat. Alonzo took the urn from my hands with marked reverence, then passed it around. No one spoke.

Missy Mae studied it for a long moment and shared with us her thoughts at this awkward, somber moment.

"Now that is one butt-ugly urn. I wouldn't be found dead in that urn."

Five

1. *Monday 10am: meet w/ Wickerby and accountant (Flores?) Reading of will. Alonzo, Virgil, Missy Mae, Harry*
2. *How dispose G's ashes at sea? Boat hire, laws . . .*
3. *Draft notice Erratica out of business, mail/post on Internet (Ask Wickerby how you sell a business)*
4. *Interview real estate agents/inspection/get appraisal*
5. ****Important! Call Scarlett to spring Baskerville from Rover's Retreat*
6. *Write column, superlatives—DUE FRIDAY 5pm OR ELSE*
7. *TAMPAX!!!!!!!!!!!!!*
8. *Where is Harry?*
9. *Friday 2pm: Take Missy Mae to podiatrist*
10. *Saturday 6pm: Memorial service, garden—food/wine (music?) Alonzo/Virgil to arrange*
11. *Find murderer*

Could my life get any weirder? Actually, it could, and would, but I was only five days into my transformation from good old Tilly Snapp to—well, I'll get to that later—as I started on my third cup of coffee at Aunt Ginger's kitchen table and looked over my to-do list. I doubted I'd be going back to Boston any time soon.

What I really wanted to do was flop back onto the red velvet couch and pull the blanket over my head. Maybe I'd wake up to find that Wickerby and Flores had done whatever the executor of a will and a certified public accountant are supposed to do when someone falls out of a parasailing harness, and I could get on a plane and go home.

Not "accidentally falls," I corrected myself. Aunt Ginger, that generous, luminous soul had been murdered. For what, when it came down to it? Greed—greed pure and simple.

I fueled my anger with visions of vengeance as I showered and pulled on white shorts and a navy blue tee. Execution would be too good for the fiend. No, he'd live out his miserable little life in a glass-walled jail cell, covered on the outside with pictures of Aunt Ginger and dildos and hundred-dollar bills. Or maybe pictures of all the wonderful things life has to offer that he'd never enjoy again: beer, a big juicy steak, an ice cream cone, fireworks, a snazzy convertible, a gorgeous sunset, a lap dancer with humongous breasts.

"What do you think of that?" I inquired of a scrawny orange tabby as I poked into cupboards looking for cat food. "You'll have to do with baked beans until I get some groceries in," I informed it.

I wandered into the living room munching on a stale rice cake and made up my bed on the couch. It seemed like sacrilege to sleep in Aunt Ginger's king-size bed, and I didn't even want to think about having to go through her personal things.

"Sufficient unto the day is the evil thereof," I told a fat black cat that was attending to its more intimate ablutions on the polished wood floor. "The Bible says so, and who are we to disagree?"

The evil assigned by the Almighty to that particular day was about to unfold. An altercation seemed to be in progress outside the living room window. I opened the doors that led to a charming little ironwork balcony that was somehow clinging to the crumbling facade on the Española Way side of the building. I took a tentative step, and when I didn't plunge two stories to meet my death on the paved sidewalk below, ventured out.

"Where the hell is it?" a stout man wielding a tripod was demanding of Virgil, Alonzo's on-again, off-again companion. "I always use the Botticelli."

Virgil Yenakis, a stocky person of Greek heritage with a neat droopy moustache, a rapidly receding hairline, and kind brown eyes, had disembarked from a gleaming white cruise ship in the Port of Miami one bright morning for a day of sightseeing before returning to a rather solitary life in the apartment above his tailor shop on Manhattan's Upper East Side. He had wandered into a gay Latino bar in Little Havana, mistaking it for a Cuban restaurant, and discovered the hitherto unexplored and unexpected delights of the gay life in the arms of Alonzo Campos.

Benign of countenance and ever courteous, even in the face of the photographer's bluster, Virgil said sadly, "Alas, the Botticelli is no longer on display."

"Whattaya mean, not on display? We're not talking about the goddamn Uffizi Gallery in goddamn Florence here. We're standing on a public sidewalk in Miami Beach, for Christ's sake."

Alonzo stalked down the sidewalk and took up position beside his significant other with the quivering intensity of a panther defending its wounded mate. The man took a prudent step back.

"The sidewalk's public," Alonzo announced, "but the railing's private, so if we don't want the Venus out here, it's none of your damn business."

"Sheez," said the man, "it isn't as though it's the original; it's a piece of wood some guy painted to fancy up the fence around the construction site for the new Fountainbleau up on Forty-fourth."

That raised Alonzo's artistic hackles. "For your information, that 'some guy' just happens to be the great Sidewalk Sam."

"I don't care if it was painted by the ghost of Christmas past, I want my Venus. I only have the models for two hours. We're all ready for the shoot; they got their makeup on and we're ready to roll."

"Um, hello, everyone," I called down. "What seems to be the problem, gentlemen?"

The photographer stepped back and craned his neck so he could put a body with the voice. "Where's Ginger? I want to talk to Ginger."

"I'm afraid Ginger's gone."

"Where'd she go?"

My personal jury is still out on the subject of reincarnation, but if I have it right it goes like this: You get born. You live. You die. You do it over again and again until you get it right. I'd never given much thought to where you go between lives, but this probably wasn't a good time to engage in philosophical speculation.

"She didn't go anywhere, or at least I'm not sure if she did or not. For the time being, she's dead."

"Aw hell. What'd she want to go and do something like that for?"

She didn't, of course, but I had no intention of telling anyone she'd been murdered until I figured out what to do about it. "She met with an unfortunate accident."

"Well, hell. Poor old Ginger."

By the time I located my sandals under the couch, wrestled my hair into a scrunchie, and jogged down the stairs to the sidewalk, Alonzo, Virgil, and the photographer were locked in a three-way embrace, consoling one another and extolling in ever mounting superlatives the glory that had been Ginger Snapp.

"I'm sorry about the Venus," I told the man, whose name, I learned, was Percy Coombes. "But it was Ginger's favorite; Alonzo's restoring it, and it's going to hang in the lobby when we finish the renovations."

I glanced at the two models in their itsy-bitsy, teeny-weeny string bikinis and four-inch stacked-heel silver sandals. The image of a grinning ass graced the bottom of one suit, preceded by the invitation to kiss it. The crotch of the other bore the image of a lolling tongue, no instructions necessary apparently.

"Look, Percy," I said, "why don't you go for contrast? Maybe pose these lovely ladies against the van Gogh? Better still, Munch's *The Scream.* Very eye-catching, very out-there."

I ignored Alonzo's gasp of horror as I steered Percy, his assistant, and the models around the corner to the image of what might have been an alien standing on a bridge letting loose with a primal scream beneath a lurid orange sky.

Percy studied the panel. "Might just work," he said, and began directing his assistant to set up the camera.

"What's wrong with that guy?" Tongue-bikini asked around a huge wad of gum as she studied Munch's masterpiece. "He don't look too happy."

Kiss-my-ass–bikini was examining her bee-stung lips in a handheld mirror. "Who know what goes on in a guy's head? Maybe he wrecked his car or something."

"Or couldn't get it up," suggested the other.

"Yeah, that's probably it. Really freaks a guy out, he can't get it up."

I left the little group of artists to their shoot, thinking the day might run smoothly now that I'd taken care of its allotted evil.

I should have known better. After all, I was Alice and this was Wonderland, where the unexpected and the unimaginable await the unwary traveler at every turn: a hookah-smoking caterpillar, a talking egg, a grin without a cat attached to it.

An eye-popping, mind-blowing, heart-stopping secret agent with eyes the color of fathomless pools of bittersweet chocolate, Irish coffee, and aged brandy; a god-yes mouth; and in case I forgot to mention it, testosterone in spades.

Six

I couldn't say whether I was pleased or annoyed to find Special Agent Will Maitland lounging in a patio chair with a white kitten curled up in his lap when I returned from a foray to PetSmart.

I didn't want to be pleased, so I opted for annoyed.

"This is private property," said I. "You need a warrant."

"Strictly speaking I don't, as I was invited to wait here for you."

"Like a vampire? You get what you deserve if you let him cross the threshold?"

"An unusual analogy, but yes, you could say that."

"Who invited you?" I demanded.

"A Missy Mae, I believe her name is. She offered me a tour, but I'm afraid I had to decline."

"And just why is that? What a golden opportunity. You could have called in the storm troops and searched the place from top to bottom. Not that you'd find anything, because there's nothing to find."

"A tour of her room," he clarified. "I seriously doubt there's anything I'd find of much interest in her room."

It might have been my imagination, inflamed by the hot flood of hormones surging through my body, but I could have sworn there was a slight inflection on the "her." No, don't even start down that road, I ordered my brain.

"I don't want you here," I managed. "They don't know anything about Ginger's untimely passing, and they certainly don't know anything about the pillow box of Win Win Poo. You didn't tell Missy Mae who you are, did you? I'm going to be really ticked off if you did."

He gently extracted the cat's claws from his khakis and deposited it on the brick patio. "I told her I was a friend of yours. Why don't we go sit in the café across the street. Neutral territory."

"Five minutes, I'll give you five minutes, and then I want you to stop bothering me. I don't know anything that would prove useful in your investigation and I don't have anything you're looking for."

My nose was so high in the air as we walked across the street that I almost knocked over a three-legged greyhound hopping along at the end of a red leather lead. A matching collar sparkled with rhinestones that spelled out "Bubbles."

"Any self-respecting dog in Boston would throw itself off the Tobin Bridge before he'd go out in public like that," I said as I recovered my balance and headed toward a table in the shade. "Mine would tear open my jugular, and then he'd jump."

"You own a dog?" came a voice from behind me.

Agent Maitland was actually holding the chair for me. What kind of man holds a chair for a woman in this day and age? Wow!

"A mutt I got from the animal shelter. His name is Baskerville. But you probably already knew that."

"As a matter of fact, I didn't," he said, signaling to a waitress. "You've come as somewhat of a surprise in the course of this investigation."

When we were settled with a bowl of lime-flavored corn chips, a beer for him, and iced coffee for me, I decided to get down to brass tacks right away. "What is it you want now?"

He shrugged. "Just thought I'd see how you're getting on."

"Right."

He took a swig of Dos Equis Amber. "I see Erratica is still closed. Will you reopen?"

"No. As soon as the will's read on Monday, I'm putting the whole shebang on the market and going home."

He looked over at the St. Claire, almost virginal again in the rosy gold of late afternoon. "Pity; it could be a beautiful building again with a little kindness. Tell me, do your tenants know you're going to sell?"

"I haven't told them yet." And I didn't know how I was going to break it to them when the time came. It was an eminently sensible decision on my part. What was I supposed to do, move to Miami Beach and sell sex toys—okay, *antique* sex toys—to perverts? There was absolutely no reason to feel guilty.

"I feel sort of guilty about it."

"Sounds reasonable to me, Ms. Snapp-Allenby. Once everything's squared away, you'll walk away with a tidy inheritance and get on with your life."

"That's the plan. Just so you know, I've dropped the Allenby. I just never got around to changing it on my passport. Alex wasn't too happy about the hyphenation anyhow. He wanted me to be Allenby, just Allenby; no Snapp. He's dead, so now I'm Snapp again, just Snapp; no Allenby."

Agent Maitland reached for a chip. "I understand your husband met with an unfortunate accident."

I only just managed to strangle a scream of exasperation. "What are you, some sort of conspiracy nut?"

He raised a quizzical brow, a trick I've never been able to master. I've practiced, but it's both brows at once or no brow at all.

"It was not an unfortunate accident. Well, it was, but not the way you people think. My husband died a perfectly natural death. He was struck by lightning on a golf course. If that's not natural, I don't know what is."

"Put that way, I see your point."

"Of course," I added, "if you take into account the fact that two or three million people die every year in this country and only four hundred are struck by lightning, and of those maybe a hundred die, and of those hundred maybe half are out playing golf, it's not all that natural, either. So I'd have to disagree."

Agent Maitland leaned back in his chair and smiled a killer smile that fried every pleasure receptor in my brain. "So if I understand you correctly, you're disagreeing with yourself."

"What if I am?" I sniffed. "Walt Whitman said, 'Do I contradict myself? Very well, then, I contradict myself.' Or maybe it was Thoreau. I can never remember."

"Winnie the Pooh?" he suggested.

I swear, if the man smiled again, I was going to have an orgasm on the spot.

"Look, Agent Maitland," I said briskly, "I've got a lot to do between now and Monday. You know and I know you didn't just drop by to see how I'm doing. To save us both time: No, I don't know where the box is. No, no one's tried to kill me. No again, mysterious strangers aren't lurking in the shadows or tailing me around Miami in black Lincoln Town Cars with tinted windows.

"And if you want to know the truth," I continued, gathering steam, "it bothers me more than a little that you're more interested in finding a bunch of stupid sex toys than finding out who killed my aunt."

He studied the brown bottle and finished it off. "Let me explain how it works, Ms. Snapp. Your aunt's case was initially handled by local officers of the Jamaica Constabulary Force in Negril, then transferred to the Westmoreland Parish divisional headquarters at Savanna-la-Mar. It was then taken up by the JCF national headquarters in Kingston, who in turn passed it on to the U.S. Department of Justice in Washington when it became evident there was no local connection in Jamaica, save the body in Kingston. The DOJ had PST take a look at the case, and it was transferred to the Miami office of the FBI, who contacted the USNCB—the U.S. National Central Bureau of Interpol in Washington. It was agreed the two agencies would work the case in tandem, which grants the Interpol agent the same exercise of authority as his FBI counterpart. Since the crime falls under the aegis of both the Criminal and Property Crimes divisions of Interpol, and I've worked in both at one time or another, it's been assigned to me."

"Gee, and here I thought nobody cared." I could almost taste the acid dripping off my tongue.

I could see he didn't care for that. He leaned forward and pinned me with those dark eyes. "Let me assure you, Ms. Snapp, I give every case that comes across my desk my undivided attention and best effort. Right now, I'm going after the box because it will lead me to your aunt's killer."

A case, that was all it was to him, another case. He'd solve it, or maybe he wouldn't, and then move on to the next and the next and the next. He'd keep his professional distance, because that's what he'd been trained to do, and Aunt Ginger would just become another name on a dusty case file or a blip in the vast reaches of cyberspace: *Snapp, Lorraine Louise, d.o.b. 05/08/1955, Philadelphia, PA; d. Negril, Jamaica, 09/30/2004. Cause of death: homicide. Case assignment: Special Agent Will Maitland, Property Crimes/Stolen Artifacts, US National Central Bureau Interpol/Miami Office. Case disposition: Closed ____, pending ____, dismissed [check one].*

Lorraine Louise Snapp deserved better, and Tilly Snapp was going to see that she got it.

I trotted out a sweet, sad smile. "I can't tell you how much I appreciate your dedication, Agent Maitland. I know you'll do everything in your power to see that the perpetrator is brought to justice and receives the full measure of the law." I watch a lot of *Law and Order.*

He wasn't buying it. "But."

Might as well lay it all out on the table. "You have your methods, I have mine."

Cool cop eyes held mine. "Let me warn you right now, Ms. Snapp. This case is more complicated, more dangerous than you can possibly imagine. If you've got it in that head of yours to start playing detective, you're going to be in a lot more trouble than you already are, because I won't think twice about parking you in a jail cell until I put this case to bed."

I think I actually snarled for the first time in my life. "On what charge?"

"You're a material witness in a homicide investigation."

"Witness?" My voice rocketed a full octave. "Witness? To what? I didn't see my aunt die, and I don't make it a habit to hang around brothels in Kingston."

"You don't have to actually witness a crime, Ms. Snapp. If I determine that you have pertinent information about a criminal investigation that you are withholding from the investigating officer, or if you fail to cooperate or refuse to testify, if and when a grand jury is convened, or you are considered a flight risk, I can see that you're held indefinitely."

"Oh, really? You have to have, um, to have . . ." I scrambled for the right word.

"Probable cause?" he offered.

"Right. Thank you. Probable cause. And you don't," I said smugly, "so don't mind me if I'm not shaking like a leaf."

He shrugged. "No problem. I can make an oath of affirmation and have a warrant for your arrest in an hour flat."

My eyes flashed blue fire. Well, not really, but I was building up a good head of steam. "You wouldn't dare."

He would. I knew it, and he knew I knew it.

He was going to smile; I could see the first tiny tug at the corner of that god-yes mouth. Anger I could handle, chagrin, indignation. But add unbridled lust to the mix and I was going to blow sky high.

"And don't you dare smile," I snapped. I fished

around in my bag, pulled out a five-dollar bill, and slapped it on the table. "You know what your problem is, *Special Agent* Maitland? You can't tell the good guys from the bad guys. Everyone's guilty until proven innocent. There's a skeleton in every closet. Conspiracy lurks at every turn. The whole damn KGB was on the grassy knoll in Dallas." I surged to my feet. "Well, let me tell you something. Lorraine Louise Snapp might be a case to you, but she's my aunt Ginger and I loved her, and whatever she may or may not have done, she was a real flesh-and-blood person. You do what you have to, Mr. Law and Order, and I'll do what I have to. So, you'd better get cracking on that warrant.

"Now, if you'll excuse me, I have more important things to do. I have a cat to feed."

As an exit line, I'll admit it lacked panache, but I was under a lot of pressure. I marched away, head held high. I wasn't going to look back to see how he was taking my little diatribe. I didn't want to know, really I didn't.

Of course, I just had to look.

The man was smiling, damn him.

12. Buy batteries.

Seven

Halsey Wickerby, Esq., surveyed his audience over thick bifocals which clung precariously to the tip of his long ski-slope of a nose. The chair beside his desk that was to have been occupied by the accountant, Carlotta Flores, stood empty due to a death in the family.

"The testatrix appended these codicils on 15 September, two weeks before her tragic death," he explained. "The first pertains only to the disposition of her property at Española Way, its furnishings and fittings. The second pertains to her business, namely, Erratica, Inc., its premises and assets, and certain intellectual property rights attendant to the online division of the enterprise, Erratica.com. These bequests are to be retained *in perpetuum.* Bequests to individuals other than Ms. Snapp's niece, Ms. Matilda Snapp, and the charitable institutions in the testatrix's last will and testament and of which I have already apprised you remain unchanged."

Somebody squawked. I figured it had to be me,

since it was fairly certain no one else in the room had a clue what Halsey Wickerby was talking about. Two years of marriage to a lawyer and three years of high school Latin under the steely eye of Miss Upton was more than adequate to clue me in to the fact that life, as I knew it, would never be the same.

I needed air. I needed time to think. And I needed a drink, which explains how I came to be sipping morosely at my third Frozen Melon Margarita at the historic wooden bar of the National Hotel on Collins, and brooding on the way life sneaks up on you when you aren't looking and whammies you with a custard pie right in the kisser.

When was the last time I'd hit the booze at two in the afternoon when the going got tough? Never, that's when, which says a lot about my mood after we all trooped out of Wickerby's office and piled into Aunt Ginger's red SUV. Alonzo, Virgil, and Missy Mae were in high spirits, and why shouldn't they be? Aunt Ginger had bequeathed each of them a lifetime, rent-free tenancy at the St. Claire. I'm not sure they grasped the fact that their good fortune came at the expense of my own unless I could find a loophole in those wretched codicils that would allow me to sell the place. I didn't want to burst their bubble, so I had them drop me off on Ocean Drive and Eleventh before they headed up to midbeach for a celebratory, artery-clogging binge at Jerry's Famous Deli.

The cool, quiet dark of the nearly empty bar invited intimacy. I could almost hear Frank Sinatra crooning "Set 'em up, Joe" and see Humphrey Bogart in a white sport coat and bow tie lighting up an unfiltered Lucky Strike at the end of the bar.

"Hypothetically," I began.

The bartender grinned. "It always is."

"This is different," I grumbled.

"It always is."

"I have this friend—"

"Uh-huh."

"A friend," I repeated, narrowing my eyes. "Anyhow, let's say this friend has this relative who dies and leaves her a really valuable piece of property and money and a business—maybe it's a legal business, maybe it's not, and maybe the relative died a natural death and maybe she didn't." I paused to pop a salted nut into my mouth, and munched.

"Lot of maybes in there," he observed. He moved down the bar to take an order for a Sam Adams Special Dark.

"Sounds complicated," he said when he came back.

"You haven't heard the half of it. Why she did it—God must know because I certainly don't—er, my friend doesn't—the relative—let's say it's her aunt—changes her will just before she dies so that my friend can never sell the property or the business."

"She—the aunt—must have had her reasons," the bartender observed.

"Mind if I join you?" A heavyset man with a bad comb-over wearing baggy khaki cargo shorts and a Day-Glo pink muscle shirt slid onto the stool next to me. "Another Sam Adams, if you don't mind," he said to the bartender.

"Coming right up."

Great, just what I needed, someone hitting on me.

"I couldn't help overhearing your friend's story. She lives an interesting life."

I swiveled around to face him. "See, that's the

problem. My friend doesn't want to live an interesting life. She's had it up to here"—I drew a line across my neck with my finger—"up to here with interesting. Parents fall off a mountain, grandmother finds God in a bottle, my friend ends up being Mommy at sixteen to her sister and brothers. Husband goes up in flames on the sixth hole, her mother-in-law moves in. Aunt falls out of the sky; she inherits a derelict hotel she can't sell and three tenants-for-life she wouldn't have the heart to kick out into the street even if she could. Then there's your perverts, your smugglers, shecret agents, mutilated corpses, murderers. Oh, and dildos."

I brooded on the injustice of it all. "Always left holding the bag. Ishn't fair."

"Your friend have a name?"

"Alishinwonderland."

"Uh-huh. What do you call yourself?"

I gave it some thought. "I call myself Matilda-Hear-Me-Whine."

"Well, Matilda," he said, "why don't I walk you home."

I wagged a finger at him. "Oh no, you don't. I'm not that kind of girl. I can find my own way home."

"Richie's okay," the bartender said. "I'll vouch for him."

He steadied me as I climbed off the barstool. "You're not in any condition to get home on your own."

"Am too. What are you, a shecret agent from Alcoholics Anonymous? Just what I need, another shecret agent. What do you do, hang out in bars looking for drunks sho you can drag them off to meetings?"

"You're going to find yourself under the wheels of a

bus and make some poor schmo in public works scrape you up with a spoon."

"Oh. Well, I wouldn't want to put him to all that trouble." I wasn't exactly drunk, but I had a nice little buzz going and didn't give the fact that he knew where I lived the serious thought it deserved. I zoned out as he guided me across Collins, along the sacramental way of conspicuous consumption known as Lincoln Road Mall, and left onto Drexel down to Española Way.

"The Hotel St. Claire," I announced with a sweep of my arm. "Home Shour Home."

I fumbled with the gate latch, pushed through, and came nose-to-chest with a black polo shirt. Somebody smelled spicy and sexy and tasty.

"Richie."

"Maitland."

"What the hell do you think you're doing?"

"Seeing Ms. Snapp home safely."

I twisted around and glared at him. "You knew who I was? You dirty rat," I snarled.

I pride myself on being able to trot out a movie quote for every occasion. I think I do a pretty credible James Cagney.

"You got her drunk," Will Maitland said softly. "I ought to drag your sorry ass in for obstruction. Ms. Snapp is a person of interest in an official investigation. I won't tolerate interference from a civilian."

The dirty rat shrugged.

The person of interest poked her finger into the chest of the agent in charge. "He didn't get me drunk, Shpecial Agent Whoeveryouare." I grinned up at him and tapped my own chest. "I did it all by myshelf."

"I don't know who you're working for, Richie, but I'd watch my step if I were you," Will Maitland said. "PST was looking at this. You could find yourself with your ass in a sling."

"PST? Jesus Christ."

"Hey, guys, remember me?" I interjected. "PST? What's PST?"

Will Maitland put his hands on my shoulders and aimed me towards the door. "You don't want to know. Why don't you go lie down before you fall down?"

Now, I consider myself a reasonable woman. I understand that men are estrogen-deprived and aren't entirely to blame when they act like jerks. I'll even go so far as to allow that you can take the man out of the cave but you can't take the cave out of the man, not in a mere thirty thousand years anyhow. They're doing their best, and you can't ask more than that. But even I have my little prejudices, and the man who takes it upon himself to tell me how I feel, what I think, what I want—well, that man requires a firm but gentle hand to guide him toward a more enlightened perspective on my gender.

"Listen up, you Neanderthal," I growled. "You want to know what I want to know? I'll tell you. I want to know what rock you crawled out from under. I want to know who botched your lobotomy. I want to know when you first realized you were God.

"And I want to know," I concluded through clenched teeth, "what PST is."

"All right, Ms. Snapp, I'll tell you since you ask so nicely. PST stands for the Public Safety and Terrorism Sub-Directorate."

"Public safety."

"That's right."

"Terrorism."

"Yes."

"Directorate."

"Sub-Directorate," he corrected.

"Oh. I see." I didn't, and I didn't want to. "You know, I think I'll just go lie down before I fall down," I announced.

"Ms. Snapp," Will Maitland said as I rummaged through my bag for the key. "PST has no verifiable intelligence that terrorist cells either here or abroad are even aware that the pillow box of Win Win Poo was stolen, much less that they engineered the theft in order to finance their activities."

"O-keeedokeee."

"You need have no concerns on that score. Your aunt was not murdered by terrorists."

"Uh-huh. Great. Good to know." I waved a dismissive hand and scowled into my bag—no key—and vaguely remembered I'd slipped it on the key chain of Aunt Ginger's SUV. It could be hours until Alonzo, Virgil, and Missy Mae slurped down the last globule of trans fat and rolled out of Jerry's Famous Deli. I closed my eyes and slid down the wooden door.

"What did I do to deserve this?" I inquired of the universe.

A large body hunkered down beside me, and a reassuring hand rested on my shoulder. "I'm sorry, Tilly. I didn't mean to frighten you."

"Can't frighten me, Island Boy. Shee, thish isn't happening. I'm not here. I'm in Wonderland." I held up a finger. "No, scratch that. I'm in the Looking-Glass House."

I may actually have giggled, a behavior I object to on principle.

" 'Twas brillig, and the slithy toves did gyre and gimble in the wabe,' " quoth I. "Betcha don't know what a slithy tove is," I challenged.

"Let's get you upstairs."

I opened one eye. "Can't. No key."

Will Maitland scooped me up into manly arms. "Richie, jimmy the lock."

"You got it."

" 'Beware the Jabberwock, my son, and shun the frumious Bandersnatch!' " I warned him woozily.

He grinned down at me. "Thanks, I'll be sure to do that."

I think I'd just gotten to "O frabjous day! Callooh! Callay!" when strong arms deposited me on the red velvet couch in Aunt Ginger's living room. I couldn't swear to it, but as I slipped away I thought gentle fingers smoothed a stray curl from my cheek, and a deep voice with just an echo of the Islands said, "Sleep tight, Alice."

EIGHT

One thing I know about myself: I am nothing if not a problem solver. I can do the *New York Times* Sunday crossword puzzle in twenty minutes flat. In ink. Waldo can't hide from my eagle eye.

I can rout an entrenched mother-in-law from the spare room without breaking a sweat and have her agreeing it's for the best by the time the taxi pulls up to bear her away. I can convince recalcitrant adolescents to abandon their snits and sulks and never doubt they reversed course and did the right thing of their own free will. Bureaucrats—with the possible exception of Jamaican bureaucrats, who conduct business in a fog of marijuana fumes and just don't give a hoot—quail before my relentless determination. Failure has never been an option for me, and present circumstances, as unexpected and bizarre as they appeared at the moment, would be dealt with in like manner.

* * *

"Big help you are," I grouched to the five cats ranged side by side along the back of Aunt Ginger's couch. "I'm up to my tush in alligators here, guys. I could use some ideas."

Maybe cats aren't at their problem-solving best at three o'clock in the morning. I sure wasn't. I'd somehow yanked myself out of a harrowing dream that featured a kaleidoscopic epic of me being chased all over Miami by Tweedledum and Tweedledee, who looked suspiciously like Will Maitland and Richie from the National bar. Halsey Wickerby and a headless corpse brought up the rear, with Aunt Ginger on the sidelines in full cheerleader regalia waving pompoms and shouting encouragement.

"Let's take it in order," I suggested. "Maybe something will come to you.

"First, I need to find a loophole in the will." I sipped at my coffee and tried to focus. "Next, there's the pillow box of Win Win Poo. Maybe Will Maitland is right: find the box and we find out who killed Aunt Ginger. So, let's say it's an important clue."

I checked my troops to make sure they were following my line of thought. It was hard to tell. "So, if someone is after it, they're going to come looking for it here. And what we'll do is, we'll open the shop and set a trap."

I scritched the nose of a gray kitten that had materialized in my lap. "Maybe I can get Blossom up from Key West to help with the shop. If anyone knows about sex stuff, it's Blossom." I was on a roll now. "And I bet Scarlett would come down from Boston; she's a computer whiz and an eBay addict.

"EBay," I informed my rapt audience, "is an online

auction house. You can buy anything there. We might get a lead on who's in the market for ancient Chinese sex toys."

I wandered into the kitchen. Twenty-four paws padded along behind. I poured milk into three saucers, figuring two cats per, and watched all six battle it out over one.

"Third," I said to no one in particular, as I'd lost my audience, "I need to find Harry Hungwell."

Harold Zazrewski, known to aficionados of the genre as Harry Hungwell in his salad days as a porn star, had been Aunt Ginger's husband for four months once. I didn't know the details, but they'd parted amicably enough and remained friends over the years. I myself had never seen Harry in action, but Blossom assured me that he more than lived up to his professional name and was right up there with the likes of John Holmes when it came to stamina and artistic sensibility.

Anyhow, Wickerby hadn't been able to reach Harry to tell him Aunt Ginger had passed away, and it occurred to me that she might have been inclined to confide in Harry if she was in any kind of trouble.

So I had the glimmer of a plan. Now I needed to shake off Tweedledum and Tweedledee to set it in motion.

Galvanized, I showered, set out enough food for at least ten cats for two or three days—they just kept on showing up, and who knew how many I'd find when I got back—and threw some tank tops and shorts into a bag. I scooped up the car keys Virgil had left on the table by the garden door and prepared to depart under cover of darkness. I doubted things had progressed to the point where Interpol would be staking me out twenty-four hours a day, but I wasn't taking any chances.

I let myself out, locked the door behind me, and headed toward Aunt Ginger's red Grand Cherokee, which Virgil had parked around the corner in front of Erratica. Over on Ocean Drive the glitterati would be gathering at the ultrachic Hurricane Alley for mimosas and eggs Benedict after another night parading their wares from one hot spot to another. But back here in the real world of residential hotels, apartment buildings, bodegas, and cigar kiosks, nothing ruffled the soft serenity of predawn Miami.

A pretty little Art Nouveau table lamp glowed in the window of Erratica: a ceramic nude, her body arched and head thrown back in ecstasy, backlit against etched glass in the shape of an orchid. I'd admired it the morning Alonzo showed me how to set the store alarm. The lady welcomed window-shoppers and passersby to witness her erotic thrall every night between the hours of 7 P.M. and 7 A.M. An automatic timer switched the rousing spectacle on and off and also activated motion sensors in the shop.

As I unlocked the car door, I made a mental note to ask Harry Hungwell what the world record was for longest uninterrupted orgasm. I had just settled in behind the wheel and was fiddling with the radio to find good driving music when I happened to glance over at the shop again. La Femme was now modestly clothed in absolute darkness. I checked the clock on the dash, then my watch. They concurred: It was only 5:10.

I didn't want to go over there and find out what the trouble was, really I didn't.

Of course, I just had to go. As the proprietor, albeit the unwilling proprietor, of "The Emporium of Curiosities for the Discriminating Collector," wasn't it my duty to protect my property, with my very life if necessary? Well, no, definitely not with my very life, but I wasn't thinking about overpriced antiques just at the moment; I was thinking about my aunt Ginger. An intruder might very well be after the pillow box of Win Win Poo at this very moment, and he might have something to do with her death. Or it might be a private investigator who could jimmy a lock in ten seconds flat, or a devastating secret agent who had no business sneaking around in there without a warrant.

Armed with righteous anger and a key-chain canister of pepper spray, which might or might not be legal in the state of Florida—it certainly wasn't in Massachusetts—I darted across the street, pressed my back against the wall, and inched along until I could just poke my nose around the edge of the window frame.

Nothing stirred in the darkness; no intimation of a sinister presence sent chills down my spine.

I stood there for long tense minutes until it suddenly occurred to me that alarms weren't screeching; police cruisers weren't careening through the streets of South Beach en route to big trouble at the Hotel St. Claire. The alarm hadn't gone off, which should mean that the motion sensors hadn't been tripped.

Maybe, just maybe, the little lamp needed a new bulb? That would be by far the best-case scenario.

Worst case: Someone had bypassed the code and disabled the alarm. He, she, or it might still be lurking in there.

Feeling uncharacteristically brave, I bent low and crept into the shadow of the doorway. I crouched down, shielded my eyes from ambient light, pressed my nose to the glass, then my ear. All was silent, all serene. I dithered for a bit, and finally took the easy way out by opting for the lightbulb theory, which was a lot less scary than confronting an intruder.

I stalked back to the car feeling like a fool. I stowed the peppershot under the seat and headed for the Tasty Bakery on Alton to pick up a blueberry muffin and enough coffee to hold me until I hit Mrs. Mac's Kitchen in Key Largo. But as I cruised down Route 1, one of my father's favorite Taoist sayings popped unaccountably into my head: "Just because you cannot see the cat does not mean he is not there."

Nine

Say there's a Richter scale for culture shock, and say you're fifteen and one day you're transported from the insular intellectual enclave of Berkeley, California, to the good-ol'-boy neoconservative mangrove swamps of Key Largo, Florida. And say you spent your formative years crawling around your parents' left-wing bookstore and doing your homework in the back room, and you suddenly find yourself under the supervision of an individual who believes Charles Darwin was the Antichrist—well, say all that, and you have yourself one hell of a reading on your culture-shock scale.

The details are just too ugly to recount here, but suffice it to say that somehow my siblings and I managed to crawl away from the disaster relatively unscathed. In any event, the generational pendulum was already in motion when my parents died and Grammie Jones gathered us to her bosom. Not one of the five of us had any intention of following our parents' hippie example, but neither had we swung so far to the other end of the arc that Grammie had a chance in hell of herding us into the fundamentalist fold. You could say we're a nice comfy dead center now. Matthew is in international banking; Mark is an intern in a prestigious New York law firm; Luke just finished up his doctorate in urban studies; and Johanna is a home- and baby-maker in Cincinnati. I, as you know, am a writer of sorts who is ready, willing, and able to compromise my artistic integrity at the drop of a hat for the sake of the almighty dollar.

I have three wonderful memories of my three years in Key Largo: my friend Blossom MacMorrough, working on the dive boats out of John Pennekamp State Park, and Mrs. Mac's Kitchen. Everything else is filed away under "Get Over It."

Mrs. Mac's Kitchen sits bayside at mile marker 99 on the Overseas Highway, which is actually just plain old Route 1, or "1" in local parlance. Guidebooks to the Keys refer to Mrs. Mac's Kitchen as "quaint" and "funky," if they mention it at all. To me, the comforting restaurant was a second home during the three years I lived in Key Largo. I spent all my free time at the corner table by the front window doing homework or furthering my fledgling career writing commercial copy for stores and restaurant menus up and down the length of the Keys.

Mrs. Mac's was always on my itinerary when I came down from Boston to visit Grammie at the Hope of Resurrection Home, which I tried to do two or three times a year. After eight years, the agenda for my time with Grammie was set in stone. We'd sit out in the garden on her favorite bench beneath an enormous gumbo-limbo tree, where she would read from the tattered pages of her Bible in her ongoing campaign to save my immortal soul. Then we'd have lunch at McDonald's, after which we'd visit the riverboat featured in *The African Queen*.

I had long ago given up trying to convince Grammie that as far as anyone knew, neither Bogie nor Katharine Hepburn had ever set foot in Key Largo, that the film had been shot in England. The discussion would move on to Bogie and Bacall in *Key Largo*, and I would explain that the town of Key Largo had actually changed its name from Rock Harbor to Key Largo four years after the film was shot—on a Hollywood sound stage—in order to cash in. Grammie would have none of it. I guess you could call it a draw: She couldn't convince me to accept Jesus Christ as my lord and savior, and I couldn't convince her that the ghost of Humphrey Bogart didn't walk the streets of Key Largo.

I was planning on having breakfast at Mrs. Mac's before heading down to Key West to shanghai Blossom. I'd do the grammie thing on my way back. By seven thirty a.m., I'd polished off a Swiss cheese and mushroom omelet, two baking-powder biscuits, and a slice of Key lime pie tart enough to strip the enamel from your teeth. I set up shop at my corner table: Apple PowerBook, CD player, to-do list, coffee. By 9:30, zoned out on the fabulous sexy voice of Mark Knopfler, I'd knocked off a column on the sad fate of the superlative in contemporary speech, and prepared to tackle my current dilemma.

Virgil answered on the fourth ring. "Hey, Tilly, where are you? I've been trying to reach you."

"My cell phone wasn't on. What's up?"

"Weird stuff going on here, Tilly."

This was news? "Weird how?"

"Wait a minute, I have to turn down the radio. Okay, I'm back. So, about two hours ago someone's banging on the door, and when I go to open it, this short bald guy says he's from the FBI—the FBI!—and hands me some papers, and guess what they are? A search warrant! So I tell him the owner isn't here, and he says that doesn't matter, he can still come in, and I say I'm going to call your lawyer. Then another guy shows up and says he's from Interpol, and they get into it about who's got jurisdiction over what, and while they're facing off I slam the door and lock it, and call Wickerby. He says don't do anything, don't open the door again, he's coming right over. Half an hour later he shows up. By then there's another guy out in the garden—short, stocky, in a muscle shirt—says he's your boyfriend and he just stopped by to take you out to breakfast."

I rummaged through my bag for the aspirin, and wished for Valium. "What happened then?"

Virgil took in a lungful of smoke and exhaled into the receiver. "Wickerby got on his cell phone and called some judge and started going on about the Fourth Amendment and illegal search and seizure and probable cause. I didn't hear it all because I was trying to call you, but eventually they all left—the FBI guy looked pretty pissed off—and that's about it."

"Just another day in Wonderland," I muttered.

"So what's going on, Tilly?" Virgil said. "You in some kind of trouble?"

Eventually, I'd have to confess to the residents of the St. Claire that there wasn't just some kind of trouble going on—there was big trouble going on. With federal agents and lawyers duking it out in the garden at seven thirty in the morning, it wasn't going to remain a secret for very long.

"Listen, Virgil, I can't talk about it right now, but I promise I'll tell you when I get back. Meantime, keep Wickerby on speed dial, and don't let anyone in—and I mean *anyone.* If anyone wants to know where I am, you don't know."

He laughed. "That'll be easy. I don't know."

"Thanks, Virgil. I owe you."

"No problem. Oh, by the way, just wanted to remind you to make sure all the cats are out of the shop when you lock the inside door that leads to the hallway. You left that white kitten in there last night."

"Right. Sure. I'll see you soon."

I waited until I got to the car and had the radio and air-conditioning going full blast before I let loose with a string of profanity that would have sent Grammie straight into the arms of her Maker.

I hadn't gone into the shop last night. But somebody had. And that somebody had bypassed the security code and lurked in the shadows inside, waiting me out and watching me make an ass of myself outside.

I wouldn't be opting for any easy-out lightbulb theories again.

Ten

The Overseas Highway runs approximately one hundred miles in a west-southwesterly direction from Key Largo down to Key West, last stop before Cuba and points south. You can drive it in a straight shot in two and a half to three hours at the mandated 45 miles per hour, and there are those who do. But if you've got an ounce of reverence in your soul for the grace Mother Earth bestows upon us in the colors of her seas and the sweep of her skies, you won't. You simply cannot.

I cruised from key to key in a kind of trance, tuning out the rape, pillage, and blight mankind has perpetrated on this fragile chain of islands, focusing instead on the natural, awe-inspiring beauty of the route. And I let my mind take me where it would. It had two destinations that brilliant October morning: the shooting star that had been my aunt Ginger, and one Will Maitland, who, if I let him, possessed the magnetism to drag me kicking and screaming out of my little cocoon and force me to confront my aloneness—not loneliness, mark you, which is a far different thing—which, as my friends, Scarlett and Blossom, pointed out at every possible opportunity, had become far too comfortable for my own good. The seduction of the familiar, if you like.

I suppose I grieved when Alex died, but in truth I hadn't loved him. I'd settled, which isn't necessarily a bad thing. Lots of people do and are perfectly happy. I can't say I was—content, yes, but not happy. One night about two years after Alex died, I had an epiphany over sushi on my third, and last, date with Steve Billingsgate: I wasn't going to settle ever again. It would be love or nothing. I bade Steve a fond farewell and hadn't dated since.

Since then, two simple commandments had proved remarkably successful in preventing me from simply caving and settling again when a particularly interesting, eligible, or attractive male hove into view.

One: Thou shalt protect thyself by immediately establishing emotional distance, kidding around and sending out signals that are decidedly sisterly rather than sexual.

Two: Thou shalt not allow thyself to make eye contact if or simply because thou feelest a tidal wave of animal lust sweeping over thee.

When I explained this strategy to Blossom once, she grabbed me by the shoulders and practically shook my teeth from my mouth. "You know where that gets you, you idiot? Alone, that's where. Just you and your vibrator spending a quiet evening at home together. For-*ev*-er!"

Too true, too true.

An imprudent or reckless woman might take one look at Will Maitland, throw caution to the wind, and catapult straight into daydreams of diamond rings and the happy pitter-patter of little feet. A wise woman would tiptoe ever so cautiously in the direction of his bed, hope he'd invite her to share it with him, and patiently await developments.

I pride myself on being neither imprudent nor reckless. I can be cautious when caution is called for. I can be patient.

The question was, could I give myself permission to inch in Will's direction? Would I?

Time would tell.

Blossom MacMorrough saved my life.

The roadmap of my day that first miserable week of my sophomore year ran a straight undeviating line between Tweetie Bird Lane and the front door of Coral Shores Public High School, where, invisible as a ghost, I trudged from class to class with no one to talk to; ate my lunch alone out on the grass near the fountain; and waited in the blistering sun for Grammie Jones to roll up in her beige Chrysler LeBaron to pick me up after school. I hated that car, hated everything and everyone. I hated my parents for dying and Grammie for trying so hard to make us feel welcome and safe when our lives had fallen apart. I hated the blond mafia of surfer guys and gals, the horrendous heat, palmetto bugs, my stupid clothes. My very existence.

And then Blossom MacMorrough roared into my life with her explosion of tawny hair and her gamine gap-toothed grin and fire-in-the-belly enthusiasm for everything that life has to offer, and I knew I had a friend for life. She was an Aunt Ginger in the making, no doubt about it.

We met in the Ladies' Lingerie section at JCPenney

in Islamorada. She was browsing 36C; I was in 34B. A short balding man was eyeing something in padded crimson lace in 38A.

"What do you think?" he said to me. "A bit much for a first date? Maybe I should go with the peach satin."

I couldn't think of a single word to say. But of course Blossom could.

"The red, definitely," she advised. "Go for it."

"Thank you, young lady," he said with a shy smile, and headed toward the fitting room.

"You go to Coral Shores," she told me. "Me too. I've seen you around. You spend too much time alone."

"I'm new," I admitted. "I don't know anybody."

"You do now. I'm Blossom."

And that's how I met Blossom MacMorrough, née Shannon Rose MacMorrough, and why, twelve years later, we were sitting on the tiny balcony of her tiny studio in a decidedly unfashionable corner of Key West eating yellowtail sandwiches from B.O.'s Fish Wagon and drinking iced tea and watching the sun set over the hordes of tourists who were trooping toward Mallory Square to watch the sun set over wall-to-wall yachts and cruise ships.

"Please, Blossom, I need you," I wheedled, having recounted the whole sorry tale from the morning Wickerby called through my trials in Jamaica to Virgil's blow-by-blow account of the morning's set-to in the garden of the St. Claire right up to the white kitten locked in the shop. "I can't do everything all by myself—find the damned box and Aunt Ginger's murderer and run the business and come up with a loophole in the will so I can sell. All I want to do is get back to my life," I whined.

"Hmmm."

"What do you mean, hmmm? I do," I insisted. "I just want to put all this craziness behind me and get back to my life."

Blossom slanted a glance at me. "Methinks the lady doth protest too much. What about your studly god? Do I hear the sound of self-imposed celibacy crashing and burning?"

"I am a 'person of interest' in Special Agent Maitland's case is all, not a 'woman of interest' in his life."

"You could be, Tilly. Just take off your damn widow's weeds and give yourself permission."

Rats. She had me there.

She closed her eyes, touched a finger to her temple, and intoned, "I see a tall dark stranger. I see hot sweaty sex. I see an orgasm."

"I've had orgasms," I protested.

She smirked at me. "I'm talking about the kind where the equipment is actually attached to a living person and you don't have to stock up on double-A batteries."

Got me again. I wasn't going to win this one, so I niftily steered the conversation toward my ultimate goal: Get Blossom up to South Beach to run Erratica.

"Seriously, Blossom. I loved Aunt Ginger. I don't give a tinker's damn about orgasms or codicils or the pillow box of Win Win Poo right now, but I do give a damn about the person who killed her, and if it's the last thing I ever do I'll find him. Whatever she was involved in, she . . ." I swallowed hard. "She didn't deserve to d-die like that."

Blossom scooted her chair closer to mine, took my hand, and let me cry it out.

"Let's take a walk," she suggested when the storm had passed. "What you need is a snowball."

We ambled through the darkening back streets of Key West, blessedly far removed from the gaudy excess of Duval Street and its herds of tourists, toward Roosevelt Boulevard and Tiki Beach Snowballs, purveyor of the shaved ice and cream concoction known, naturally, as snowballs. Blossom went for the Whiskey Sour. I dithered and eventually settled on Snorkleberry.

Comfortably ensconced on a wall on Garrison Bight, we slurped at our melting cones and watched the sport boats heading out to the reefs for night dives. The great thing about real friendship is the ease of shared silence, and it was a long time before Blossom spoke.

"Charlie would kill me if I asked for time off during Fantasy Fest week. We're already short a driver on the Conch Train."

I nodded. "Uh-huh."

"And there'd be the problem of subletting my place."

"True."

"I have this sort-of thing going with this guy who's really built."

"I see."

She was weakening. Time to close the deal.

"Did I mention that the shop's full of weird sex stuff?"

"Sold."

By ten the next morning, I was humming along. I'd edited and e-mailed my column to the syndicate office, checked with Virgil that nothing untoward had occurred at the St. Claire in the past twenty-four hours (it hadn't), and launched the assault on Codicils A and B of Aunt Ginger's last will and testament.

Arthur Kelso, scion of Michael Arthur Kelso; elder brother of Michael Arthur Kelso, II; and the second Kelso of Kelso, Kelso & Kelso, Attorneys at Law, School Street, Boston, was delighted to hear from me and how was I getting on and Alex's wife should always feel free to contact him with any inquiries of a legal nature, etc., etc., etc. Arthur had good reason to think fondly of Alex. He'd ceded the first putt to my husband on the sixth hole of Greenways Country Club that June afternoon three years before while he trotted off to a sand trap some fifty feet away in search of his own ball, thereby escaping instantaneous incineration at the hand of the Almighty.

After a goodly amount of throat-clearing and hemming and hawing about distinctions in estate law from one state to another, Arthur suggested I fax a copy of the will to him, and he'd have a look-see and get back to me. It might take a few days. He was glad to be of assistance and they all missed Alex and what a fine young man he'd been and God bless me and have a nice day.

"Have I got a proposition for *you!*" I announced as soon as Scarlett answered her cell phone. I could hear horns blaring in the background.

"You're on the Southeast Expressway, right?"

"How did you guess?" Scarlett admitted in that sad resigned way of South Shore commuters during morning rush hour. "Are you still in Miami? When are you coming back?"

"I've been in Key West with Blossom, but I'm in a

gas station in Marathon right now on my way back. So, do you have a moment?"

Scarlett sighed. "I'm sitting in a traffic jam just outside the South Station tunnel. I've probably got all morning. What's this proposition?"

"How would you like," I crooned in the smarmy tones of a huckster about to peddle a patch of prime swampland at the edge of the Everglades, "an *all-expenses-paid* vacation in beautiful *Mi-am-i Beach, Florida!?*"

Scarlett Cecilia Snow is a twenty-six-year-old carb addict with a cap of thick, ruler-straight brown hair and olive green eyes that peer out at the world from behind enormous glasses. She is your quintessential computer geek. She does things I couldn't possibly comprehend with computer software that put her firmly in the six-figure income bracket, and she certainly didn't need an all-expenses-paid vacation to Miami Beach or anywhere else.

I met Scarlett at the Back Bay YWCA in a self-defense class that sought to nurture the self-esteem of the timid, inept, and unfit. We were assigned to be partners and we snarled, screeched, bit, scratched, kicked, and kneed our way to a firm friendship. At the end of six weeks, we were still unfit, but considerably more courageous and almost ept.

"Hold on a sec, I think I can just squeeze into the left lane," Scarlett said. "Okay, what's going on? Hey, that guy just gave me the finger!"

"Look, this is a bad time—"

"No, it's as good a time as any; I've got a long day ahead of me. Are you in some kind of trouble, Tilly?"

"You could say that. I'm, um, trying to solve a murder. Would you be willing to come down and help me?"

"*A murder?* Who died?"

"Well, Aunt Ginger died, of course—"

"I know, sweetie," Scarlett said gently, "but she wasn't murdered. Er, was she?"

"Actually—"

I heard the sound of breaking glass, and someone going berserk, screaming obscenities.

"I have to go, Tilly. There's a man running around with a baseball bat in the breakdown lane."

"Will you come?"

"Yes!" she shouted through the din.

"Bring Baskerville!" I yelled. "His vaccination papers are in the kitchen drawer, and you'll have to—"

"Yikes! He just took out the rear window of a BMW and he's heading this way. Here come the cops. Gotta go, sweetie. Call you later." And she was gone.

A safe, sensible life in Boston? Who was I kidding?

Eleven

Everyone knows SUVs are heavier and ride higher than passenger cars, and are three times more likely to topple in a high wind or roll over in an accident. No person in her right mind will take a corner on two wheels in a Grand Cherokee.

Unless, of course, that person's grammie has disappeared from her nursing home in the company of a mysterious stranger. In which case, she might be forgiven not only for failing to exercise due caution, but even for doing so with only one hand on the wheel while yelling into a cell phone clutched in the other.

"You *what?* She *what? He did?* When? Where? Are you *insane?*"

By the time I hit the parking lot, tires squealing, I was loaded for bear and shaking from head to toe with fury and fear.

The receptionist took a prudent step back when I stormed up to the counter in the lobby. "I'm so very sorry, Ms. Snapp. But he seemed like such a nice young man," she stammered, "and your grandmother was just giggling and chattering away when they went out, and he said he was your fiancé, so I thought—"

"Call 911," I ordered. "No, wait. Where's Lucille?"

"She's on vacation. Hiking in Nepal. She'll be back in a few weeks."

"Who's in charge, then?" I snapped.

"Consuela?"

"Get her."

The girl scurried away. I spent the next few minutes pacing circles around the lobby, too angry, too terrified to cry. I had researched this place thoroughly when it became evident Grammie could no longer manage on her own on Tweetie Bird Lane. They knew better than to release her into the custody of anyone whose name did not appear on the list of permitted visitors, who were required to show identification, sign in, indicate time of departure and expected return, and destination.

The register! I grabbed it off the counter and flipped through the pages to today's date. There it was, the second-to-last entry.

Resident: Marilyn Jones. Visitor . . .

Special Agent Will Maitland was toast.

"Tilly dear, did you know *Key Largo* wasn't filmed here in Key Largo at all?" Grammie Jones chirped as I stalked up to the orange plastic booth by the front window of McDonald's. "Isn't that amazing? William says it was all done in Hollywood."

I slid in beside her and sent "William" my blackest look.

"I know, Grammie."

"And," she continued, flourishing a cold fry, "Key Largo wasn't even Key Largo! It was some other name, and the town stole it."

"I know, Grammie," I said, glaring at Will Maitland. I nearly vaulted across the table when he cocked one despicable brow.

Grammie reached for a paper napkin and patted her lips. "Watch this, William. Lauren Bacall." She angled her head and gave him a coy look. " 'You know how to whistle, don't you, Steve? You just put your lips together—and blow.' "

He laughed. "Very good. Not everyone can do Bacall."

Grammie giggled and preened. "Now you do Bogie, William."

"I'm afraid I'm not very good at impersonations, Mrs. Jones," he said.

"Oh, I wouldn't say that," I interjected silkily. "Last time I checked, I didn't have a *fiancé.* Tell me, *dear,* how did you know where to find me?"

"I say it's about time you got married again, young lady," Grammie said as she began shoveling dozens of sugar packets into her bag.

Will grinned. "Missy Mae was kind enough to suggest you might be visiting your grandmother. I called ahead, and lo and behold discovered you were expected. Whither thou goest I will go, *my love.*"

Better watch out, I cautioned myself. A playful Special Agent Will Maitland was making an appearance, and he was too adorable by half.

"Glory be!" Grammie exclaimed. "A man who knows his Bible! Ruth 1:16. 'And Ruth said, Entreat me not to leave thee: for whither thou goest, I will go; and where thou lodgest, I will lodge; thy people shall be my people, and thy God my god. Where thou diest—' "

"Oops, nature calls," I said, and fled to the ladies' room, leaving Will Maitland to suffer through the interminable recitation of Ruth's adventures gleaning in the Field of Boaz, as he so richly deserved. By the time I emerged a few minutes later, he was wearing the fixed smile of a truly desperate man, which I have to admit afforded me no little pleasure.

I also have to admit that the extraordinary tableau—my studly god and my winsome, wrinkled grammie smiling at one another across a table strewn with the remains of two Happy Meals in the neon-lit orange plastic wasteland of McDonald's—sent a little ripple of warmth straight to my heart.

Uh-uh, Tilly, I told myself. Don't even start.

"I'll take her home," I said to him gruffly as we guided Grammie out of the restaurant. "It's too hot to do the African Queen today."

"I'll meet you there. We need to talk."

We stepped out of the stale, overchilled air into searing heat and helped Grammie toward my car.

"I can never decide who I like better, Oprah or Dr. Phil," she was telling us. "Judge Judy's pretty good too."

I was only half listening when I saw him. It wasn't so much the man himself that caught my attention as the T-shirt he wore: a tie-dyed number in the national colors of Jamaica—green, black, and gold. Along with the Rasta tie-dyed shirts of red, gold, and green, you saw these tops everywhere in south Florida and the Caribbean, but this one bore the logo of the Jamaican national bird, the "doctor bird," known more commonly as a hummingbird. I'd seen that bird on a T-shirt on the corner of Duval and Fleming in Key West a few hours ago.

Will touched my arm. "What?"

"Nothing," I muttered. "Let's get Grammie into the car, or she's going to die of heatstroke."

While he lifted her up into the seat and fastened the seat belt, I cranked up the air-conditioning to arctic.

Will came round to the driver's-side door. "Get out," he said in a low voice.

"I most certainly will not. Just because you're some hotshot secret agent doesn't mean you can order me around."

"Get out, Tilly. Now."

His arms came around me the moment my feet touched the pavement.

"Hey! What do you think you're doing?"

"I'm going to kiss you; try to look like you're enjoying it."

"I'm going to do no such—"

"Shut up, Tilly, and just do it."

Now, I imagine you'd agree that a woman wants a little romance with her kisses—a gentle touch, a few soft words. And I'm pretty sure you'd agree that "Shut up, Tilly, and just do it" does not meet the minimum quality standards for such a moment.

The woman who would give a tinker's damn about minimum quality standards when a studly god takes her mouth in a kiss that blows every circuit between her mouth and her knees would be a blithering idiot.

"Who is he?" he said into my hair after he gently eased his lips from mine.

"Huh?"

"The guy by the Subaru."

"Guy?" I managed as feeling started to return to my tongue.

"Snap out of it, Tilly. The guy standing by the blue Subaru. You recognized him."

So much for the magic of the moment. "I'm not sure," I mumbled into his chest. "I think he's the one who tried to grab my tote at the airport in Montego Bay. And I saw a man in Key West this morning; he had his back to me, but I'm pretty sure he was wearing the same T-shirt because I bought three of them for my brothers when I was in Jamaica."

Will cradled my face in his hands. "This is what you're going to do, Tilly. Get in the car—don't look at him—and drive your grandmother straight home; don't stop anywhere along the way. Take her inside and don't set a foot outside until I come to get you. You understand?"

I nodded. "Do you think he's the one who—?"

"Just do what I say, Tilly."

"Okay. Er, maybe you should kiss me again, like you're kissing me goodbye?"

"Good idea."

Grammie dozed off just after the second angel poured his golden vial of God's wrath upon the waters of the sea. I marked her place in the Book of Revelations, tucked the blue-and-yellow afghan around her, and tiptoed away. I spent the next anxious hour in the "visitors' parlor" just off the lobby, thumbing through old issues of *Modern Maturity* and *Florida Senior.* I decided to shoot myself the day the AARP tracked me down when I turned fifty-five.

I had the grace and good sense to apologize profusely to the receptionist for my earlier behavior. I opted for the PMS defense. PMS will excuse just about any bad behavior, right up through manslaughter; it is exceeded in firepower only by the Twinkie Defense and rarely fails to acquit.

Apparently I was forgiven, because the girl brought me a glass of iced tea, a plate with three graham cracker squares on it, and a cheery little pamphlet that advised me to "Repent or Die." I expect she thought I needed reminding. I read it from cover to cover, and decided I'd rather go to hell than spend eternity sitting on a cloud with nothing much to do.

I crunched the last ice cube in the glass, sucked what juice remained in the soggy slice of lemon, and wandered to the window to peer out through the lacy curtains for the umpteenth time. It was going on two hours now, and I was beginning to think I'd been stood up. When my cell phone rang, I sprinted across the room and barked, "Where the hell have you been?"

"And hello and how's-your-day-going to you too," Blossom said.

"Great, my day's going great. What do you want?"

"You're barking, sweetie."

"Sorry, Blossom, I'm not myself."

"Who is? Let's hear it."

Blossom MacMorrough possesses that rare ability to winnow the wheat from the chaff; discover order where others see only chaos; zero in on the heart of the matter.

"Did you have an orgasm?"

I blinked. "Orgasm?"

"He used his tongue, right? That can do it under the right circumstances."

"'Right circumstances'? 'Right circumstances'?" I

stomped around the parlor waving my arm in the air. "For God's sake, Blossom, the man practically kidnaps my grandmother. Some maniac is stalking me from Montego Bay to Miami Beach to Key West to Key Largo. I've got federal agents standing in line waiting to serve me with warrants. I've been threatened with arrest for obstruction of justice. I've got a hotel I can't sell; I've got tenants I can't evict; I've got cats coming out of the woodwork. I'm standing in a McDonald's parking lot in ninety-five-degree heat kissing a man who's trying to nail me—for smuggling, that is—with my aunt Ginger's killer thirty feet away, and you want to know if I had an *orgasm?*"

"Well?"

"No," I muttered.

"Early days yet, sweetie, early days."

Will Maitland did stand me up. I gave him another half hour, and when he didn't show I stalked out to my car, turned the reggae station out of Coral Gables to top volume, and headed back to South Beach.

"Iiiiii shot the sheriff, but I didn't shoot no dep-u-ty, oh no! oh!" I caroled. "Iiiiii shot the sheriff, but I swear it was in self-defense, oh! oh! oh!"

"Where the hell are you," the sheriff I had in mind demanded when I finally heard my cell phone ringing.

"I just passed Homestead."

"Will you turn down the damn radio? Better. I thought I told you to stay put."

"If I'd stayed put until you showed up," I snarled, "I'd have been seventy and ready to check myself into the nursing home."

"I'm sorry about that," he said. "I should have called sooner. He followed you back to the home. I followed him. He waited for ten minutes, and when you didn't come out, he took off. I'm still with him. I put a trace on the car; it's a rental out of Orlando to a Joseph Alvarez. Ring any bells?"

"Nope. No bells."

"I want you to get in touch with me if you remember anything else about him."

"Don't sit by the phone," I snapped. "I am not in charity with you at the moment."

"I can tell."

"I just have two questions for you. One, is my grandmother in any danger? It's not like an eighty-four-year-old woman's got the pillow box of Win Win Poo stashed under the bed."

"No. He was following you; you happened to stop by to visit her. Next question?"

Only lunatics and sociopaths who plan on taking a whole lot of other people with them when they go, use their cell phones at sixty miles an hour. I signaled for an exit and pulled over.

"Do you still think I'm involved in the theft of the pillow box?"

He didn't say anything for a moment. "I'm afraid I can't share that information with you."

My teeth were clenched so tight I halfway expected the words to pop out of my ears. "So you do?"

I could almost hear his shrug bouncing off a telecommunications satellite up there in the ionosphere and beaming straight down into my ear. "You remain a person of interest in an ongoing investigation."

"A suspect."

"I didn't say you're a suspect. I said you're a person of interest, Tilly."

I wonder if I would have caved right then and there

if he'd said something more along the lines of "person of interest, Tilly, *to me.*" He didn't of course, and the "Tilly" might or might not have been included to indicate interest of a more personal nature.

Get hold of yourself, girl, I told myself. You're grasping at straws.

"You cop, me person of interest," I said à la Tarzan.

"You don't do a very good Johnny Weissmuller."

"But you do a very convincing cop, Special Agent Maitland."

"Thank you, Ms. Snapp. And you do a very credible person of interest."

See, here's the problem with cell phones. When a conversation has gone downhill to the point that you are bereft of words, you cannot enjoy the emotional release to be found in slamming down the receiver to signal that rational discourse is no longer an option. Thumbing the "off" button simply cannot compare. You therefore have to make do with your best parting shot and hope it hits home.

"Bureaucrat!"

I swear he was laughing as I hit the "off" button.

TWELVE

You think of three kick-ass gals on a mission, you think *Charlie's Angels.* You think Drew Barrymore, Cameron Diaz, Lucy Liu in the film of 2000; or maybe Farrah Fawcett, Kate Jackson, and Jaclyn Smith from the 1970s television show. Beauteous, brainy, bodacious babes gettin' down, gettin' it on; gettin' their man.

No one is ever going to mistake me for Drew Barrymore. Blossom is no Cameron Diaz, but she might be Farrah Fawcett—they both have a lot of hair. If you took away Scarlett's glasses, she and Kate Jackson could pass for cousins twice removed, but then she wouldn't be able to see ten feet in front of her face and wouldn't be much help when the time came to take down our man.

Call us babes at your peril. I suggest you don't. But you could call us angels too.

Ginger's Angels.

Late Friday night, I folded my hands on the beechwood Art Nouveau desk in Aunt Ginger's office and cleared my throat. "Your mission, should you choose to accept it—"

"That's from *Mission: Impossible*," Blossom observed.

"Whatever. As I see it we have three sub-missions we must address before we can embark on the big one, which is—"

"Apprehend the person or persons who carried out, or caused to be carried out, the assassination of your aunt Ginger, and bring him, her, or them to justice."

"Well put, Scarlett."

"How about, 'Get the bastard and hang him on a lamppost by his teeny-weeny wienie,' " Blossom offered.

I nodded. "That's good too."

I waited for other suggestions from the troops, but most of them were asleep or tending to some portion of their anatomy. There were twelve feline residents of the Hotel St. Claire at last count, eight of them kittens, and I was starting to think I might be living in a Stephen King novel.

"Mission One," I said. "Reopen Erratica. That's your assignment, Blossom. Take it away."

Apparently Blossom had given it a good deal of thought on the drive up from Key West. We had to establish credibility as worthy and competent successors to Aunt Ginger, she said, or at the very least put on a good show. Most of the daily business would be tourists on the hunt for South Beach eccentricity and most of the sales impulse buys. We'd need a cheat sheet behind the counter until we could familiarize ourselves with the stock. We should do some reorganizing, display the kinky stuff all together to make it easier to identify customers who dropped in specifically looking for that kind of merchandise. We needed high visibility to lure the weirdos into the shop. Blossom had a friend whose cousin might be persuaded to do an article for the *Miami Herald* if given the right incentive, say a pair of tickets to a Dolphins playoff game: "Tragic death of eccentric but beloved South Beach resident, niece to carry on in her footsteps," and so on.

Mission Two: Aunt Ginger's computer files. Scarlett said she'd be able to deal with password protection, but if Aunt Ginger had installed sophisticated firewall protection and antispyware programs it might take days before she could hack into whatever business Aunt Ginger might have preferred to keep to herself. Meanwhile she'd be looking at recent sales and purchase orders, supplier and customer databases, and e-mail correspondence. She would also maintain the Erratica.com Web site and surf the Internet auction houses to monitor cyberchat.

I had a sudden thought. "Scarlett, can you access her bank records? Maybe she had a safe deposit box somewhere. Oh, and she traveled back and forth to Jamaica a lot, so we need to find out what she was up to there. Other than nude parasailing," I added.

Blossom perked right up. "She was nude? That is so cool."

By two a.m., Scarlett was in the full throes of carbohydrate withdrawal. We trooped upstairs to Aunt Ginger's kitchen, where I'd laid in a supply of Ben & Jerry's for just such an emergency.

"Mission Three," I continued when Scarlett had regained some metabolic equilibrium and set her pancreas pumping out enough insulin to handle a pint of Cherry Garcia.

"Find the pillow box of Win Win Poo. We'll start

right here at the St. Claire, although I seriously doubt it's on the premises. It may be in Timbuktu for all we know, but we have to start somewhere. We'll draft Alonzo, Virgil, and Missy Mae to help, but I don't want them to know Aunt Ginger was murdered—only that a valuable antique is missing."

"What are you going to do about the FBI? How are you going to keep them out?" Blossom wanted to know. "Eventually they're going to get a warrant that will stick. Your lawyer isn't going to be able to stonewall them forever."

"I honestly don't know," I admitted.

"I do." Scarlett said. "We keep them out by letting them in.

"We're pretty sure the box isn't here," she continued, "but we'll institute a thorough search just to be sure. Then we invite them in and give them the run of the place. They won't find anything either. We can even suggest they take Ginger's computer to assist them in their investigation."

Scarlett sat back and grinned.

I waited a beat. "We give them Aunt Ginger's computer. And we do this because . . . ?" I held out my hands palms up, inviting edification.

"No, Tilly, we give them *a* computer."

I frowned. "We give them a . . . Scarlett, you're a genius!"

"Shucks, ain't nothin'."

"I don't get it," Blossom said.

"We buy a computer just like the one in the office—she's got a Mac G5," Scarlett explained patiently. "We copy everything from Ginger's hard drive onto the new computer. Then we edit the files or purge the ones we don't want them to know about on the one we hand over. They'll figure out they've been had eventually, but for the time being we're upstanding citizens, eager to cooperate with federal officers in the performance of their duty."

"What about you, Tilly?" Blossom asked.

I tossed the empty ice cream tubs into the trash, gathered up dishes and spoons, and plucked a black kitten out of the sink so I could wash up. "I guess I'm command central. I've got the legal stuff to deal with too, and I want to find Harry Hungwell. He didn't show up for the reading of the will, which worries me. I think he spends a lot of time in LA; I hope I don't have to go out there to track him down. And I'm going to do some research on pillow boxes. All I know is what Will Maitland told me. I'm thinking I might try to trace the Win Win Poo box from the time it was stolen in Singapore."

"How come you get to have all the fun?" Blossom pouted.

"Huh?"

"While you're out there hunting down porn stars and playing with sex toys and kissing gorgeous secret agents, we're stuck back here holding the fort."

"Someone has to investigate," Scarlett reminded her.

Blossom hooted. "I love this!" She leaped to her feet and spread her arms wide. "*La*-dies and gentlemen, boys and girls, we give you—big drum roll—Tilly Snapp, Sex Detective!"

Thirteen

Long after Blossom and Scarlett dragged themselves off to bed, I lay sleepless in Aunt Ginger's big bed staring up at the vintage paddle fan, nearly mesmerized by the lazy revolution of the blades and the soft hum of the motor. For once I wasn't covered by a quilt of cats; I'd left them in full possession of the couch and dragged a limp, chastened Baskerville into Aunt Ginger's room to forestall an all-out turf war.

"Don't think of it as defeat," I consoled him. "Think of it more in terms of a strategic retreat. Look on the bright side. We've got this huge bed for just the two of us, and the toilet's just a few feet away if you need a drink."

Baskerville had not taken well to his first experience flying the friendly skies. Scarlett had had to dose him twice with the vet's sedative: first to get him into the pet carrier and again at the United check-in counter when his plaintive howls of discontent brought a phalanx of security guards on the run with weapons drawn. If I'd expected a drooling ecstatic reunion when I unlatched the carrier door, I was in for a disappointment. Baskerville staggered out, eyed me reproachfully for a long moment, and rolled over with his four paws in the air. He'd been semicomatose ever since.

Baskerville is a fearsome sight—mostly Rottweiler, some Doberman, the rest generic; he's big, black, and sharp of tooth and claw. He is also one hundred percent wuss. He fainted dead away once when he craned his neck around and saw his own shadow nipping at his heels. I swear.

I met Baskerville at the SPCA shelter in Boston; he was an abused, abandoned stray. He smiled at me through the bars of his cage, hope evident in his big brown eyes, and I was his for life. It's fortunate I wasn't in the market for a guard dog. Baskerville's idea of protecting me is to launch himself at everyone, irrespective of age, size, gender, race, creed, or party affiliation, yapping and yipping and slobbering with joyful abandon. A friend bearing doggie treats or an axe murderer, it's all the same to him.

I toyed with one droopy velvet ear and was rewarded with a wet nose nuzzling my palm. "Thanks for coming down, big fella. It means a lot to me. We need a fierce guard dog like you to keep the bad guys away.

"I promise it won't be all work and no play," I went on to assure him. "There's a great beach and the boardwalk—we'll take our chances on getting a ticket from the doggie police—and we'll find some dog-friendly parks. The dog watching is super; just wait 'til you get a load of the locals."

Baskerville isn't much of a talker, but he's a great listener. I was feeling just mellow enough, what with the hypnotic whir of the fan, the scent of night-blooming jasmine drifting up through the open French doors, and the luxury of real goosedown pillows and silky Egyptian cotton sheets to let go some of the tension of the past two weeks and share a few girlish confidences with him.

I set the scene with a few deft strokes, then came straight to the point. "The thing is, he didn't have to kiss me the first time around; he could have just leaned in close and whispered, and the Subaru guy wouldn't have been able to hear us. But he did kiss me. And he didn't have to kiss me the second time either just because I suggested it. He could have said it wasn't necessary. But he didn't say it was unnecessary."

I paused to give Baskerville an opportunity to comment.

"It's not as though he couldn't keep his tongue in his own mouth if he wanted to," I pointed out, wondering where I was going with this. "And he didn't have to plaster me up against him like that so I could feel his . . ." I caught myself just in time; poor old Baskerville didn't need to be reminded of his own limitations in that regard.

"I'm reading more into this than there is, aren't I?" I said glumly. "James Bond does that sort of thing all the time. He's kissing the girl, but all the while he's checking out the scene, looking for the bad guys or some way to escape the peril they're in.

"I bet they teach them to do that in Interpol school," I grouched. " 'Take the person of interest in the ongoing investigation in your arms. Your objective is to bring her to the brink of orgasm but no further; the tongue is especially recommended for the purpose. You may signal your own presumed arousal in the usual way, but only if absolutely necessary, as it may impede mobility in the event of sudden attack or the need to initiate a pursuit. Agent Maitland, perhaps you'd like to demonstrate for the class.' "

Let it go, I counseled myself. You'll never know what he had in mind; hell, you don't know what's going on in your own head most of the time. He kissed you; you kissed him back. You kissed him; he kissed you back. Move on.

Heeding this excellent advice, I slipped out of bed and padded over to the French doors. Baskerville joined me, and we stood for some minutes in companionable silence looking out at the night. When we got bored with that, we decided to go for a walk and catch the sunrise.

Baskerville must have smelled the man before we even turned the corner onto Española Way. Claws scrabbled over pavement as he dragged me toward the shadowed doorway of Erratica, where I could just make out a darker shadow and the ruby glow of a burning cigarette. Digging in my heels, I managed to haul him in before he became airborne and took me with him.

It must have been a full minute before I realized the screeching alarm was coming from inside my head, not from inside the shop. That roar was blood rampaging through veins and arteries; the thunder, my heart crashing against my rib cage. The yipping and yapping, Baskerville. At least I think it was Baskerville.

Here you had your classic fight-or-flight scenario. I figured I could probably make it back into the hotel if I didn't have to outrun a speeding bullet and

Baskerville cooperated. I wasn't entirely defenseless if it came to a fight—again assuming firearms would not be brought into play. The peppershot was already in my hand and Baskerville was on the launch pad.

In the end, common sense gave way to curiosity, and I heard myself say in my best B-movie mode, "Show yourself or my dog will rip out your throat."

The burning cigarette arced out of the doorway into the gutter and the lurker stepped forward. I recognized him at once as the snarky little man at Montego Bay Airport who tried to steal my tote, the hummingbird-T-shirt-wearer in Key West, and the Subaru guy at McDonald's: the man Will had pegged as Joseph Alvarez.

"Please, there is no need. I am only window-shopping."

"Window-shopping," I said. "At five o'clock in the morning."

He shrugged. "I am an early riser, like yourself. You are the owner? You appear to carry some very interesting merchandise. Some very old, very valuable, no?"

Evidently he didn't realize I recognized him. He was trying out friendly-chatty-ordinary-guy to see if I was buying it. I wasn't, and frankly, something about his eyes—hard and assessing, in a curiously soft, almost babyish face—was making me very nervous.

He pulled a pack of Marlboros out of his shirt pocket and held it out. "Cigarette? No? It is a bad habit, I know. I have tried to give it up, but you know how it is."

He stepped towards me and offered his hand. "My name is Jose. Perhaps you would care to join me for a cup of coffee?"

I'll never know why Baskerville chose that moment to introduce himself to our new acquaintance, but as he leaped up and planted his big paws on the man's chest, the sudden tension on the leash jerked my feet right out from under me. A second later the guy came crashing down on top of me, followed by Baskerville, who saw no reason not to join in the fun.

What happened next is pretty fuzzy—they say that's not unusual with a concussion, even a very mild one—but I do vaguely remember seeing Richie lumbering down the street toward us, and the guy kicking out at Baskerville and Baskerville yelping in pain, and then I'm on my knees planting my fist in his crotch—the guy's crotch, not Baskerville's—and he's screaming, and then a car screeches to a stop and a woman leaps out with a stun gun in her hand, and the next thing I know a nurse is asking me what day it is and who's president of the United States.

FOURTEEN

"He didn't attack me," I explained for the tenth time. "Baskerville lunged, I fell, the guy fell, Baskerville pounced."

"You don't know that," Blossom pointed out. "Maybe Baskerville picked up on this guy's bad vibes and sprang to your defense."

Whatever Baskerville's intentions had been, I would treasure to my dying day my brief glimpse of the unspeakable horror on that man's face as Baskerville hurtled toward him. I might even go so far as to forgive a guy for trying to defend himself against the onslaught of a slavering beast, except for the fact that the slavering beast in question was *my* slavering beast, which is why Joseph Alvarez was going to be waddling around like a duck for a few days, having felt the full measure of my wrath in the form of a quick jab to the balls.

"He come around here again, chica, me'n Virgil take care of him," Alonzo promised as he snagged the last piece of pepperoni pizza and went back to supervising the delivery of chairs and tables he'd rented for Aunt Ginger's memorial service the next day.

Alonzo Campos grew up in the slums of Havana and arrived on our shores in the 1980 Mariel boatlift, Fidel Castro's magnanimous gift to the people of the United States of every psychopath, criminal, lowlife, and troublemaker, among the last group, Alonzo Campos. Joseph Alvarez probably thought of himself as a pretty tough customer, but if poor old Baskerville could put the fear of God into him, heaven only knows how he'd react if he ran across Alonzo in a dark alley.

I reached for the coffee carafe. Scarlett slapped my hand away. "No coffee. The doctor said to lay off the caffeine for a few days. That includes soda," she added as I made a grab for the Coke. She sorted through the small pile of tea bags she'd brought out to the garden. "Here, try the decaf Thai Spice."

"I don't want decaf Thai Spice," I whined. "I want caffeine."

I make a lousy invalid and an even lousier patient, as the doctors in the emergency room at the South Shore Medical Center now had reason to know. They were still stonewalling to keep me from signing myself out against medical advice when Scarlett, Blossom, and Alonzo finally swept into the emergency room a little after nine. I wanted to sign myself out because I was in a panic about Baskerville. Was he running loose in the streets of South Beach? Had he been dognapped? Had Joseph Alvarez stomped him to death? I hadn't exactly blacked out in the woman's car—it was more of a brownout—but Baskerville cannot be ignored in a confined space and I would have known if he were there. He wasn't, so where was he?

As it turned out, he was tied to the railing by the

van Gogh self-portrait and howling like the, well, hound of the Baskervilles. When Blossom shot out of bed and rushed to the window, she'd seen Richie staggering away clutching his shoulder and Joseph Alvarez curled up on the ground in agony clutching his crotch, but I was nowhere in sight.

The doctors didn't want me walking out of the hospital and dropping dead in the parking lot, not on their watch. The woman who had dropped me off stayed only long enough to make sure I'd be seen to; she told the receptionist she had a plane to catch.

"I wish I knew who she was," I said. "I never even got to thank her. She didn't leave her name at the hospital."

Missy Mae scraped up a blob of congealed mozzarella from the bottom of the pizza box. "Not gonna find her no matter how hard you look," she said.

"Why do you say that? I could put an ad in the paper; maybe she'd see it when she came back from her trip."

"No need," Missy Mae said, " 'cause I already know who she is."

"You do? Who?"

"Ginger, of course."

I looked at Scarlett; Scarlett looked at Blossom; Blossom looked at me; we all stared at Missy Mae.

"You think I'm crazy, but you got a guardian angel up there in heaven now, Tilly. Ginger's your guardian angel, and she sees you're in trouble and she come flying down and zap that Alvarez fellow and poor old Richie, who was probably just trying to help, and take you to the hospital and then fly right back up to heaven again."

"I don't know, Missy Mae," I said. "Angels armed with stun guns? I can't see it."

"I don't know why not. A woman got to protect herself, don't she?"

"In heaven?"

A loud crash brought Missy Mae to her feet. A dolly stacked five feet high with chairs had collided with a huge ceramic urn overflowing with crimson bougainvillea and golden creeping Jenny. She bore down on the offender, shouting, "You there, you broke that planter, you gonna wish your mama drowned you at birth!"

Aspirin wasn't making a dent on the headache I wouldn't admit to having. I was going to have to relent and take the Tylenol with codeine the doctors had given me. "I guess I could use some sleep," I said. I stood up, clutched the edge of the table, and plopped back down with a grunt. "No, don't worry. Just a little dizzy is all," I assured everyone, waving them off. "Okay, here I go."

I did go, but with Blossom on one side, Scarlett on the other, and Virgil bringing up the rear in case we all went crashing backwards down the stairs. Almost before I knew it, I'd been tucked up in Aunt Ginger's bed, dosed with codeine, and soundly scolded for being a jerk.

"It's a bump on the head," I grouched. "I bet Joseph Alvarez is in a lot worse shape than I am. Go fuss over him."

Scarlett took off her glasses. When Scarlett takes off her glasses and pinches the bridge of her cute little nose, you know she's about to get serious.

"Tilly, you're not going to get away with making a joke out of this. I expect you're right, Alvarez didn't know you recognized him, and probably thought he could make nice and pump you for information. He could just be another agent or private investigator, but—"

"Or," Blossom interrupted, "he could be a hit man."

"True," Scarlett allowed, "but whoever he is, this is serious business, Tilly, and I think it's time we took steps to ensure your safety."

I held up a hand. "Before you go on, I have something to say. I've been thinking—"

Blossom rolled her eyes. "Not good."

"Now who's not being serious?" I snapped. "Listen, you two, I can't tell you how grateful I am that you were willing to just pick up and come to Miami to help me out, but I realize now I was overreacting. I didn't think it through. Once we get the shop open and running again, I can manage things on my own, and I don't want to . . ."

Put you in danger too.

". . . take advantage of your friendship. If it turns out I really am in danger, I'm sure the police would . . ."

Take me into protective custody.

". . . keep an eye out for me. I'm only a 'person of interest' to Interpol, a means to an end. They'll probably only . . ."

End up arresting me as a material witness in a double homicide.

". . . hassle me until they finally realize I don't know anything. The same goes for . . ."

The maniac who killed Aunt Ginger.

". . . Alvarez and his ilk. So you see, there's absolutely no need for you to worry about me. I want you to get back to your own lives as soon as possible."

Scarlett put her glasses back on. "I'll get my phone," she told Blossom.

"Don't bother; I'm already on it," Blossom replied, whipping her cell phone from her back pocket.

I made a grab for the phone. "Hey, what are you doing?"

"Calling the police."

"What? Why?"

"Obviously you've lost your mind," Scarlett said. "You need to be placed in protective custody."

"That, or we could let Will Maitland haul you off to jail as a material witness," Blossom suggested. "You should be safe enough there."

I fell back against the pillows and glared at them. "What, you're mind readers now?"

Blossom flicked the phone shut and patted my hand. "We're your friends, sweetie, and we're not going anywhere. Now be a good girl and go to sleep."

I did, or rather the codeine did it for me, and I woke up with sunlight slanting across the bed and Baskerville breathing doggie breath in my face. I vaguely remembered crawling out of bed with a bladder full to bursting and staggering into the bathroom in the peachy glow of a nightlight, but otherwise Miami Beach could have been under attack by creatures from outer space during the past fifteen hours and I wouldn't have known a thing about it.

If I wake up dead and find there's no hot water in the showers, I'll know I'm in hell. That goes for caffeine as well. Fortunately, Aunt Ginger was prepared for such an emergency. Her apartment had hot water and strong coffee in spades. Forty-five minutes later I was sitting on the little balcony that looked out over the garden, all squeaky-clean with my hair piled in a careless topknot, comfortable in a loose light blue cotton sundress, savoring my first sip of extra dark organic French roast.

The garden was a jumble of folding metal chairs and tables, coolers, boxes of plastic glasses and tableware, cases of beer, soda, and snacks. What better way to memorialize Aunt Ginger than to throw a party? If Missy Mae had it right, she'd be flying down from heaven with her trusty stun gun to join in the festivities.

I doubted the little catch at my heart when I thought about her would ever go away entirely. As I was growing up, Aunt Ginger would blow into my life three or four times a year like some contrary Mary Poppins. "Just checking in," she'd say, and sail away again on the east wind. She always arrived bearing wonderful gifts: a fan of fragrant sandalwood intricately carved with mythical beasts, a Chinese doll made of porcelain so delicate you could almost see through it, a child-size kimono of yellow silk, a white marble pebble from the gardens of the Taj Mahal.

You never knew when Aunt Ginger would arrive, but after a few days or a week she'd get this wistful look in her eyes and then you'd know she was about to go, needed to go. She'd hug us tightly and tell us she loved us and then she'd be gone. And I'd be sad for a while, and maybe a little angry that she didn't want to stay with us, that there was something more important that she needed out there in the world.

"Don't let Scarlett catch you drinking coffee," Blossom advised as she dropped down beside me. "Feeling better?"

"Much. I still have the lump, and my wrist hurts, but the headache's pretty much gone. Where is she, by the way?"

"She's working on Ginger's computer. We went out last night and bought another Mac G5. Ginger probably had a laptop too, but we couldn't find it."

"It wasn't with her stuff at Sin and Sand. Maybe it was stolen when she was . . ." It always hurt to say "murdered."

"There's nothing we can do about it now," Blossom said briskly. "We'll work with what we have. Hungry?"

I was, so we collected Scarlett and walked over to the Eleventh Street Diner and sat out on the shaded patio and ate a mountain of their great Waldorf salad and drank iced tea—decaf for me, under Scarlett's watchful eye. By the time we got back, Alonzo, Virgil, and Missy Mae were setting up in the garden. Scarlett went back to the computers, and Blossom and I pitched in to help. By four we were pretty much done. Virgil went off in the SUV to get ice and pick up the flowers; Alonzo fussed with the sound system he'd rigged up; and Missy Mae retired to her room to rest and get gussied up, as she put it.

I never quite got the story straight of how Missy Mae came to be living in the St. Claire. Apparently she ran a scam of some sort for years, rolling around Miami Beach in a wheelchair she didn't need. She liked to wheel herself over to the St. Claire and pose in front of the panel featuring Whistler's mother; apparently tourists were willing to pay $10 a pop to photograph the odd tableau. Aunt Ginger would bring her iced tea in the heat of the day, and one morning Missy Mae wheeled herself over and never wheeled herself away.

"How many are we expecting?" Blossom asked.

"I haven't any idea," I said as I adjusted the drape

of the beautiful batik sarongs I'd appropriated from Ginger's closet to cover the "altar" table. I had flatly vetoed Virgil's idea of putting the urn there in pride of place, opting instead for a display of the "Ginger Botticelli" and framed pictures of her from babyhood to the last digital shot of Aunt Ginger clowning for the camera on the beach at Negril. And flowers of course. Bold brilliant flowers, not the lugubrious spikes of gladioli, snapdragons, and saccharine lilies people heap around their dead.

"I hope it's not more than a hundred, or we'll have to take over the street," I said

"Hey, check out the talent!" Blossom whispered. By "talent" Blossom usually meant a particularly notable specimen of the male gender.

"Ms. Snapp, I'd like a word with you."

I knew that voice. I looked over to see Will looming on the other side of the garden fence. I think I actually groaned.

"Is that *him?*" Scarlett inquired.

"Of course it is," Blossom answered for me. "My God, Tilly, you actually kissed that beautiful man and didn't have even one orgasm?"

Will Maitland crooked a finger at me. I couldn't believe it: The man actually crooked a finger at me. I resisted the urge to return the gesture with a finger of my own.

"What do you want? It's Sunday. Don't you ever take a day off from harassing people? Watch a little football, do your laundry, call your mom?"

"We need to talk. Now."

I stalked across the street to Zephyr Café without so much as a glance in Will's direction, and plopped down at the same table we'd sat at before. I didn't wait for him to hold my chair for me this time, and he didn't try. Neither of us was in the mood to observe the social niceties.

"Coke," I told the waitress. He opted for Dos Equis again.

He came right to the point. "Tell me about last night."

"Is this on the front page of the *Herald*?" I asked no one in particular.

"Hold the wisecracks, Tilly. This is serious. Tell me everything that happened, everything."

"Nothing happened! Well, something happened, but it's not such a big deal as everyone's making it out to be.

"I took Baskerville for a walk," I recited. "We—"

"At five o'clock in the morning?"

"Yes. We thought we'd enjoy the sunrise. I saw someone standing in the doorway of Erratica smoking a cigarette. I asked him what he was doing there. He said window-shopping. He offered me a cigarette, a Marlboro. I said no. He told me his name was Jose. He asked me if I'd like to go for coffee and—"

"Was he the same guy?" Will interrupted. "Jamaica, Key West, McDonald's?"

I nodded.

"Did he threaten you?"

"No, he didn't threaten me. It was obvious he didn't know I recognized him."

The catering truck pulled up across the street. "Can we finish this up? I can't believe I'm sitting here explaining what happened for the umpteenth time, and I have to get ready for the memorial service."

"Keep talking."

I took up where I'd left off. "As I was saying, he asked

me if I'd like to go for coffee. Baskerville has what my vet calls a 'greeting disorder.' He goes a little nuts when I open the door or start talking to someone on the street. A lot nuts, actually. It's his way of saying hello. He jumped up on the guy and knocked him over. I tripped on the leash. Baskerville thought it was a game and pounced on us. The guy kicked him and I punched him in the crotch—the guy, not poor Baskerville—and then I saw Richie running down the street toward us. . . . By the way, who *is* Richie, anyhow?"

"Richard Ott, alias Richie the Ratfink. Small-time, hires himself out for surveillance jobs. He's annoying but harmless."

"Oh. Anyhow, then a car came screeching to a stop and a woman jumped out. She must have thought I was being attacked, because she zapped Alvarez with one of those little personal stun guns, and I guess she must have zapped Richie too, because Blossom saw him staggering away holding his shoulder. Then she took me to the emergency room. I have a mild concussion and a sprained wrist. The end."

Will reached over and cradled my left wrist in his big hand. "He do this?" he said softly, running a finger over the Ace wrist support.

I shook my head. "I fell on it." My wrist didn't hurt when he held it like that; it started humming a happy little wrist song.

"Why the hell did you just stand there talking to him, Tilly? You know he's been tailing you for weeks. I ran his priors after I followed him to the rental car place in Orlando. He's bad news. I don't want you messing with guys like that."

"I wasn't messing with him. I told you, he didn't know I recognized him."

"Sweet Christ," Will muttered. "You're playing detective again, aren't you?"

"Well, what if I am? I thought I'd try to get some information out of him. Why he was following me, who he worked for. You don't have to be a hotshot secret agent with a shiny badge to do that. In fact, I could probably learn more over a cup of coffee in an hour than you could grilling him all night under a bare bulb in a cement cell."

"For God's sake, Tilly," he groaned, "just use your common sense for once, will you? People are dying because of that damned pillow box. Did it occur to you for even one millisecond that he might have had a lot more in mind than a cozy chat over a cup of coffee?"

"Of course it occurred to me," I retorted. "I do have a bit more common sense than your average village idiot, you know. I didn't have any intention of going anywhere with him. Besides, I can protect myself. I took a class at the YWCA."

He settled back in his chair and gestured with his bottle of Dos Equis. "Oh well, now that I know you've taken a self-defense class at the Y, I can stop worrying about you."

I bristled. "It was a very good class, I'll have you know. I would have gotten an A, except I couldn't make myself do the fingers-in-the-eyes thing, so I only got a B-plus. And don't forget I had Baskerville to protect me, and pepper spray."

"Right, I see your point. A thug with a Glock 9 wouldn't stand a chance against you."

"There's no need to get sarcastic."

One straight, dark brow went up.

I poked at the melting ice cubes in my Coke with

the straw. "You, um, worry about me?" I didn't dare look up.

Dumb, dumb, dumb, Tilly, I scolded myself. Of course he worries about you; you're his best bet to find the pillow box; just a means to an end. What do you expect him to say?

"Yes."

"Huh?"

"You asked if I worry about you. Yes, I worry about you."

"Your investment, you mean."

"Investment?"

"You worry about me—me being your investment—because I'm your best bet to find the box, a means to your end. Now, if someone else got hold of me, then I'd be their best bet to find the box, a means to their end," I jabbered on, "and they'd be doing the worrying about me, me being their investment. So what I'm saying is, you'd rather do the worrying about your investment than have them do the worrying about their investment."

I swear, if I had a third foot, it would be right there in my mouth with the other two.

Will tilted his head and regarded me in much the same way an intake psychiatrist at an institute for the terminally loony might when deciding which ward to stick me in.

"I'm not sure what the hell you just said, Tilly, but to answer your question again, yes, I do worry about you."

"Me. Just me, not me as—?"

He held up a hand. "Please, not again. I worry about you, Tilly, just you."

"Oh." He worried about me. Me.

He finished off his beer. "What about the woman who zapped Alvarez and Richie? Did you recognize her?"

I jerked my attention back to business. "No. Do you think she was watching the shop too, and that's why she saw what was happening and thought I was being attacked?"

"Hola, chica," Alonzo shouted from across the street. "We need you over here."

Will stood up and tossed a ten on the table. "I expect so. There are a number of women in the illegal art trade. Your aunt Ginger, for example."

"You don't know that," I protested as he walked me back to the garden gate. "You haven't offered me one iota of proof she stole that box or knew who did. It could have been stolen by yak herders from Outer Mongolia, for all you know."

"But you think she did, don't you?"

He had me there. I did think Aunt Ginger was involved, because I knew one thing no one else knew—not Will Maitland or the FBI or Richie or Halsey Wickerby, not even Scarlett and Blossom.

There was a very good chance Aunt Ginger had been in Singapore in May when the pillow box of Win Win Poo was stolen.

Fifteen

Lime green is not my color. You will not find halter dresses with spaghetti straps and plunging necklines that stop just short of a person's belly button in my closet. Nor will you see gracing my earlobes anything more daring than simple studs and modest hoops. Heels higher than one inch are right up there with foot binding as far as I'm concerned, and the men who design them can look forward to tottering around hell on spiked heels for all eternity.

Blossom knows these things about me, which is precisely why, when I rang a little silver dinner bell and said, "I want to welcome you to GingerFest, the first annual celebration of the life of Ginger Snapp," I was clad in a lime green halter dress, wearing two-inch strappy gold-tone sandals on my feet with long gold thingamabobs studded with chunks of green sea glass dangling from my ears.

I had fought the good fight as Blossom marched me from boutique to boutique along the Lincoln Road Mall, down Collins, up Washington, and over to

Ocean Drive. "What's wrong with a nice navy blue skirt and a white blouse?" I demanded.

She stopped abruptly in the middle of the sidewalk outside Armani Exchange. "You're not in Kansas anymore, Dorothy, you're in South Beach. Look around," she said with a sweep of her arm. "Do you see anyone wearing navy blue skirts and white blouses?"

"But I'm not the South Beach sort," I protested. "I'm Eddie Bauer, L.L. Bean, Lands' End."

Blossom clutched at her heart. "*Lands' End*?"

"J. Jill?" I added hastily, hoping to redeem myself.

My only comfort was that Scarlett hadn't fared much better. She came away from the expedition with a sleeveless wrap dress in a wild tropical print and pink flamingo earrings.

Blossom, who lacked only the flesh and blood big cat itself to round out her latest fashion obsession with all things spotted, chose a leopard skin–patterned tube dress that aspired to make it to midthigh, and matching bikini panties and ankle boots with two-inch heels.

A few people showed up at GingerFest in traditional dark colors—Halsey Wickerby and Carlotta Flores among them—but otherwise the crowd looked pretty much like an explosion in a paint factory.

I raised a plastic champagne flute. "To Ginger!" I proclaimed.

"To Ginger!" the crowd echoed.

I swallowed the big lump in my throat and went on quickly, "I know she touched the lives of each and every one of you. So . . ." I picked up the dinner bell. "If you're inspired at some point in the evening to share your thoughts or memories of her with us, just ring this bell and speak up."

I needed a few minutes to collect myself, so I left

Alonzo plucking out a song on his ukulele in honor of Ginger and went inside. Except for Missy Mae's room and bath, the ground floor hadn't seen much progress in the way of renovation yet.

Although the charming lobby of the old hotel had long ago been partitioned and reduced to a mean little vestibule, Alonzo had miraculously found the original floor plan in a derelict bureau in the basement. Two of the offending walls had been knocked out and the foul dung-brown linoleum taken up to reveal a lovely tile floor. It was Virgil who found the original brass chandelier and ceiling moldings under a pile of junk. Bringing the St. Claire to life again would truly be a labor of love, and it saddened me to realize Aunt Ginger would never see it accomplished.

I wandered down the hall to the door that led into the shop, keyed the code to turn off the alarm, and stepped into the dim interior.

Some people die and are considerate enough to close the door behind them on their way out. Other people hang around for a while sulking and hoping maybe there's some been some sort of mistake. Eventually God sends them an eviction notice and they pack up and move on.

And then there are those who see no reason why they should stop living just because they died. They've got life force in spades.

I could feel every ounce of Aunt Ginger's life force there in Erratica, could almost smell the sandalwood perfume she favored. "Hey, Aunt Ginger," I said. "Where are you?"

"Meow," she replied.

My stomach executed a neat half nelson and plummeted straight down to my shoes. It rebounded up into my throat and eventually came to rest more or less where God had put it in the first place.

I bent down, felt around, and came up with a handful of kitten.

"Oh, there you are," Scarlett exclaimed from the doorway. "I've been looking all over for you. We've got trouble. So many people showed up that there isn't room for them in the garden or over at Zephyr and they're spilling out onto Española Way. The police are here."

In Wonderland the fun just goes on and on.

I have to give the Bicycle Unit of the Miami Beach Police Department high marks for patience and restraint. Under similar circumstances, Boston's men and women in blue would probably have called out the riot squad.

Flanked by Blossom and Scarlett, with Alonzo, Virgil and the photographer Percy Coombes running interference and Missy Mae at rear guard, I managed to plow my way through the cheerful throng, which had by now grown by a factor of three, toward the patrolman standing beside a sleek black Trek racing bike.

"Is there a problem, Officer Narducci?" I inquired, peering at his badge and trying to look ingenuous.

Of course there was a problem. A person would have to be blind, deaf, dead drunk, or stoned out of his mind to miss the fact that Aunt Ginger's memorial service had turned into a street party.

"Wow, check out the legs," I heard Blossom mutter behind me, referring to Officer Marco Narducci's long, lean, tanned legs, revealed by his navy blue riding shorts.

"Not now, Blossom," I said out of the corner of my mouth. "We've got a situation here."

"This your party?" he said to me.

"Not exactly, sir. It's a funeral."

"Ooooeeee!" someone in the crowd yelled. "Yeah, baby, take it off!" A roar of approval went up as a stripper friend of Aunt Ginger's evidently complied. I suppose it was too much to hope she'd have anything on under her orange bustier.

"A funeral, huh?"

"Er, not exactly. We don't have a dead body in the garden or anything like that."

"I still think we should have put her ashes out on the altar," Virgil grumbled.

"Ugliest cremation urn I ever seen," Missy Mae informed Officer Narducci. "Ginger'd die of shame she wake up and find herself in that tin box. What we oughta do is—"

"We're holding a memorial service for my aunt Ginger," I interjected desperately, hoping he hadn't gotten a whiff of the faint but unmistakable aroma of marijuana smoke wafting across the street from Zephyr. "She met with an unfortunate accident in Jamaica, and we wanted to celebrate her life. We're calling it GingerFest, and I guess it's gotten a little rowdy. I'm really sorry."

"You got a permit, Ms. . . . ?"

"Snapp," I supplied. "Tilly Snapp. I'm her niece. A permit? I didn't know I needed one."

"You need a special event permit issued by the city manager to close off a public street, and a police detail to keep traffic moving and maintain order. The permit has to be applied for thirty days in advance of the event, forwarded to the FDOT, and signed by the chief of police."

"Ride 'em, cowboy!" someone hooted from the direction of the Sistine Chapel panel at the far end of the arcade. Who was riding whom or what was riding what, I really did not want to know.

"I didn't expect so many people," I confessed.

"We got a right to assemble," Missy Mae declared. "It's in the Constitution."

"Er, Missy Mae—" I began.

"First Amendment of the Bill of Rights says so," she went on. " 'Congress shall make no law respecting an establishment of religion, or prohibiting the free exercise thereof; or abridging the freedom of speech, or of the press; or the right of the people peaceably to assemble, and to petition the government for a redress of grievances.' "

"Please, Missy Mae," I begged, "perhaps this isn't the best time to—"

" 'The right of the people peaceably to assemble,' " she repeated, glowering at Officer Narducci. "If a memorial service ain't a peaceable assembly, I don't know what is."

An assembly that featured strippers, Class II proscribed drugs, and possibly unnatural acts being committed on a public sidewalk probably hadn't occurred to the Founding Fathers when they sat down to draft the Bill of Rights, and I seriously doubted Officer Narducci was going to think so either. GingerFest was lurching toward disaster.

"Marco, how's it going?" Will Maitland said, unaccountably materializing at my side.

"Maitland," Officer Narducci acknowledged. "You a friend of the deceased?"

Will slid a reassuring arm around my shoulder. "More like a professional association. Tilly's just down from Boston. She's been pretty upset about her aunt. Maybe you could cut her a little slack this time."

Will Maitland, my knight in shining armor?

"We'd really appreciate it, Officer Narducci," Blossom purred, making a tiny adjustment to the bustline of her leopard skin–spotted tube dress.

Scarlett slipped off her glasses and peered at him with myopic solemnity. "Please be assured, Officer Narducci, that in future we will comply fully with all city government rules and regulations."

I tried to look bereaved, contrite, hopeful, and grateful all at once, no mean feat when you only have one face.

Officer Narducci threw one long, lean, tanned leg over his bike, settled himself on the narrow saddle seat, and set his white helmet on his black buzz-cut. For a split second before he donned a pair of mirrored Ray-Bans, I thought I saw an amused gleam in his eye.

"I could cite you on any number of charges, Ms. Snapp," he informed me in that flat law-and-order tone of voice I'd become all too familiar with since I tumbled down the rabbit hole, "but as you're in mourning I'll let it go. This time."

"Thank you, that's very kind of you," I said.

With a quick sidelong glance at Blossom's provocative bosom, he pedaled off to keep the streets of South Beach safe for decent citizens and big-spending tourists.

I turned around to thank my knight in shining armor, but he'd disappeared as mysteriously as he'd arrived.

* * *

"Missy Mae?"

"Uh-uh."

"Blossom?"

"No."

"Virgil?"

"Nope."

"You're sure you locked it and reset the code, Scarlett?"

"Absolutely."

"Alonzo, you checked for holes in the wall, or vents a kitten could squeeze through?"

"Nada, chica."

"The front door?"

"Locked. Didn't see no sign of forced entry."

We all looked considerably the worse for wear in the soft glow of the paper lanterns strung round the garden. We sat or sprawled in various stages of exhaustion amid post-GingerFest flotsam, jetsam, and disorder.

I folded my arms, tapped a toe. "Here's what we have. On at least two occasions in the past week someone who is not one of us has been in the shop."

"Or some thing," Missy Mae muttered darkly. "Maybe Ginger fly down—"

"Please, let's not go there again, Missy Mae," I interrupted. "This is not an angel or a ghost. It is a flesh-and-blood human being who can bypass the security code and come and go at will."

"Could be that Interpol fellow," Virgil suggested. "Or FBI, cops, that Richie fellow."

"A cat burglar?" Scarlett said. "Like Cary Grant in *To Catch a Thief.*"

Richie the Ratfink didn't strike me as the Cary Grant type.

I paced back and forth. "It's hard to tell if anything's been stolen, since we haven't done an inventory yet, but I think we can assume they're looking for the box, since they've been back at least twice."

Scarlett, ever practical and well grounded, held up a hand. "Let's not get ahead of ourselves here. We have another problem. If he got into the shop from the inside hallway, that means he—"

I stuck my fingers in my ears. "I do not want to hear this."

"He's been in the building," she finished. "We're going to have to change the locks on the outside doors."

"He been spyin' on me when I'm in my birthday suit," Missy Mae growled, "he gonna be singin' soprano."

I plopped into a chair and buried my head in my arms on the table. Seeing that I was out of commission for the moment, Blossom assumed command. "First thing tomorrow Alonzo changes all the locks. We contact the security company to get a new code. Tilly, pull yourself together."

I sat up. "Okay, okay."

"We'll work in two teams and divvy up the building to look for the box," she continued. "Alonzo and Virgil will take the basement; there's a lot of heavy stuff down there that will need to be moved around. Missy Mae, Tilly, and I will do the upper floors. Scarlett, do you think you can finish up with the hard drives by tomorrow night?"

"I should be able to."

I was getting my bearings back. "I'll call Wickerby and tell him to contact the FBI, Interpol, whomever, that they can come in without a warrant on Tuesday morning. Then we concentrate on getting the shop open."

We had a plan. Everyone else trooped off to bed, but Baskerville and I sat out in the garden for a while, enjoying a warm breeze that brought with it the promise of rain. I let him take care of business behind a huge stand of bamboo. We had talked it over and agreed we wouldn't be taking any strolls through the dark streets of South Beach for the foreseeable future.

I closed my eyes and tried to picture myself in my flannel jammies, curled up snug as a bug on the couch in the high-ceilinged living room of my comfortable condo in the South End of Boston, as the sky spit shards of sleet against my window.

That's where I belonged, right?

Not sitting here in a ridiculous lime green halter dress in the garden of the Hotel St. Claire in South Beach, as the first drops of sweet warm rain began to fall.

"Is it? Where you belong?" whispered a doubting little voice from somewhere deep in my subconscious. "Are you sure?"

SIXTEEN

"I warned you," he said.

A key grated in the lock. Heavy footsteps faded away down the long, dark corridor. In the far distance another door slammed shut.

My nemesis leered down at me where I huddled on the hard bunk of my cell. "I told you, 'If you've got it in that head of yours to start playing detective, you're going to be in a lot more trouble than you already are, because I won't think twice about parking you in a jail cell until I put this case to bed.' "

He pulled a small key from his pocket and tossed it from hand to hand. "I'm not required to unlock the cuffs, you understand. It's optional when dealing with a recalcitrant, possibly violent material witness in a double homicide."

He pulled me to my feet, turned me around, and tested the wrist restraints—red leather sparkling with rhinestones that spelled out "Alice."

"No, I don't think I will take off the cuffs," he decided. "You need to learn that we play by different rules here in Wonderland."

He stood just close enough that I could feel the heat of him at my back, his big body not quite touching mine, his breath a rough whisper against my neck. The air around us rippled with the scent of warm leather, freshly picked limes, and yes, just a soupçon of jerk-goat rub.

"You tell me where they are," he said, "I might cut you some slack, talk to some people, get you out of this hole before menopause sets in."

He moved a fraction closer. I might not have eyes in the back of my head, but I can appreciate a well-favored gentleman when he presses a very, very impressive package of masculine distinction against me. I felt a stroke coming on.

"Not talking, Alice? You'll be spilling your guts by the time I get through with you, you better believe it." His words were unbelievably arousing. "Smuggling ants is a capital offense here in Wonderland."

Somewhere a kitten meowed.

"You're forcing me to play rough, Alice. That what you want?" he whispered, his lips a millimeter from my right ear. "You want me to play rough?"

He would, and he knew I knew he would.

Fortunately I was in no position to stop him.

He sighed in mock regret as he tied a blindfold over my eyes. "Have it your way."

A moment later he had me backed against a cold cement wall.

"Last chance," he said. "Give up the ants, this stops right now."

No way I was going to give up my ants. A person's got to do what she's got to do to protect her ants. I took a deep breath. I could take whatever terrible torture he had in mind; I would take it for my ants, and rejoice.

It was bad, hideous, worse than I ever could have imagined. He towered over me, the male ascendant, confident in his strength, in his God-given right to bring the female under his hot hard dominion. He would break me, bend me to his will, make me beg.

I would do whatever I could to help. My ants deserved no less.

Barely breathing and unbearably aroused because I could not see him, I trembled, awaited my fate.

"You want me," he murmured. "You know you do."

I shook my head vehemently.

He released the straps of my lime green halter dress and let it slide down my body. I shivered in the damp, cold dungeon air. I craved the heat of that powerful body, only inches away, but he made no move to touch me. I wouldn't beg; I wouldn't.

"Ask nicely, Alice," he said as though he could read my thoughts.

I couldn't help myself, strained toward him. "That will do." He leaned into me; my knees would have buckled if his denim-clad hips weren't pinning my naked body to the wall.

His mouth hovered above mine. "Open."

I turned my head to the side, but he jerked it back, teased open my lips with his clever tongue, and took possession.

That god-yes mouth sent shock waves arrowing straight to my center. He plunged, pillaged, and plundered, traced a fiery path along my jaw.

I wanted more, craved more and more and more, knowing I would die if he stopped now. As he lapped at my ear, licked, and laved, I lost control, shuddering, panting, inhaling greedily the intoxicating scent of . . .

Alpo.

"Damn it, Baskerville, get off of me," I snarled, shoving the big goofball away. I pulled the pillow over my head and dived back into the dream.

My body throbbed with need only an agent in charge could satisfy. "Please," I begged, "you can have the ants if only you'll let me finish."

He began to fade slowly, inexorably until only a mocking grin remained on his god-yes mouth. "Too late, Alice."

"No!" I cried.

He laughed softly. "You forgot to buy batteries."

And he was gone.

"Aaaaaaaaagh!"

SEVENTEEN

The pillow box of Win Win Poo was lying around somewhere in the vast reaches of the known universe, but it wasn't in the Hotel St. Claire in South Beach, Miami, Florida, USofA, that's for sure. My crew scoured the building from top to bottom, from wall to wall. We searched high and we searched low.

No pillow box and not one scintilla of proof that it had ever passed this way. Let the FBI do its worst on the morrow, they wouldn't be leaving the St. Claire with the pillow box of Win Win Poo. I would of course be handing over Aunt Ginger's computer with my blessings.

Halsey Wickerby and Carlotta Flores came by around noon to see if we'd found the box yet. Wickerby deeply regretted that Ginger had not seen fit to confide to him the combination to the large safe in her office; we would have to bring in the company that had installed it in order to open it. Ginger had been a wonderful woman, somewhat unusual of course, and yes, he had heard rumors that she might be dabbling in, er, certain activities that might straddle that fine line between legal and, er, not quite legal, but he himself had never seen any evidence of such with his own eyes.

Carlotta said Aunt Ginger kept meticulous records. She—Carlotta—reconciled the books monthly and saw to the timely filing of all state and federal taxes. Beyond that, she knew nothing of Aunt Ginger's business affairs. She lamented what a terrible shame it was she had met with such an unfortunate accident and in the prime of life too.

By nightfall, new locks had been installed, the security alarm code reset, and the transfer of sensitive data from one Mac G5 to another completed. Blossom, Scarlett, Virgil, Missy Mae, and Alonzo headed out for pizza and a movie. I opted to stay home with the four adult cats and the single kitten that remained with us after GingerFest.

It was Scarlett, of course, who came up with a brilliant idea to reduce the ever-growing feline population of the St. Claire. We placed eight winsome kittens, each with a little colored bow around its neck, in an old guinea pig cage Virgil unearthed from somewhere, and set it out on a table in the garden. We had only one condition for adoption: Each kitten had to be named Ginger regardless of gender. They'd gone like wildfire. I took the tiny orange furball I'd found in Erratica. She was, naturally, named Gingersnap. Baskerville approved my choice.

My little family gathered in the kitchen for a light supper, and I got to work with Baskerville snoozing at my feet and Gingersnap rolled up like a miniature orange hedgehog in the white wicker fruit basket on the table. Alongside a map of Singapore I'd printed off the Internet I laid down a creased piece of white paper approximately three by six inches.

It was a receipt from Borders Books and Music, #01-00 Wheelock Place, 501 Orchard Road, Singapore, 238880, dated May 16, 2004, for the purchase of two paperbacks—*Deep South* by Nevada Barr and *Immortal in Death* by J.D. Robb—a box of notepaper, three Lindt dark chocolate truffles, and a soy latte.

The receipt, which I had come across in a pocket of a creamy yellow shantung silk jacket hanging in Aunt Ginger's closet, was not proof positive that she herself had purchased these items and must therefore have been in Singapore on that date. No, what caught my attention was the cryptic notation on the reverse, scrawled in a spiky hand I knew well: "Orch r bide to cairn 77 66 62350882 wong 195 lim 2 firm yee 203. Perp sing!"

There could be no doubt; the handwriting was Aunt Ginger's. I had received hundreds of postcards mailed from every nook and cranny on the planet from the time I could puzzle out "cat." I still had every one of them packed into shoe boxes in my closet.

"Okay, here we go," I said to Gingersnap.

" 'Orch,' 'bide,' and 'cairn' might be street names." I consulted the map. "Yes, there's an Orchard Road. A Bideford Road turns into Cairnhill. So let's say these are directions: Take a right off Orchard onto Bideford Road and go on to Cairnhill Road. Seventy-seven might be the street number, sixty-six possibly an apartment number."

On a hunch I checked the front of the receipt for the telephone number of Borders. It started with 6235, so 62350882 would be a telephone number.

"So far so good," I told Gingersnap, who expressed

her opinion of the whole game with a sweet little yawn. "Wong, Lim and Yee are Chinese surnames, but I don't know what the numbers after each one means. 'Firm?' like a company: Wong, Lim & Yee? Perp. Perpendicular? Perpetual? Perpetrator? Sing has to be Singapore."

I hadn't been sure whether to tell Blossom and Scarlett about the receipt when I first found it. They were in deep enough as it was; I didn't want them sharing a jail cell with me as material witnesses if it should turn out that Aunt Ginger actually had stolen the pillow box of Win Win Poo. Now, as I tried to puzzle out the meaning of the note, I realized I was going to need more brainpower. Scarlett could probably locate the Holy Grail using the Internet if she put her mind to it, and Blossom was no slouch in the intuition department. Besides, they always knew when I was hiding something. They would hound me until I broke down and confessed, and then read me the riot act for leaving them out of the loop.

Everyone should have friends like Blossom MacMorrough and Scarlett Snow.

I gave it up for the night and took myself off to bed, where I lay awake thinking about Will Maitland for a long time. While not exactly the enemy, he wasn't an ally either. We were both after the same thing in the short run, but beyond that, we parted company. He wanted to smash an international art and antiquity smuggling operation, and if that meant branding Lorraine Louise Snapp as a thief and swindler for all eternity, it didn't signify so long as he could put his precious case to bed.

I, Tilly Snapp, Sex Detective, would see to it that Aunt Ginger's reputation was not ruined, even if she turned out to be as guilty as all get out. And if that meant reining in my libido and passing on Will Maitland, then so be it.

"How sweet! Thank you, Matilda dear, but really, that won't be necessary."

I shot straight up in bed. "Is that you, Aunt Ginger?"

"Meow," Gingersnap replied.

Eighteen

Wickerby arrived on Friday morning at 8:00 on the dot, fastidious, as was his wont, in a gray suit, a white shirt, and a bow tie patterned in a daring paisley print of gray and navy and more gray.

"Up to now, you have been protected by the Fourth Amendment of the Bill of Rights," he instructed me. "To wit, 'The right of the people to be secure in their persons, houses, papers, and effects, against unreasonable searches and seizures, shall not be violated, and no warrants shall issue, but upon probable cause, supported by oath or affirmation, and particularly describing the place to be searched, and the persons or things to be seized.' "

He set a classic black leather attaché case on the table, unlocked it, and began laying out with military precision yellow legal pads, no. 2 pencils, a Sheaffer fountain pen embossed with the initials HBW, miscellaneous papers, three reference books, a cell phone, an appointment book, and a tin of wintergreen Altoids.

"Ain't no one seizin' nothin' or nobody," Missy Mae informed him.

Wickerby adjusted his spectacles and peered up at her. "By admitting federal, state, or municipal agents onto the property, Ms. Snapp acknowledges the determination of probable cause in the warrant signed by Judge Pinkett and waives certain of her rights, which include but are not limited to seizure of property or, *in extremis*, her person."

Missy Mae, who had, unaccountably, proved to possess a legal turn of mind when she challenged Sgt. Narducci over our First Amendment right to assemble peaceably at GingerFest, shook her head. "Tilly agreed to this here search of her own free will before that judge signed the warrant. She didn't acknowledge nothin'. She still protected under that amendment."

Wickerby fired up his legal thrusters. "No, no, Ms. Quarles. She may or may not acknowledge the validity of the affirmation which led to the issuance of the warrant, but as she has agreed to the search of her property, she therefore acknowledges that said search is not unreasonable and—"

Missy Mae folded her arms across her chest and narrowed her eyes. "You one of them strict constitutional constructionist nuts. In 1991, the Supreme Court upheld the judgment of the Fifth Circuit Court in the matter of—"

"Missy Mae," I interjected, "perhaps you could fetch coffee for Mr. Wickerby. Since you'll both be stationed here by the garden door all morning, there should be ample time to delve into the finer points of constitutional law later on."

Missy Mae never misses a minute of Court TV. Wickerby didn't have a clue what he was up against.

"I can't understand why the security company hasn't arrived yet to open the safe," he fretted, moving a legal pad a scant sixteenth of an inch in order to align it perfectly with the appointment book. "I specifically told them eight fifteen, not a minute sooner, not a minute later."

I dragged Baskerville from beneath the table, where he could only be up to no good. "I meant to tell you. I had them come by yesterday evening."

It was the first time I'd seen Wickerby off-kilter. "I don't think that was wise, not wise at all," he scolded. "You are in a most delicate position. There are dire legal ramifications, of which you are surely unaware, when a warrant has been issued and you intentionally remove or hide evidence. At the very least, you can be found in contempt of court."

Better to be found in contempt of court than in possession of the pillow box of Win Win Poo, I thought.

"I didn't remove or hide anything, Mr. Wickerby. I didn't expect to find the box in the safe, and I didn't find the box in the safe. There are a number of items in there that must be very valuable, all with proper bills of provenance, some inventory that Aunt Ginger might not have wanted to display openly in the shop, if you know what I mean, and personal letters. That was all."

Wickerby drummed his fingers on the table, for him the equivalent of blowing his top. "You should have consulted me first, Ms. Snapp. I am most displeased."

I didn't take well to being lectured when I was six, and I appreciated it far, far less at the age of twenty-six. I admit I was surprised and annoyed at Wickerby's uncharacteristic display of pique, but I wasn't going to get into it with him with the FBI about to storm the gates.

"I appreciate your concern, Mr. Wickerby," I said,

trotting out a conciliatory smile. "I know you have my best interests at heart. We can discuss this at some other time, but the authorities are going to be here any minute and I need to make sure everything is organized inside."

"Of course, of course," he said quickly. "I do apologize, my dear. Please understand: My practice is confined to family and estate law, and I admit I'm somewhat out of my comfort zone in this matter. I can't help feeling there's more to this business of the pillow box than meets the eye. Oh dear, here they are. Good morning, gentlemen."

If television teaches us anything, it promises that sooner or later every household in America will be able to boast of its very own raid by grim-faced agents of one law enforcement agency or another. Doors will be kicked in, warrants thrust into trembling hands, the elderly and the lame pushed aside, and children herded into corners where they will cower and cry and clutch their teddy bears. Men and women clad in unrelieved black with FBI/ATF/Police—or, if we really luck out, CSI—emblazoned across the back of their jackets will stampede from room to room, paw through our personal effects, empty fifty-pound bags of dog food onto the kitchen floor, and tear up the tulips in the front yard. We will object that our civil rights are being violated and threaten to call our lawyer. The agents will find nothing, warn us not to leave town, and disappear into the night to return to the casting office whence they came. A good time will have been had by all, and we can return to our regularly scheduled lives.

In the event, the actual search of the St. Claire that morning was something of a disappointment. David

Duchovny, Val Kilmer, and Kevin Costner must have been out on other assignments; the agent in charge, one George Grimes, wouldn't be starring in anyone's sexual fantasies anytime soon. Agents from the FBI's Art Theft and Money Laundering Units appeared in suit and tie, were unfailingly polite, and took care not to let the cats out of the bathroom. A gray kitten that had somehow evaded the roundup for GingerFest was discovered in a broom closet and rode off to a new life in the pocket of a detective from the Miami-Dade Police Department Division of Investigative Services.

Nothing was seized that was not specified in the warrant as pertinent to the current investigation, and receipts were provided with the assurance that everything would be returned in due course. Among the items loaded into a black van were Aunt Ginger's computer, four banker's boxes filled with files, and six artifacts with suspect bills of provenance.

I was surprised and, yes, I'll admit it, more than a little disappointed not to see Will among the phalanx of agents trooping in and out of the St. Claire. I expect he already knew that the pillow box wasn't on the premises. Still, the least he could have done was hang around to make sure the FBI didn't haul his material witness off to the slammer before he could, because, frankly, I couldn't picture George Grimes playing the starring role in my erotic dreams.

The entire episode was all very civilized and would have passed unremarked but for the fact that by ten o'clock half the residents of South Beach and a horde of tourists were milling around outside the hotel, bringing traffic to a standstill throughout the historic district and threatening to create gridlock from the Julia Tuttle Causeway clear down to Fifth

Street and the access ramp to the MacArthur.

Miami has more than its share of resident celebrities—J.Lo, Shaq, P. Diddy, Sly, Gloria—and a horde of wannabes, flavors-of-the-month, and has-beens shuttling in and out from LA and New York daily. But nothing brings out the mob like a film shoot. Somehow a rumor took hold and ran like wild-fire through the streets of South Beach that *CSI: Miami* was shooting on Española Way. There might be a very real possibility of witnessing with one's own eyes David Caruso, in the flesh, looking philosophical and donning his Ray-Bans with the precision of a neuro-surgeon as he did at the end of every episode.

That the show is filmed almost exclusively on a soundstage in El Segundo, California, and beaches south of Los Angeles would have done little to dampen the crowd's enthusiasm, which reached fever pitch when the local Fox affiliate deemed the situation worthy of breaking-news status and had a helicopter hovering overhead and its news team on the spot in under fifteen minutes, with CNN and WSVN-TV 7 not far behind. Not to mention a grim-faced Sgt. Marco Narducci, who happened to be pedaling through the historic district on his appointed rounds when he found himself swept toward the St. Claire on the crest of a wave of squealing Japanese schoolgirls.

In the entire span of my twenty-six years in the real world in the persona of Good Old Tilly Snapp, my entire experience of law enforcement of any sort had consisted of a visit to a police station with my sixth grade class, the arrival of two somber policewomen on the doorstep of the house Alex and I had just purchased to inform me of his untimely demise, and two ten-dollar parking tickets.

After only two weeks, six days, eleven hours, and forty-three minutes in Wonderland, I had gone *mano a mano* with the Jamaica Constabulary Force over a *pro forma* permit to transport my aunt's remains back to the United States. I had been detained, marched away by AK-47–wielding military personnel, questioned, and suffered my person and luggage to be searched by an agent of U.S. Customs and Immigration Enforcement. I had been interrogated, threatened with indefinite detention under the mandate of the Homeland Security Act, placed under surveillance, scolded, harassed, and generally discombobulated by a special agent of the International Criminal Police Organization.

With Sgt. Marco Narducci's arrival on my doorstep for the second time in less than a week because of a public disturbance at the Hotel St. Claire, I could now look forward to a bright future as a troublemaker in the eyes of the Miami Beach Police Department. Fortunately, the FBI takes precedence in the pecking order of law enforcement agencies over the Bicycle Unit of the Miami Beach Police Department, and Sgt. Narducci was forced to pedal away once more without issuing the citation he felt I so richly deserved.

When the hue and cry finally faded away around noon, the crowds dispersed, and life in and around the Hotel St. Claire was restored to a semblance of normality, Baskerville and I decided we needed some breathing and romping room. Alonzo suggested Hobie Beach off the Rickenbacker Causeway, one of the few that allowed dogs to run free. I loaded him—Baskerville, not Alonzo—into the back of the Grand Cherokee and we headed off for some well-deserved rest and relaxation.

Nineteen

Baskerville is not one to hide his feelings, and running free for the first time since that vicious Scarlett Snow drugged him, stuffed him into a cage, and subjected him to one indignity after another catapulted him out of his usual manic behavior when off-leash straight into the hyperecstatic. For a while I trailed after him as he charged up and down the beach and ran frantic circles around me. We played toss with a soggy green tennis ball, and I admired the little gifts he deposited at my feet—a faded sock, fast food containers, and various detritus of undetermined origin.

Eventually, I left him happily sniffing the hindquarters of a fox terrier, settled down in the soft white sand, shut my eyes, and allowed my thoughts to drift where they would as the hot sun sank deep into my bones and the gulls wheeled overhead.

They drifted straight in the direction of Will Maitland, of course. They usually did these days.

Heaven knows there are hordes of Mr. Wrongs out there, but I've always suspected Mr. Right was a delusional construct visited on the female psyche to ensure the survival of the species. I suppose that's why a neon sign didn't light up over Will Maitland's head flashing, "MR. RIGHT, MR. RIGHT!"

"You wouldn't know Mr. Right if he fell out of the sky right at your feet," Good Old Tilly Snapp would have said.

"Maybe you have to fall down a rabbit hole to see it," the new Tilly Snapp, Sex Detective, responded.

"Okay, I'll concede it's possible—he's sexy enough—but that's probably all there is to it."

"I bet if he'd take off his cop hat for two seconds, he'd be funny and warm and nice to a person's grammie."

"Okay, so he'd be nice to Grammie, but you have to admit the timing stinks," Old Tilly would point out. "Eventually you're going to get this mess sorted out. You'll find the box and clear Aunt Ginger's name; find a loophole in the will and sell Erratica and the St. Claire; and go home to Boston where you belong. That's the plan and you're going to stick to it, right? So where exactly does Will Maitland fit in?"

Good Old Tilly Snapp would be correct about the timing—it did stink—and right about the box and Aunt Ginger and the will and maybe even closing Erratica. Selling the St. Claire and going back to Boston? Maybe, maybe not. Probably not.

As for where Will Maitland fit into all this? God only knew, because I sure didn't.

"You're looking relaxed for a change."

I shaded my eyes as I peered up at the figure of a man framed against the dark blue sky. He wore a white shirt with the sleeves rolled up nearly to the elbow, revealing sleekly muscled forearms sprinkled with dark hair; a black belt; and pleated black trousers. He was barefoot. He had nice feet, big feet. A pair of sunglasses dangled from one hand.

My heart tattooed a welcoming riff. Other parts of me bubbled, buzzed, and hummed according to their respective functions.

"I am," I said. "Was." I didn't want to sound too easy.

"Mind if I join you?"

I sat up, brushed sand from my white tank top, and retied the red bandana over my unruly hair. "Yes. I mean no." Start over, Tilly. "No, I don't mind. Yes, you may join me, Agent Maitland."

He dropped down beside me. "How about I be Will and you be Tilly today."

Okay, I could be Tilly to his Will today. Let tomorrow bring what it would.

"How did you know where to find me?" I said.

"Your friend Blossom told me. I had court this morning, or I would have come by to make sure Grimes didn't haul you off to the slammer as a material witness."

I wiggled my toes in the sand. "I wouldn't have gone along quietly. You've got first dibs."

He laughed. "I doubt you'd go along quietly with me either, but thanks anyhow. They didn't find it, of course. You knew they wouldn't."

I shrugged. "Call it intuition."

His big body shifted as he leaned back on his elbows, crossed his ankles, and stared out over the bay. "Uh-huh, intuition."

I started to scoot away from him on the pretense of retrieving Baskerville's soggy tennis ball. A girl doesn't want to start getting ideas of the romantic sort when an alpha male is stretched out next to her on a sandy beach, all splendid and stunning and godly, or her hopes up that he might roll onto his side and prop his chin on his hand and maybe look down at her with an enigmatic little smile, like he's thinking about kissing her and then . . .

"Tilly."

"Huh?"

I don't know how he managed it, but one moment I was reaching for the tennis ball and the next I was looking up into those dark eyes, and he was looking down at me with an enigmatic little smile, like he was thinking about kissing me, and then . . .

"Let's take this off," he said, and I felt my hair tumble free as he slid the bandana off and tossed it aside. He moved a shade closer. "I'm probably going to regret this."

That was about as romantic as, "Shut up, Tilly, and just do it."

"Oh well, we wouldn't want that, would we?" I said somewhat tartly.

"Probably was the operative word there."

"Why doesn't that make me feel any better?"

"You could say no, Tilly."

"I could."

"But you won't?"

No, I wouldn't, couldn't. At that moment, I didn't give a damn whether Will Maitland was Mr. Right or Mr. Wrong, or whether the timing was good or bad, or where he fit into my plans or into my life.

I slid my arms around his neck. "No," I said. "I won't."

"Hey, lady!" someone shouted. "Is that your dog?"

Reluctantly I wriggled out of Will's arms, rolled over, and shot to my feet. "Oh, hell. He's at it again."

I took off running down the beach. In the distance I could see a woman beating at Baskerville with a floppy pink hat. Somewhere in the fracas I suspected a female fox terrier was being compromised.

"Get your dog off my Princess," the red-faced woman screamed.

I grabbed Baskerville's collar and dragged him off the quivering little terrier.

"He was . . . He was . . . violating her!"

Actually he wasn't—couldn't. But Baskerville couldn't seem to get it into his head that he was no longer equipped for the task of passing on his genes to the next generation; there would be no little Baskervilles in his future.

"Someone call 911!" The woman pointed an impassioned finger at me. "I want her arrested," she cried to the gathering crowd, as though I were the offending party.

Will sauntered up, surveyed the situation with cool cop eyes, and pulled out his badge. "Perhaps I can be of help, ma'am," he said solemnly. "What seems to be the problem?"

"Th-that mongrel was, you know, on top of her, my Princess," she cried. "I want him arrested. I want her put down."

Nobody calls my dog a mongrel, even if he is a mongrel. "Little Princess didn't seem to mind," I shot back.

"Tilly," Will said under his breath. "Let me handle this."

I picked up Baskerville's hind leg and pointed. "Have a good look," I snarled. "If anyone was doing any fornicating, it was your precious Princess."

Will took me by the shoulders and gave me a little shove. "Go away, Tilly."

Baskerville and I departed in a huff.

He caught up with us a few minutes later. "Quite a temper you have there."

"She was a doofus. Her dog was a doofus. Put Baskerville down," I muttered darkly.

"I believe what she actually said was, she wanted *you* put down. I explained that you were deranged and I'd make arrangements to have you taken into protective custody. That seemed to mollify her somewhat."

"What is it with everyone wanting to put me behind bars?" I inquired of the universe.

Baskerville bounced toward us across the sand and skidded to a stop with the entire length of his tongue hanging out.

"He needs water," I said. "I've got some in the car."

We walked back to the parking lot in silence. I wondered what he was thinking, wondered why I felt so empty. I wished he would say something, wished I could think of something to say.

I knew it would be stupid to tell him how right it felt to be with him when he was Will and I was Tilly and ask him if he thought so too, and how lousy the timing was and if he thought so too, and how I knew in my heart this wasn't going to work out and if he thought so too. I'd just be asking for trouble if I said something stupid like that.

"This isn't going to work," I blurted out before my sense of self-preservation could shut my mouth down. "You of all people should know that."

The brow went up.

I faced him squarely, and spelled it out. "You're the cop. I'm the suspect. There are rules about that sort of thing: not getting involved, keeping your professional distance. If the suspect has a brain in her head, she's going to wonder what the cop is up to and not allow herself to be seduced into cooperating or confessing. There's no place for libido in the mix."

The other brow joined the first.

I poked a finger in his direction. "You yourself said it was a bad idea."

Worse and worse. I was leaving myself wide open to get whammied. He'd confirm that it had indeed been a bad idea, and then I'd have to agree with him that it had been a bad idea, even if I thought it had been the best idea since sliced bread, and then he'd say it would be best to forget it ever happened, and I'd have to agree with that too, even if I knew I never would, and we'd shake hands and return to our respective corners. I braced myself for the worst.

He regarded me for a long thoughtful moment. "You've been watching too many cop shows, Tilly."

"Have not!" I called after him as he strolled away toward a gleaming black Audi a few spaces down.

What was I, five? I couldn't believe it: Tilly Snapp, an accomplished literary professional reduced to a verbal comeback worthy of a petulant preschooler.

Thoroughly disgusted with myself—and secretly relieved that he hadn't stayed with the script—I climbed into the Jeep, ordered Baskerville to the back of the cargo space, and lowered the window to let the superheated air out while the air conditioner pumped cold air in.

The Audi headed for the exit onto the Rickenbacker, circled around, and drew up beside me again. The tinted window slid down.

"I said I was probably going to regret kissing you."

I knew I shouldn't ask, didn't want to know.

Of course I just had to ask, had to know.

"Do you? Regret it?"
"Do you?"
I shook my head. "No."
He aimed that killer smile at me. "Neither do I."

Twenty

Scarlett peered at the small ivory index card.

```
Item No. 643-02
Sacred Purging Bone
Pre-Columbian, ca. 1000-1400 AD
Taino Culture, Caribbean Islands
Bone, probably manatee
Extremely rare.
From a private collection. Bids only.
```

"Let's see." She consulted the log. "Here it is. 'Also known as a Purging Spatula or Vomit Stick.' "

"Oh, yuck!" Blossom shoved the velvet-lined box back into the glass display case. "That's about all the information I think I need to know," she announced, and headed off to the bathroom to wash her hands.

Intrigued, Scarlett read on. "Employed by Taino shamans during sacred rituals to induce vomiting in order to purge the body and spirit of impurities. *Nota bene:* The status of the manatee is now listed as critical under the Endangered Species Act. Please see manager for more information."

I smiled. "That is so like Aunt Ginger. She loved manatees. On my sixteenth birthday she took me out on a manatee dive."

"From the manatee to the Middle Ages," Scarlett said.

Items No. 882-99 & 883-99
Two Medieval Bat Boxes
Devon/Cornwall, England
Pewter
Provenance unknown
Best offer.

Scarlett frowned and nibbled on the end of her Bic. "I'm beginning to suspect that 'provenance unknown' is antique-speak for a reproduction or a forgery, which is why there's no firm price. Maybe we should change it to *Caveat Emptor,* 'Buyer Beware.' This is turning out to be really interesting, don't you think, Tilly?"

I did, but she'd have to saw my tongue out with a plastic picnic knife to get me to admit it. Erratica was growing on me. It might sell the weird to the weird and the kinky to the kinky, but oddly enough, it was a little island of sanity in the fetid swamp of corporate greed, consumer gullibility, and mind-numbing mediocrity of South Beach. A person buys a vomit stick because he wants a vomit stick in his life, not because someone else convinces him that he'll never be able to claw his way to the top, nurture his inner child, or get laid without one. Madison Avenue types aren't sitting around a conference table right now working up an advertising campaign for Taino vomit sticks. But if you wake up one morning and decide you can't live without one, you know where to go.

Blossom returned. "Are we almost done for today? I've about had it with opium weights and Billy the Kid's silver toothpick. I want to get to the good stuff."

Scarlett consulted her list. "Not too much more. We should be able to finish up this part in the morning, and then we can get to the 'good stuff,' by which I assume you mean the sex stuff."

"I guess I can wait one more day," Blossom conceded.

"Class dismissed," I announced.

"What we need," Blossom said, "is to spend the afternoon at the beach, get take-out from Big Pink, and spend the evening watching *Sex and the City* reruns."

Scarlett and I agreed that was just what we needed. We'd been holed up in Erratica for most of the past two days, acquainting ourselves with the nonkinky items on display, most of which were oddball collectibles, albeit pretty high-end. Ernest Hemingway's beard trimmings, for instance—"From the proprietor's personal collection"—could be had for a mere $125.00.

My goal was to have the shop up and running before mid-November when the first snowbirds set down in Miami, a harbinger of the hordes to come. Blossom's friend's cousin had come through with a nice little piece about Aunt Ginger in the *Herald* and promised that opening day would be listed in the "Let's Go" section of *Weekend.* Two alternative South Beach weeklies would be covering it too.

Scarlett was monitoring the Web site, handling orders and inquiries as best she could and keeping an eye out for suspect e-mail. We decided not to announce Aunt Ginger's passing, in order to see what silence on the subject might bring our way.

"You go on ahead; I'll meet you in the usual place," I told them. "I have to finish this bee thing by Monday."

The bee thing was commercial copy for a catalogue company that leased out fruit and nut trees and beehives. You got the harvest—maple syrup or dates or honey from your tree for a season. They did cows and sheep too, but you didn't get a steak or lamb chops; you got Brie or a wool blanket. I wrote cute little brochures about how things were going with your tree or your bees or your cow. I wasn't going to win a Pulitzer for it, but it helped pay the bills. Today was bees.

I changed into a red tank suit and long batik-style cotton wrap skirt, grabbed a yellow beach towel, and headed downstairs to set up my laptop on a table in the garden and finish editing the damn thing so I could head over to the beach. I settled on Bonnie Raitt as best suited for music-to-write-about-bees-by and got to it. I was humming right along when a familiar hand—nice, big—appeared before my eyes and snapped its fingers.

I pulled off the headphones, saved the document, and tried to cock a casual, inquiring brow.

He slouched in the chair opposite, his long legs stretched out before him. "Everything going okay?"

I shrugged. "Of course, why wouldn't it be?" No need to muddy the water with the news that there had been two sightings of Richie the Ratfink in the past three days.

"Baskerville behaving himself?"

"We had a talk."

Couldn't the man show a little compassion and wear something that didn't make a woman want to leap over a table and tear it off? Maybe chew tobacco, sport a nose ring? Better still, wear a mask.

It is my opinion that there are men who shouldn't be allowed out in public unless they're wearing bells around their necks to warn susceptible women they're in the vicinity and give them the chance to save themselves if they choose to. Harrison Ford and Sean Connery are such men, if you go for the more mature type. Brad Pitt, Orlando Bloom, and Leonardo DiCaprio are such men. Ben Affleck, Will Smith, and Colin Farrell are not, no matter what they may think or their publicists, *People* magazine, and their mommies tell them.

Beauty may be in the eye of the beholder, but base animal magnetism is assessed and appreciated in an organ considerably to the south. Both were online and in perfect working order there in the garden, and I suspect Will knew it.

Men like Will Maitland would have to be brain-dead not to know the effect they have on women, and frankly the whole dynamic stinks. He knew I wanted him; I knew I wanted him. The problem was, did he want me? For how long? And was I ready to take that kind of risk?

"Earth to Tilly," said the man causing my current angst.

"Oh, sorry. You were saying?"

"I wasn't. I was watching you think. You're cute when you think."

My libido shifted into third. Something had to be done. "Would you like a beer?"

"You'd actually invite me in? Without a warrant?"

I shrugged. "Why not? You've probably been in already. There's nothing interesting in there anyhow. Come on."

I closed the laptop and led the way.

"Oh, I don't know about that," I thought I heard him say as I trudged up the stairs to Aunt Ginger's flat.

"Sorry, we don't stock Dos Equis. Amstel Light or Rolling Rock?" I made a mental note to stock Dos Equis.

"Rolling Rock's fine."

"Bottle, glass?"

"Bottle."

While I got a glass for myself, Will flicked off the cap and took a swig, glanced around, and wandered over to the window. Richie had better be on a coffee break or there was going to be trouble.

"So," I said.

He leaned back against the counter and smiled. "So."

Here's the problem. Say the studly god broke the rules like Will had on Hobie Beach—maybe his genes have mutated or he suffered a blow to the head—and he turns his divine gaze, not to mention his divine lips, upon a woman who has been conditioned from age thirteen not to expect it because, obviously, there is something wrong with her. What is she to think? Naturally she will think that there must be something wrong with her because he *is* noticing her.

"What?" I demanded, feeling unaccountably peevish.

"I'm making you nervous. Why is that?"

"You're looking at me," I muttered.

"You don't want me looking at you?"

No, yes. *Yes.*

"I can never tell what you're thinking, or whether you're Special Agent Maitland thinking or just a guy standing in my kitchen drinking beer thinking."

He set his bottle down on the counter. His eyes were darker, his voice deeper. "To answer your question, I'm the guy standing in your kitchen drinking beer thinking. Why don't you come here, Tilly, and I'll tell you exactly what he's thinking."

"I'm fine here."

"What is wrong with you?" Blossom said. "Go for it."

"I'm thinking, I'm thinking," I said.

"Stop thinking," she ordered.

"You're thinking again," Will observed.

"Now or never," Blossom warned.

"Please, Blossom, will you shut up? I've got a situation here."

"Tilly," Will said, "Blossom's at the beach."

I swear I heard a vertebra pop out of alignment as I jerked around. No Blossom.

"Come here," he said again, his voice a little rough around the edges. "Don't you want to know what I'm thinking?"

"Say yes, you idiot," Blossom whispered.

Go. Away.

"That's my girl. Have fun."

"Yes," I said to Will.

"Closer."

"Okay."

"You never felt like this about me," Alex said. "What was I, chopped liver?"

"Not now," I said.

"Yes, now," Will said, pulling me against him and kissing the breath right out of me.

"It's because I had a small penis, isn't it?" Alex

persisted. "It's not like a guy can do anything about his penis, Tilly. You have to use the equipment God gave you."

God had been kind to Will Maitland—very, very kind.

"The Viagra helped," Alex said.

"This is not a good time," I told him. "I can't talk now. Can't you see I've got two tongues in my mouth?"

"Stop talking, Tilly," Will growled. In about ten seconds the sarong slid to the floor, followed by my swimsuit.

His dark eyes traveled down my body, slowly. "Nice," he murmured.

He pulled off his black T-shirt, peeled down his faded jeans, slipped off his sneakers. I swear I went into cardiac arrest for a few seconds.

A girl can only take so much. I tried to back away. "Maybe this isn't such a good idea. You, me. Under the circumstances."

He folded his arms across his chest and smiled. "Scared?"

I sprang to my own defense. "No, I am not scared. It's just not going to work, that's all."

He looked down at himself, then grinned up at me. "Seems to be working just fine."

"That's not what I meant," I blustered as he scooped me up and headed for the couch.

"Yes, it is, and you're just a little bit scared. It's been, what, three years? We'll start off easy, like this." His tongue traced a wide circle around my left breast, moving in slow spirals toward the center until I couldn't stand it any longer and grabbed the back of his head and arched up against his clever mouth. I heard him laugh softly.

"Not the couch, dear," Aunt Ginger said. "You're going to want a nice big bed for this one."

"What is this, Grand Central Station?" I demanded. "And I don't want this one; I don't want anyone."

"Liar," Will said. "You want me. Allow me to demonstrate." He moved lower and almost slid off the end of the couch.

"For pity's sake, Matilda, the poor man's going to be on the floor in a minute. He needs room to work."

She was right, of course. Aunt Ginger had a lot of experience when it came to this sort of thing. I didn't know how I was going to be able to stand up, let alone drag him twenty feet down the hall to my bedroom.

"We can't do this here," I gasped as his tongue touched on a particularly sensitive spot.

"Sure we can."

"Better get a move on," Aunt Ginger advised. "Neither of you is going to last much longer."

I managed to wriggle away from him and roll off the couch. "We don't have a lot of time here," I warned him.

"You've got that right." He lunged.

Somehow I fended him off and darted down the hall.

"Well done, Matilda!" Aunt Ginger cheered.

The bedroom door hadn't even slammed shut behind us when he brought me down on the big bed in a tackle worthy of an NFL linebacker.

"Why can't anything be easy with you, Tilly?" he growled. "Now here's what we're going to do. You're going to stop muttering to yourself and give me your undivided attention. In case you've forgotten how it goes after three years—"

I glared up at him. "Hey, wait just a minute. You don't know that. Maybe I've been doing the guys at Rizzo's Pool Hall every Saturday night for the past three years."

"It's possible," he allowed.

"Lots of sailors down at Boston Harbor when the fleet comes in."

"I expect there are."

"You can find some pretty decent talent at Gold's Gym," I went on. "Let's see. The pizza delivery guy's always horny." I was running out of ideas. "Um, my neighbor has a foot fetish—"

He put a finger to my lips and shook his head. "Repeat after me.

"Will, you are the first man I've had in three years."

"Will, you are the first man I've had in three years."

"You are the first man I've wanted in three years."

"You are the first man I've wanted in three years."

"I desire only to be your love slave and serve your every base, perverted fantasy."

I bit down on the finger, hard.

He laughed. "It was worth a try. For now, let's just go with the basics and see where it takes us."

Sounded good to me.

"I think I'm losing count," I gasped, still reeling from the explosion of stars as he slid up my body and slipped one arm beneath me to raise me to him. "How many times—?"

"Twice."

"Twice? I thought . . . What about the shower?"

"Trust me, math was always my strong subject."

The phone on the bedside table was ringing.

"Will, the phone's ringing."

"I don't hear any phone."

The ringing stopped, then started up again immediately. Stopped; rang insistently.

I groaned in frustration and stretched over to grab the receiver with my free hand. Will was still buried deep inside me, hard as a steel beam and fighting not to move.

"Tilly? It's Blossom. You sound out of breath."

I managed to form a nearly coherent sentence. "Run, had to, phone."

"What are you doing? We've been waiting for you for hours."

For a moment I simply could not find my voice. "Writer's block," I rasped.

I was shaking beneath him, my muscles clenching around him. He slid his hand between us and caressed the spot where our bodies were joined.

"No, stop," I gasped.

"Are you okay?" Blossom asked.

"I can't talk right now, Blossom. Just had a stroke of, um, stroke of . . . inspiration, that's it, inspiration. Get me something at Big Pink," I croaked and slammed down the phone.

"Three," Will groaned as he moved hard against me one last time, let go, and took me with him over the edge.

"Four, actually," I murmured against his neck a few minutes later.

TWENTY-ONE

You have to be really careful around Scarlett. She can pick up on a little clue here and a little clue there that no one else sees, feed the data into that analytical mind of hers, and she *knows.*

I thought I was doing remarkably well by the time they arrived home loaded down with goodies from Big Pink, but my studied nonchalance was no match for those shrewd olive green eyes.

"So, did you finish writing the piece?" she inquired as we set out the feast in the garden.

I emptied a huge bag of chips into a bowl. "Pretty much. Needs a little tweaking here and there, but it's about ready to go."

"Writer's block, huh?"

"Yup."

She nodded her head towards Will, who was playing catch with Baskerville. "He help you?"

I tried to look puzzled. "Help me?"

"You know, get unblocked."

"Tilly, you're rolling your eyes again," Blossom

scolded as she emerged from the hotel carrying two six packs of Amstel Light. "Remember the sharks. What happened to the Rolling Rock? I could have sworn there were two bottles left.

"You really should have given it a rest and come to the beach," she went on. "There was some good talent there today."

"Blossom, men who wear Speedos are not talent," Scarlett said. "They're dorks."

Blossom stared at Will and nudged me. "Lots of talent here too."

"I wouldn't know," I replied.

Oh yes, you would, Scarlett's eyes said.

"That man should be wearin' one of them chastity belts Ginger got in the store," Missy Mae said, "on account of all the women who wanna jump his bone."

"Bones," I corrected her, "it's plural. Jump his bones."

Missy Mae positively cackled. "I say bone, child, I mean bone."

"Onion ring, anyone?" I said brightly.

Virgil appeared with a sizzling platter of Buffalo wings, and everyone started loading up their plates. "I didn't expect to see you here, Agent Maitland," Virgil said. "Tilly finally decide to let you in?"

"Yes, Tilly," Scarlett said, "tell us what made you decide to let Agent Maitland in. Without a warrant," she added with a perfectly straight face.

I set my plate down on the table, dabbed daintily at my mouth with a paper napkin, and smiled at her. "Scarlett, dear, could I have a word with you?"

". . . third time this week we caught that Richie the Ratfink out there spyin' on us," Missy Mae was saying when we returned ten minutes later. "There's another one too. Sits over at the Zephyr. We call him Mr. Clean on account he bald as a baby's butt." She looked at Will. "Might be one of yours I told Tilly, so she marches right over and asks to see his badge but he don't got one, says he just like hangin' out there."

Remain calm, I instructed myself.

"Virgil, Alonzo, maybe you and Missy Mae could run down to the liquor store and pick up some Rolling Rock. Blossom says we're out." Somehow I didn't think I was going to need to stock up on Dos Equis after all.

Silence comes in many moods from contemplative right up to postapocalyptic. The silence that settled over the garden was uncomfortable verging on ominous.

Blossom doesn't intimidate easily. "It isn't as bad as it sounds," she said to Will.

"No?"

Scarlett jumped right in. "Absolutely not. If we thought we were in any danger, we would have called you, wouldn't we?"

Clever, Scarlett, I thought, but he's not going to buy it.

"Would you?" Will inquired softly.

"Of course we would," Blossom said "All we're trying to do is keep the business going until Tilly can figure out what to do about Ginger's will. Everyone knows now that the pillow box isn't here. Tilly even posted a sign on the front of the shop saying so."

"I'll get it." Scarlett disappeared into the hotel.

"We haven't received threatening phone calls or anything like that," Blossom told Will.

"I know. We've had a tap on the office phone for a while."

We'd taken that possibility into consideration since the FBI and Interpol had been keeping Aunt Ginger under surveillance, but the idea that popped into my mind at that moment froze my blood.

"Here we are," Scarlett announced. " 'On the advice of the FBI and the Property Crime Division of Interpol, Erratica will no longer stock pillow boxes and similar items on the premises. We invite inquiries, however, and regret any inconvenience our new policy may occasion. Please see manager for further information.' "

"It was Tilly's idea," Blossom said. "Sort of a preemptive strike in case anyone thought we had the pillow box. Since we put it up, no one's tried to break in again."

Scarlett scrambled into damage-control mode. "We aren't absolutely certain someone tried to break in," she said, looking daggers at Blossom. "Nothing was disturbed or stolen. We had a lot of cats around at the time and they tend to get into mischief. The alarm didn't even go off." She smiled at Will. "You told Tilly we had to be careful, so we got a new alarm code just in case and had new locks installed."

"The man at Zephyr hasn't been around for days," Blossom added, trying to stack the deck in our favor.

"So there you have it," Scarlett concluded like a lawyer summing up before the jury. "We've done everything possible to cooperate with you and the FBI, and to ensure our own safety."

I have to say Scarlett and Blossom can put on a pretty good show, but it was too much to hope he'd buy it.

"I am only going to say this once," Will said slowly. "Whatever you three are up to, I promise you that I will close you down if it interferes in this investigation."

"You mean you'll close down Erratica," Scarlett said.

"No, I will close down the whole place. You, Ms. Snow, will go back to Boston. Ms. MacMorrough, you will return to Key West and stay there. The others will have to find somewhere else to live for the time being."

"And where will I be going?" I said.

He looked at me for the first time since Missy Mae opened her big mouth. "You will be going to jail as a material witness, as I believe I have already explained."

I looked at Blossom and Scarlett. "We'll have to behave ourselves then, won't we, girls?"

"Yes, Tilly," they chorused.

I turned back to him. "Is there anything else you'd like to say, Agent Maitland?"

"No."

"Then if you're done with Scarlett and Blossom," I said sweetly, "perhaps they can be excused so I could have a word with you in private?"

"Uh-oh," I heard Blossom mutter. "Not good."

"Um, Tilly, this might not be the best time—"

I didn't take my eyes off Will's face. "No, Scarlett, I think this is the perfect time."

Nobody said a word as they loaded up the trays and trooped off.

I cleared my throat, feeling strangely calm. I'd ask the question, and then perhaps I'd know what kind of man Will Maitland really was.

"Just for the record, since you say the office phone is tapped—which, by the way, we already guessed—did you also obtain a warrant to plant listening devices on this property before or since my aunt died? In Erratica or Alonzo's studio or Missy Mae's room or the spare rooms on the third floor?"

"No."

"Aunt Ginger's apartment?"

He had to know what I was thinking.

I waited for the answer, looking him straight in the eye.

"No."

"Do you know if the FBI did?"

"No, but I'll find out. If they did, I'll make sure they're removed."

I nodded, satisfied he was telling the truth, but feeling empty and sad. "Thank you."

He leaned across the table and took my hand. "I'm sorry, Tilly."

I shrugged. "There's nothing to be sorry about. You have a job to do. This afternoon shouldn't have happened. You know: business, pleasure. Cop, suspect; oil, water. Special Agent Will Maitland thinking, guy standing in my kitchen drinking beer thinking."

"Are you sorry?" he said softly.

I shook my head. "You?"

"Definitely not."

He let go of my hand and stood up. "Let's see what happens when I get back."

"Oh, you're going away?" Will was going away.

"I have to go to Kingston. I should be back in a week or so. If you need to get in touch with me, call the office. And for God's sake, Tilly, stay out of trouble."

"I'll try."

"Try harder."

Blossom folded her arms and tapped a toe. "Out with it."

I gave a greasy plate a quick rinse and set it in the dishwasher. "What do you want me to say?"

"Tilly, this is Blossom you're talking to. You don't expect me to buy this 'he dropped by and we had a beer' stuff, do you?"

"I'm not asking you to buy anything," I said testily. "He did drop by and we did have a beer."

"Hold on, Blossom," Scarlett said. "We're not going to get it out of her this way by asking questions. I already tried. Let's tell her what happened. Sit down, Tilly."

I wiped my hands on a towel. "I have to finish the bees copy and e-mail it out tonight."

"Oh, no, you don't," Blossom said, beating me to the door.

"Blossom," I growled. "I don't have time for this."

"Then we'll make it quick."

I turned around, looking for help from Scarlett. She was holding a chair for me.

"So," she began when we were all settled. "Here's what happened. You take your laptop out to the garden to work; it's a nice day, not too hot, good to be outside. He appears. You're annoyed at the interruption, yes—you want to get your piece written and go to the beach—but excited to see him. You've been having dreams, fantasies about him, maybe a little kinky. He apologizes for interrupting. You offer him a beer."

I started to get up. "That's what I said. Now can I—"

"I'm not finished," Scarlett said.

"Let me tell," Blossom said. "You offer him a beer. He's looking at you; you're uncomfortable. You know he's going to make a move, but you haven't had a man in three years and you're scared. A man like that doesn't take no for an answer. You worry; he can have any woman he wants, so why you? He scoops you up and carries you to the bed."

"Couch," I said under my breath.

"He's hung—a blind grandmother can see that—and the man knows what he's doing. You start to relax, let go. The earth moves. You've gone two rounds. I call. Disaster! We'll be back soon. Will there be time for a third round? Is he up to it? *Yes and yes!*"

"So, Tilly," Scarlett said, "that's what happened. Would you care to fill us in on the details?"

"No, I would not." Gathering the shreds of my dignity about me, I marched out of the kitchen and down the hall, changed my mind and marched back.

"Three times," Blossom was saying. "Holy hell, three times!"

I poked my head in. "Four, actually." I could hear Blossom moaning as I sauntered away.

Revenge can be soooo sweet.

TWENTY-TWO

The following day I decided it was time to show Blossom and Scarlett the Singapore receipt. Will was on his way to Kingston, and I had to kick my own investigation into high gear.

"I told you she's been hiding something," Blossom said to Scarlett.

"I know," Scarlett said. "She doesn't want us to get in any deeper than we already are. She's worried we're going to end up in jail with her."

How did they *know* these things?

"Orch r bide to cairn 77 66 62350882 wong 195 lim 2 firm yee 203. Perp sing!"

"I think the three names might be a company," I said. "You know, Wong, Lim & Yee. A firm."

It took Scarlett all of five seconds to pull up the Singapore white pages on-screen. "There's a Wong & Yee, a Wong Wong & Lim, two Lim & Lims, and a Yee Yee Yee & Lim. I don't see a Wong, Lim & Yee. Did you know there are only about five hundred basic Chinese surnames?" Scarlett's brain attracts factoids like a giant magnet picks up iron filings.

"So the only link between the names is the fact that all three have numbers after them," Blossom said. "Maybe it's 'firm' like in the price of something. Firm: that's the price and you can't bargain or you won't change your mind." Like Scarlett, Blossom is addicted to eBay.

"Blossom, you're brilliant!" Scarlett said. "I bet Wong, Lim, and Yee were in a bidding war for the pillow box. Wong was in for 195, Lim for 200—he was firm on that—and Yee for 203."

"Thousand dollars?" I squeaked. "That can't be right."

Blossom shook her head. "No way."

"I can't think of any other interpretation," Scarlett said.

She frowned. "Of course, that doesn't tell us who was selling it, only who was willing to pay a fortune for it."

"Do we know the name of the collector it was stolen from?" Blossom asked me. "Maybe he's 'Perp.' "

"Will never said."

Scarlett turned over the receipt. "Now for the signature. It's almost illegible, but you can see it's not Lorraine Snapp or 'Ginger Snapp.' "

"There's an *h*, or maybe it's an *n*," Blossom said, "and that looks like *ng*."

Blossom took off her glasses and held the paper a scant inch in front of her eyes. "The initials could be 'S.S.' or maybe 'F.F.' I'll see if I can find a magnifying glass in Ginger's office."

"Don't bother," I said, "I know who it is. "It's an *h* and the initials are 'L.L.'

"L. L. Hungwell. Lorraine Louise Hungwell."

* * *

Baskerville needed a walk and I needed some thinking time alone. We decided to take in the ultrahip scene along Ocean Drive.

I guess I hadn't thought it through. Of course Interpol's first step would be to find out if Aunt Ginger had been in Singapore in May when the pillow box of Win Win Poo was stolen. But she'd been traveling on a fake passport under the name Hungwell and they hadn't been able to trace her movements. Will suspected there was a connection between Aunt Ginger and the man who'd been murdered in the brothel in Kingston shortly after arriving in Jamaica from Singapore, but since he didn't know Aunt Ginger had been in Singapore, the only connection he could make was that they were both in Jamaica at the same time and she died a week after the mystery man did.

I stopped dead in my tracks. Could Will possibly believe that Aunt Ginger murdered the man in Kingston and then was murdered herself? Worse still, could I?

Could he be "Perp"? Had Aunt Ginger seen "Perp" in Singapore? Had there been a falling out among thieves?

"Really, Matilda, you're watching too many cop shows," Aunt Ginger observed from the Great Beyond.

My knees went weak. I looked around for somewhere to sit down, spotted an empty table at an outdoor café across the street, and made a beeline for it.

It was only when I'd plopped down and ordered iced tea from a snotty waiter who introduced himself somewhat reluctantly as "Jason, your server today," and who regarded me as though I were something the cat dragged in, that I realized I'd staggered into Hurricane Alley, Ocean Drive's preferred watering hole for the beyond-rich-and-famous and the beyond-boring-and-bored.

"I wonder if you could pass me a few packets of your Splenda," a husky female voice said. "We can't seem to get the waiter's attention."

I'd have to have spent the past year on Mars not to know who the woman at the next table was. In the No-One-Ever-Said-Life-Was-Fair department of ordinary women's lives, "Artemis" was as stunning in person as she was on the cover of every fashion magazine and celebrity tabloid in the known universe.

Mirrored bronze wrap sunglasses could not conceal the identity of her superstar companion, Lincoln Steele, nor, I suspected, were they intended to.

Even among the herd of glitterati that stampeded up and down Ocean Drive from morning to night and night to morning, Artemis and "Linc" blazed like the sun. Which is why, of course, everyone studiously ignored them, including their waiter. Gawking is way uncool, in the parlance of the young.

Everyone except Baskerville, that is, who disdains cool and was eyeing the white bichon frise on Artemis's lap with suspicious intent.

"Thanks," Lincoln Steele said as I passed him the cut-glass bowl of sugar and artificial sweetener packets.

"There's Lenny K.," Artemis exclaimed. "I'll be right back. Hold Biscuit, Linc."

"Your dog is drooling on my shoe."

I leaned down and peered under the table. Without my noticing—a person can be excused for not being her usual alert self when a cinema god is sitting at the next table—Baskerville had inched over and was poking his big wet black nose at a pair of shoes that must have cost more than my snotty waiter earned in a week.

I could just see tomorrow's headlines in *Variety*:

!!!DOG DROOLS ON LINC'S SHOE!!!
DreamWorks stock down eight points
Spielberg: "No comment."
Full report p. 8

I crawled under the table and hauled Baskerville back by the collar.

"Am I going to need a lawyer?"

Lincoln Steele laughed. "I'll let it pass. This time."

The waiter bustled over and handed me the check. "Will that be all, *madam?*"

Obviously, I wasn't just something the cat dragged in, in my baggy shorts and Boston Red Sox T-shirt and ratty sneakers. I was the creature from the Black Lagoon that had slithered out of its fetid swamp and somehow ended up on the patio of Hurricane Alley in superchic South Beach and needed to be dispatched before it scared off the denizens of Botox Nation.

And it had the nerve to bring its dog with it.

I pointed to my iced tea, which I'd barely touched, and smiled sweetly. "Actually, no. And would you be kind enough to bring my dog a bowl of water?" I said in my best Grace Kelly manner.

The battle lines were drawn.

"I regret to say," he sniffed, "that we do not serve dogs at Hurricane Alley."

Someone cleared his throat at the next table. "While you're at it, bring my dog a bowl of water too. Perrier."

The waiter took one look at Lincoln Steele stroking Artemis's little Biscuit, and said, "Of course, Mr. Steele, I'll see to it right away."

He turned to me. "Perrier as well, madam?"

I considered for a moment and couldn't resist. "He prefers Evian. Room temperature, please."

"Of course, madam." Jason bustled away.

Lincoln Steele threw back his head and laughed. "Well played."

I'm pretty sure I blushed. "Thanks. I guess I can't blame him. I look like something the cat dragged in."

He reached over and extended his hand. "Lincoln Steele."

Like the man needed to introduce himself, but it was rather sweet of him, I thought. "It's nice to meet you. Tilly Snapp."

"More like something the dog dragged in," he said with a laugh. "You still look a little green around the gills."

"I beg your pardon?"

"When I saw you hotfooting it over here, you looked like you'd seen a ghost."

Artemis returned, casting a cool look in my direction, cooed over her little "Biscuitbabykins," and informed Linc that she had to go to the little girls' room and then they really had to get moving or she'd be late for her fitting.

I reached down to untie Baskerville's leash from the table leg. "I'd better get him out of here, or your dog is going to suffer a fate worse than death."

"It's a he," Linc said.

"Baskerville doesn't discriminate on the basis of gender. Better safe than sorry."

I rummaged through my backpack for my wallet.

"Damn, damn, damn," I muttered when I found it contained exactly $2.37. Jason was going to have a field day with this.

"Problem?" Lincoln Steele said.

"I forgot to stop at the ATM."

"I'll get it." He leaned over and dropped a twenty on my table, which would just about cover a glass of iced tea in a place like Hurricane Alley.

"Please, that's not necessary," I protested. "I've got my credit card."

"I insist."

People were staring at us.

"Um, okay, thanks. Drop by and I'll give you a discount."

He leered charmingly, a talent that earned him fifteen million a picture plus a percentage of the gross. "What are you selling, sweetheart?"

I rolled my eyes. "Not what you're thinking." I rummaged in my bag again and pulled out a business card. "The shop is called Erratica, 'The Emporium of Curiosities for the Discriminating Collector.' On Española Way. We'll be reopening on Sunday."

"I might just do that. I'm a curious guy."

I noticed Artemis heading back with a decidedly unfriendly gleam in her eye, and dragged Baskerville away.

"Don't be daft, Tilly," Scarlett said. "Your aunt Ginger didn't murder anyone. She was a kook, not a psychopath."

I gave the little ceramic satyr a final wipe and set it

back on the shelf. "I know, but I can't help feeling that I'm not seeing something that's staring me right in the face."

"You have to understand the victim before you can find the killer," said Blossom, who has read more mysteries than any other human being I've ever known. "They're two sides of the same coin."

"See, there's the problem," I said. "I can't see Aunt Ginger as a killer, but I can't see her as a victim either. I might be able to understand how she got herself into this mess in the first place, but I'll never understand how she let herself get killed."

"After the opening, I think we should sit down and work up a timeline," the ever-practical and organized Scarlett said. "Try to trace her movements from the day she was at Borders in Singapore until the night she died. I'll download all the e-mails between May 16 and September 30. The telephone messages in the office were erased up through September 18. I expect she did that before she left for Jamaica. It's a shame her cell phone disappeared when they ransacked her room at the resort; we might have gotten her speed-dial numbers and been able to access the messages on that phone."

"Have you heard from Harry Hungwell?" Blossom asked.

I sighed. "No. Wickerby's been trying to reach him too, but no luck."

After ten days' hard work, the shop was finally coming together. We started out reorganizing by taking each item and assigning it a rating—G, PG, PG-13, R, NC-17, X, XX, and XXX—then shelving it accordingly. G, PG, and PG-13 were displayed for anyone to see. The customer had to find his way to a screened-off area at the rear of the store if he was in the market for R and NC-17; I expected a lot of traffic back there. X through XXX were not on public display, but a sign on the wall above the long glass counter read PLEASE APPLY TO THE MANAGER FOR A FULL LIST OF SPECIALIZED MERCHANDISE.

We discovered things in a storeroom in the basement that defied categorization and, for that matter, comprehension. We came up with a special rating for them: C-a-H, which stood for Creepy-as-Hell. I intended to douse them with gasoline and light a match at the earliest opportunity.

"Can't people read the sign?" Blossom complained when a skinny man of about sixty wearing a baker's apron rapped on the glass.

I unlocked the door. "I'm sorry, we're closed. We'll be reopening on Sunday."

"Heard about Ginger," he said. "Rotten shame. Thought I'd come by, see if you want us to continue deliveries. Name's Eddie."

"Deliveries?"

"Cookies, every Tuesday morning."

"I wondered about that," said Scarlett. "I saw the invoices."

Blossom perked up. "Did someone say cookies?"

"Best in South Beach. Hold on, I've got some left on the truck."

He returned with a large white bakery box. "I put in a variety so you choose what you want to order. Ginger, now, she'd order a mix of penises, breasts, and mouths most weeks; hearts and flowers on Valentine's Day, of course; naked Santas at Christmas. Last year when she was running a special on fetish items, we did up some nice feet for her. We usually throw in a half dozen Winnie the Poohs or Elmos in case someone brings their kids in with them."

"Here, try one," Blossom said to me. "Mmmm, real butter. These are great, Eddie."

"All natural ingredients."

I had come a fair distance down the long and winding road that led through Wonderland, but I wasn't quite ready yet for shortbread penises. I opted for a mouth.

I asked Eddie if they could make a special delivery in time for the opening on Sunday. They could. "Let's hold off on the penises for the moment," I told him, "but I'll take the mouths and breasts. Moons and stars and flowers might be nice. We'll go with Winnie the Pooh for the children. No feet."

We got back down to the business of where to put what.

"What about the potty-chairs?" I asked Blossom, who seemed to have a knack for finding exactly the right place for everything.

These potty-chairs were definitely not your ordinary K-Mart models. Two had heated gold-plated seats, one played "The Itsy Bitsy Spider" when sat upon, and the other bore the monogram *HRH Gregor IV.* They were marked with red tags as sold, but we couldn't find the actual record of the sale. I expect anyone who collects potty-chairs would choose to do so as discreetly as possible. Blossom suggested they would make a cute window display, so we put them in the kitsch window to the left of the front door.

"We have two love swings of the Dowager Empress Takamiya," Scarlett reported. "NC-17?"

Blossom frowned. "How about the nice leather one with the padded velvet straps in NC-17, and the rope number in XXX—it's got more of a bondage feel about it. And I think the walking sticks would make a nice grouping in the window too," she added.

The walking sticks made me a bit queasy. A lot queasy actually. I'm pretty certain I wouldn't want to be seen parading down Fifth Avenue on the arm of a gentleman sporting a walking stick made from a bull's penis. Of course, if I were carrying a shoulder bag made from a bull's ballock, I couldn't very well cavil.

Scarlett informed me that they were guaranteed "Made in the USA," which you have to agree is suitably patriotic and likely a strong selling point. I suppose if you're going to slice off some poor bull's pride and joy, trot it over to your friendly neighborhood taxidermist to be sterilized and cured, stretch it over a metal rod, and cap it with brass knob—in the shape of a bull's head, of course—it would be churlish to sneak off to snatch one from, say, Namibia or Iceland.

These canes also come in boar and antelope, which are native, and elephant, which is not. I imagine zookeepers across the land keep a pretty close lookout when the canemakers' convention comes to town.

"Someone sent an e-mail asking if we had any musical condoms," Scarlett said as she put the finishing touches on "The Wonderful World of Condoms" display in a glass case near the door that led to the office.

"Musical condoms?" I gasped.

"Believe it or not," Scarlett said. "I looked it up on the Internet."

"What a great idea!" Blossom enthused. "What kind of music?"

"All kinds. 'Happy Birthday to You,' 'The Wedding March,' 'Twinkle Twinkle Little Star,' 'Old MacDonald Had a Farm.' "

"How about the 'Hallelujah' chorus?" Blossom asked.

"I didn't see that, but I'll check it out. The music gets louder as things heat up, so there's bound to be a hallelujah chorus somewhere. They don't run on batteries, but they're guaranteed not to electrocute you.

"You'd be surprised what you can find if you poke around," Scarlett continued. "I found a site that lists two hundred euphemisms for male masturbation. And there's even a site for electric-chair fetishists."

And just when I thought Wonderland couldn't get any weirder.

As we worked our way through the inventory, I made a mental list of things my friends especially liked. Virgil seemed taken with a bra, size 42-DD, autographed by Anna Nicole Smith. Missy Mae expressed interest in a set of Victorian grave bells; they might come in handy to summon assistance if by chance she were buried alive. Alonzo became engrossed in a how-to manual entitled *Visual Guide to Lock-Picking*. Blossom had her eye on a set of ivory and ebony chess pieces in the shape of phalluses, and Scarlett ooohed and aaahed—a thing she rarely does—over an Art Nouveau lamp with a white shag glass shade hand-painted with scenes of Victorian couples cavorting *au naturel* amid England's green and leafy bowers. To make sure these things weren't sold on opening day, I secretly altered the display cards to read "sale pending."

By late Saturday night, we were ready to roll.

The trap was baited and the spring set. Now all we needed was the rat.

Twenty-three

"I've already told you, sir, it's not for sale," I said.

The less than pleased customer drew himself up to his full five feet three inches, extracted a wad of bills from a crocodile-skin wallet, and slapped them down on the counter. "Name your price."

"There is no price, sir. It's not for sale."

"I demand to see the owner."

"I *am* the owner."

"Do you know who I am, young woman?"

No, I didn't know who he was and I didn't want to. We'd been going back and forth for ten minutes, and I was running short on patience.

"I am Stuart Highsmith," he informed me. "I own the largest collection of cremation urns in the country, if not the world, and I am the president of Necropher-nalia Collectors of America. The former proprietor of this shop would not have displayed an item that she did not intend to sell."

"Excuse me, miss," an elderly gentleman in madras

shorts and an orange polo shirt said. "Do you have any more of the breasts?"

"Let me check," I said, profoundly grateful for the interruption. I really wasn't up to explaining to Mr. Highsmith that the former proprietor presently occupied the urn in question, which was precisely why it wasn't for sale.

"You're in luck, there's one left," I told the old gentleman, handing over the sugar cookie on a napkin.

"I'm a breast man," he said shyly as he nibbled. "I'm almost eighty, but I still like a good breast."

"We've got some lovely marble breasts right over there," I said, pointing to a shelf against the far wall. A good salesperson would have accompanied him, but I wasn't going to leave Mr. Highsmith alone with Aunt Ginger's urn. He couldn't get to it easily—he would need a ladder to reach the shelf high on the wall behind the counter—but I didn't like the look in his eyes. Seeing that I wasn't going to budge, he took his leave in a huff.

The opening was proving to be a great success. Some of the people who trooped in and out all afternoon were acquaintances of Aunt Ginger's or regular customers. Others had read about Erratica in the paper and come to check it out, and we attracted a good number of tourists on their way from the street market to Lincoln Road Mall. Even the weather cooperated with a brief downpour around three that had people running for shelter.

No one asked about pillow boxes, but X to XXX did a brisk trade. Whips seemed especially popular. Alonzo had to escort a group of sniggering teenagers out of R and NC-17, and Virgil followed a woman out onto the sidewalk and returned with a life-size bronze Indian phallus of impressive proportions, ca. seventeenth century, that had somehow found its way into her purse without her having any idea how it got there.

"It's going well, don't you think?" said Scarlett.

Blossom joined us. "You look great, Tilly. I like the tube top; it's a good color for you. You're starting to look très South Beach. It suits you.

"Wow, is that who I think it is?" she suddenly exclaimed.

I looked around the shop. "Who?"

"No, outside. My God, it is! Lincoln Steele! And Artemis is with him."

"Oh right," I said. "He said he might drop by."

"He said . . . ? You *know* Lincoln Steele?"

"No, Blossom, I don't know him. He paid for my iced tea and Baskerville's water because I forgot to go to the ATM, and I offered him a discount if he ever came by the shop. I never thought he would."

"You amaze me," Blossom said shaking her head. "You're only in South Beach for a month and you're hanging out with Lincoln Steele. I think I've been underestimating you, Tilly."

"I am not hanging out—"

"Uh-oh," Scarlett said. "I think we may have a situation developing out there."

"God, I hope not," I said. "We're going to end up in court if the police have to come out to restore order one more time. Sgt. Narducci was pretty understanding about Aunt Ginger's memorial service, but he really pitched a fit during the FBI/*CSI: Miami* mix-up. He had to call in the Motorcycle Squad to clear the street, and while that was going on someone stole his bike. He told me he'd arrest me on the spot if he had to—"

"Oh, dear," Scarlett said. "People are starting to push and shove to get a look at them and ask for autographs. I think those must be their bodyguards moving in to protect them. Here come the news vans. Hold on, I think I hear a helicopter."

Bad dream, not happening, I told myself.

"Look, they're coming in," Blossom said. She urged me forward. "Go say hello."

"Um, hi," I said to Linc. "I didn't think you'd show up."

"I told you, I'm a curious guy."

"Well, just have a look around. If there's anything I can help you with let me know."

The phone in the office was ringing. "Excuse me."

I ran to the back of the store and picked up the receiver. "Erratica. Can I help you?"

"Yes, hello. I understand you've reopened your shop. Hello, hello?"

"We seem to have a bad line," I said. "Where are you calling from?"

"I am calling from Singapore."

I sat down with a thud.

"Do you hear me?" the man said.

"Yes, I hear you."

"My name is Robert Lu. I found your web site on the Internet. I'd be interested to know what other merchandise you have in your shop in Miami. I'm particularly interested in ancient Chinese—" His voice was fading in and out.

"Mr. Lu, I'm afraid I can't hear you very well. If you'll give me your number, I'll call you back."

"What? I don't hear you."

"Your number, Mr. Lu. I need your telephone number."

"I will send an e-mail."

"Can you just give me a better idea of what you're looking for?" I shouted, but he was gone.

I slammed the phone down. "Damn, damn, damn."

Scarlett appeared at the office door looking anxious. "What's wrong? Who was that on the phone?"

"A man named Robert Lu, calling from Singapore. He said he saw us on the Internet. But the connection was terrible and he wouldn't give me his phone number to call him back. He said he'd send an e-mail telling me what he's looking for."

"Well, at least that's something. We'll have an e-mail address to work with. I might be able to trace it back. This is good, Tilly; we got our first nibble."

Blossom poked her head in. "Linc wants to talk to you."

The phone rang again. I grabbed it. "Yes? Mr. Lu?"

"Staying out of trouble?"

Zing! went the strings of my heart.

Scarlett poked me. "Mr. Lu?"

I shook my head and mouthed, "Will." Scarlett grinned.

"How are you, Will?"

"Aren't you going to ask what I've learned in Kingston?"

It would have been my second question. The identity of the man in the brothel was a crucial clue in discovering who killed Aunt Ginger.

"Well, since you bring it up, what have you learned?"

"I'm afraid I can't share that information with you."

"You're pond scum, Will Maitland."

"I asked you if you wanted to know," he said with an evil chuckle. "I didn't say I'd tell you."

I have a fairly well-developed malicious streak myself.

"Well, thank you for calling. I'm sorry I can't stay to chat but I really can't keep him waiting."

"Who can't you keep waiting?" Will demanded.

"Linc."

"Linc? Who the hell is Linc?"

"Lincoln Steele," I said brightly. "You know, the movie star?"

"He a friend of yours?"

"Uh-huh."

"A close friend?"

"I'm afraid I can't share that information with you."

"Tilly—"

"Gotta run, Will. Have a nice day."

Put that in your pipe and smoke it, Agent Maitland.

Artemis wanted to buy Scarlett's Art Nouveau lamp. I told her it was sold.

"It doesn't say sold," she pointed out. "It says 'sale pending.' "

"I know, but I'm holding it."

Artemis looked to Linc. "I love it. I really want it."

Linc took me aside and turned on the charm. "The woman will make my life a living hell if she can't have it. Do you want that on your conscience?"

"Oh, I think I'll be able to sleep at night."

"You're a hard woman, Tilly."

"I have an idea. Artemis, I've got another lamp that I think you might like."

I took her into the office and showed her La

Femme, which I was considering keeping for myself. "She's beautiful, don't you think?" I said. "She reminds me of you; I thought so the first time I saw her."

I thought no such thing. I had never given Artemis a single thought in my life. But it did the trick. Linc took me aside again, pledged his eternal gratitude, kissed my hand, and told me if I ever needed anything to leave a message for him under the name Jimmy Crane at the Fisher Island Club.

Scarlett nudged me. "Uh-oh."

I groaned. Sgt. Narducci stood in the doorway glowering at me, and behind him I could see the two bodyguards and three police officers trying to push back the excited crowd that had gathered when news got out that Lincoln Steele and Artemis were on a shopping spree at Erratica.

"Looks like ya got a heap o' trouble, Miz Tilly," Linc drawled in a remarkably good imitation of John Wayne.

"You don't know the half of it," I muttered.

"Now, don't you go worryin' about it, little lady," he said. "You just stay right here and let Linc handle it."

The royal couple departed a few minutes later, smiled and waved at their adoring subjects, and drove off in a black Porsche Cabriolet back to the celestial realm wherein they dwelt. In their wake they left a flustered Sgt. Narducci clutching their autographs and looking forward to seeing his picture, posing for the camera with a grinning Lincoln Steele's arm thrown around his shoulder, on the evening news.

"Man, you can't buy that kind of publicity," Blossom enthused. "We'll be on the news and get written up in the papers, and word will be out all over Miami that Erratica is hot, hot, hot. Maybe one of the TV tabloid shows will check us out. We could really make something of Erratica, don't you think, Tilly?"

I did think so, but then again I didn't want to think about the implications. As far as I was concerned, Erratica was only a means to an end: intended to lure players in the pillow box affair out into the open and ultimately expose the person who killed Aunt Ginger.

"When the renovations are finished and the arcade is restored," Blossom went on, "we could expand, maybe organize the merchandise in separate, connecting shops, so we wouldn't have the problem of displaying G next to XXX. The high-end merchandise needs its own display space too."

Blossom was launched and I didn't have the heart to burst her bubble by reminding her that I intended to sell. "I see branches in Palm Beach and Key West!" she said.

Scarlett was getting into it too. "The Web site's okay, but I could really make it sing," she chimed in. "Position it better on the search engines and create a better link network. We'd have to be careful not to lose the ambiance. That's what kills small businesses when they become successful. They buy into bigger-is-better and end up being blah."

"Blah is the kiss of death," Blossom agreed. "What do you think, Tilly?"

Since conscience does indeed make cowards of us all, I slunk off to relieve Missy Mae, who had been keeping an eye on things behind the screens in R and NC-17.

"Ginger would be real proud of you," she told me. "She knew what she was doing when she put them codicils in her will."

"I beg your pardon?"

" 'Missy Mae,' she says to me, 'I'm worried about Matilda. She's unhappy—' "

"What? She thought I was unhappy?" I said. "That's ridiculous. Well, maybe when Alex died and I had to sell the house, and afterwards for a while, but that was over three years ago. I'm not unhappy."

"Some people don't know when they're unhappy," Missy Mae informed me.

"I think I would know if I was unhappy," I said stiffly.

"Ginger seen something in you you don't see in yourself, and that's why she left you everything. I'm thinking she knew you'd just try to go back up there to Boston and hide your light under a bushel again, like the Bible says, so she made it so you couldn't sell."

"What's going on?" Scarlett said from the doorway. "Tilly, what's wrong?"

"I just give her something to think about," Missy Mae replied. "She'll be fine once she takes it in. I better get back."

Scarlett put a comforting hand on my arm. "Tilly?"

I told her what Missy Mae had said.

"Oh that. We'd already figured it out."

" 'We'?"

"Blossom and I."

"You and Blossom think," I said very slowly, "that Aunt Ginger fixed it so I'd have to move to Florida and sell weird stuff to degenerates."

"No, Tilly," Scarlett said gently. "She fixed it so you would finally understand your true nature."

"But I know who I am!" I protested. "I'm a twenty-six-year-old widow who likes her safe, uncomplicated life, and would never in a million years think of moving to Florida and selling weird stuff to degenerates."

Scarlett nodded her head. "Exactly."

* * *

By eight-thirty that night, the living room looked as though a herd of elephants had run amok in a Chinese restaurant. By the time we closed the store for the night, everyone was exhausted and starving, but no one could agree what to order. I had pretty much given up trying to pick and choose from Yeung's take-out menu, and ended up ordering all the appetizers, anything sweet and sour, ten cartons of General Gau's chicken, plain rice, fried rice, plain noodles, fried noodles, and enough boneless honey ribs to feed the Miami Dolphins' backfield. We'd be eating leftovers for a week, but we wouldn't be fighting over the Peking Dumplings.

Beverages of choice included beer for Alonzo, Jack Daniel's for Missy Mae, milk for the cats, water for Baskerville, red wine for Blossom and Virgil, white for Scarlett and me.

I picked up a chopstick and rapped on a glass. "Ladies and gentlemen, may I have your attention, please?"

The cats continued to pick their way delicately through the debris and Baskerville had eaten so much he couldn't even raise his head, but everyone else complied.

"First, I want to propose a toast to the person who really deserves the credit for this great day. My aunt and your friend, Lorraine Louise Snapp! To Ginger!"

"To Ginger!" they shouted.

"Gone but not forgotten!" Virgil proclaimed.

"Gone but not forgotten!"

"I keep telling you," Missy Mae said, "she ain't gone."

"Here but not forgotten!" Alonzo thundered.

"Here but not forgotten!"

"I know Ginger would be proud of each and every one of you—"

"And you too, Tilly," Scarlett said.

Blossom raised her glass. "To Tilly Snapp, the new owner of Erratica, the Emporium of Curiosities for the Discriminating Collector!"

"To Tilly!"

"I have a few little things here I'd like to give you to thank you for all your hard work these past few weeks.

"Alonzo, this is for you."

He looked startled, then blushed.

"Open it," Missy Mae ordered.

"Hey, it's the *Visual Guide to Lock-Picking*. Thanks, Tilly."

"Just don't make me have to come down to the police station at four in the morning to bail you out."

"Virgil. I don't know what you intend to do with this, but I hope you'll let us take pictures when you do."

"Hoo-eeeee!" Missy Mae yelled when Virgil held up the bra. "You gonna need implants you wanna wear that."

"Now you, Missy Mae," I said. "I hope you won't be needing these any time soon."

"Better safe than sorry," she said when she opened the box of grave bells. "Don't you laugh, Alonzo. You gonna wish you had some of these when you wake up in a coffin and realize you got six feet of dirt between you and oxygen."

"Scarlett, I don't think I've ever heard you oooh and aaah before, so I guess you must really like this."

"Oh, Tilly! How did you know?" she exclaimed, holding up the beautiful Art Nouveau lamp.

"I think it must have been the drool that gave you away.

"And last but never least, Blossom. If these chess pieces aren't incentive to learn to play chess, I don't know what is."

"What about you, Tilly? Isn't there something you really want?"

I looked around at my friends, old and new, my big dumb dog, and my cats. "I think I may already have it."

Morning, noon, or night, rain or shine, in sickness and in health, when your dog has to go, he has to go. Baskerville had to go in the middle of the night—or to be more accurate, at three fifteen in the morning—and as it happened to be raining at the time, I opted for a quick trip to the garden. I pulled on my sweats and trotted downstairs. I lounged in the doorway out of the rain while he picked his spot—never a simple matter with Baskerville, there being so many fascinating spots to check out before making a final decision.

We trudged back upstairs, detoured to the kitchen for a drink of water, and crawled back into bed. Baskerville conked out straightaway, of course. Gingersnap rearranged herself on my pillow in a little ball and drifted off purring.

I lay awake for a long time listening to the rain, thinking about the opening and how Aunt Ginger had set in motion the bizarre series of events that brought me to South Beach and catapulted me into a life and a world I never could have imagined just a few weeks before. And the more I thought about it, the more bizarre it seemed. Not just bizarre—

improbable. And that odd feeling came creeping back that I was missing something, some one element that would make sense of it all.

So I dozed, drifting through that strange landscape that lies between the conscious world and the dreaming, where the bits and pieces of our waking lives wait patiently for us to fit them together, and without warning, we leap from our bath like Archimedes, shouting, "Eureka!"

Gingersnap tagged along as I dragged the stepladder out of the utility closet in the hallway, carried it into the shop, and set it against the wall behind the long glass display counter.

Erratica's curiosities, like books in a darkened library, reposed on their shelves, waiting to tell their stories, share their secrets when the morning should come.

I steadied myself and reached for the gaudy heart-shaped urn, climbed down, and set it on the counter.

"So, Gingersnap, are you a betting cat?"

"Meow."

"Me too. Here goes," I said as I carefully opened the clasp and peered inside.

It was empty.

TWENTY-FOUR

"Where are you? We've been worried sick. Wait a minute, Blossom's getting on the other line."

I heard a click. "Okay, I'm here, Scarlett," Blossom said. "Tilly Snapp, where the hell are you?"

"How's Baskerville?" I asked.

"Moping," Scarlett said. "Tilly, we haven't heard from you for three days! Are you all right?"

"I'm fine, really."

"But where are you? When are you coming back?"

I picked up my iced tea and gazed out over the impossible turquoise of the Caribbean. "I can't tell you and I don't know."

"You don't know where you *are?*" Scarlett said.

"No, Scarlett, she knows where she is, but she doesn't know when she's coming back," Blossom explained. "Look, Tilly, enough with the woman of mystery thing. You leave us a note on the kitchen table saying 'something's come up' and you disappear off the face of the earth. No explanation, nothing. We're your friends; we deserve more consideration."

Blossom has always played the guilt card very well. And she was right: they did deserve more consideration. "Something's come up. I'll call soon. Don't worry. Love you" wasn't going to satisfy two women who probably knew me better than I knew myself and who could read me like a book.

It wasn't intended to. The less they knew about where I was and what I was up to, the better.

"Well?" Blossom demanded.

"Look, you're going to have to trust me—"

"She's in trouble, Blossom," Scarlett said.

"I know. You're in trouble, Tilly," Blossom told me.

"I am not in trouble."

"Who's that laughing?" Scarlett asked. "I hear someone laughing."

"She's in a bar," Blossom said.

"Are you in a bar, Tilly?"

I could see trouble heading my way in the form of a paunchy middle-aged man crammed into a red Speedo and sporting a goatee. He'd been checking me out from the other side of the tiki bar and evidently decided I might be worth a closer look. I picked up my drink and headed for an empty table on the far side of the pool.

"What's been going on there?" I asked, hoping to forestall further interrogation.

"I don't see why we should tell you anything," Blossom said, "since you won't even let us know where you are."

"Blossom, please," I said. "I know you're annoyed with me—"

"Damn straight I am."

Speedo wasn't giving up. He strutted over to the low diving board, stepped up, and made a show of stretching and preparing to dive. With a quick glance in my direction to make sure I was taking in all his masculine charms, he launched himself into the crystalline water.

"Are you in Boston, Tilly?" Scarlett asked. "Will called and wanted to know where you were, and I told him we didn't know and we were worried about you. He blew his stack and said that when he got back he was going to put you in jail and throw away the key."

Uh-oh, not good, I thought.

"And there's something else, Tilly. It's really weird. Do you remember that little man who was at the opening who wanted to buy Ginger's urn? He came back today."

I already knew what was coming.

"And do you know what? The urn is gone. We looked everywhere. It's disappeared."

"Right, well, I'm sure it will turn up. Gotta go now. Please don't be angry with me. I'll explain when I can. I love you. Kiss Baskerville for me."

"I don't know who this Baskerville is, but he sure is one lucky guy." Speedo held out a hand. "Chip Stearns, Cincinnati, Pisces, real estate, divorced. Mind if I sit down?"

I did; I really did.

Chip settled down to make his pitch. "Fortunate for me that I'm here and he's not, wouldn't you say?"

No, I definitely would not say.

"I don't remember seeing you here before. I come down two, three times a year, check out the action if you know what I mean. I'd have remembered."

I was halfway out of my chair, intent on making a run for it, but changed my mind. "Wow, two or three times a year. You must know everyone."

He tilted back his chair, waggled his brows. "You could say that."

I smiled charmingly. "I'm Matty. A friend of my mother's told me about this place. She always said you could get anything you want at Sin and Sand. Anything."

"Sure can. What would a beautiful woman like you be looking for? Maybe I could help you find it."

I tried to look coy. "Maybe you could. Time will tell. Hey, maybe you knew my mother's friend. She used to come here a lot. Ginger Snapp?"

"Ginger? Sure I knew her. Everyone knew Ginger. She was one hot dish, always up for a good time. I heard about the accident—damnedest thing, really threw me for a loop. That was, what, a couple of months ago?"

"September thirtieth."

"Right. Hey, let me get you another drink. Iced tea?"

"I'd love to, but some other time," I said. "I need to lie down for a bit; I had a long flight."

"Where do you hail from?" Speedo asked, trying to prolong the conversation. "No, let me guess." He checked me out, or rather I should say, checked out my breasts. I could almost hear him debating between 34-B or C. I think I was supposed to be flattered.

"Upper midwest," he said after due consideration. "Wisconsin. Madison?"

I smiled brightly. "You got it."

He gave the table a good rap with his fist. "Hot damn, I'm never wrong."

I stood up. "You must be very proud."

"So, Matty, will I be seeing you at the luau tonight?"

"Luau?"

"Oh, you have to come to the luau." He leered up at me. "Dress optional. The guy who sets his dick on fire is going to be there," he added as incentive.

Wonderland had just gotten a whole lot weirder.

Everyone did love Ginger, from the manager, Curtis Marley, proud second cousin to *the* Bob Marley on his mother's side, right down to the boy who raked the beach every morning. Death was fast turning her into a Sin and Sand legend, and the manner of that death was proclaimed to be—depending on the religious or philosophical inclination of the person doing the proclaiming—unfortunate, tragic, senseless, litigable, the work of the devil, the way of all flesh, the final joke of an indifferent universe, or the will of God. She was a nice woman, a good tipper, a real piece of ass, the reincarnation of Catherine the Great, an Upa-Guru, a saint.

I ventured back out to the tiki bar around three, having made certain Speedo the Wonder Stud was aboard a boat headed for a reef dive. Uncle Jimmie, as the tiki bartender was known, wiped his hands on his spotless white apron and grinned when I settled onto a stool and asked him about Aunt Ginger. He pulled a chilled glass out of a little refrigerator under the bar, filled it with ice, and poured in iced tea.

"Lemon, no sugar, right?"

"You have a good memory."

"Got to. The guests feel good you remember what they like."

He looked over toward the dock where two giggling women were being strapped into a parasailing harness. The red, green and gold parachute was laid out ready to catch the wind and take them as close to flying as they would ever get.

"A fine woman, Ginger," he said quietly. "You a friend of hers?"

"Family. She was my aunt."

"You be Matilda?"

I smiled. "I be."

He stuck out his hand. "Uncle Jimmie. It's an honor to meet you, Miss Matilda."

"You were a friend of hers?"

"Ginger be everyone's friend," he said. "Everyone be hers." I waited for him to set off down Memory Lane, but he went quietly about his work, wiping down the bar, setting out napkins, and filling little bowls with heavily salted bar nuts. "Why did you come here, Miss Matilda?" he said suddenly.

The question caught me by surprise. I had to think fast. "Um, well, she always talked about this place, and I thought . . . I wanted to . . ."

"She said you would. 'Jimmie,' she said, 'my Matilda will know what to do.' "

"Do?" My mind went absolutely blank for a moment, then switched into high gear.

"When?" I demanded. "When did she say I'd be coming? What am I supposed to be doing?"

He moved away down the bar. "Come on down to the luau tonight. There's a friend of Ginger's you might want to talk to."

Speedo the Wonder Stud practically glued himself to my side the minute I arrived at the huge bonfire on the beach. To my everlasting relief, "dress optional" was not so dire a prospect as I had feared. Only a few women in the large crowd came topless, although quite a few abandoned their inhibitions as the liquor flowed and joints were surreptitiously passed around.

I decided against wearing my lime green halter-top dress, now a staple in my wardrobe, and opted for a white tank top and simple ankle-length cotton skirt I'd picked up in the gift shop for a paltry eighty dollars. I hadn't had time to go shopping in Miami—"go SoBe" as Blossom put it, "SoBe" being shorthand for South Beach. The truly hip had to distance themselves from the hoi polloi, who couldn't afford a thousand dollars a night for a room at the Raleigh or $75 for a manicure, and called it simply "the Beach," so I suppose I would have to say "go Beach"—that is, if I were truly hip, which I most definitely am not.

There might just be a column there, I thought, as a faux-Rastaman dressed in a leopard-skin loincloth spread a blanket of broken glass on the sand and, barefoot, began gyrating wildly to the pounding beat of a steel drum.

"If you think the bottle dancer is great," Speedo enthused, "wait 'til you see the fire guy."

I surreptitiously poured the Stinger Speedo had insisted on buying for me into the sand, the third in less than an hour. Evidently he had romance on his mind.

"I can't wait," I said. *To get out of here before some maniac burns his penis to a crisp in front of my eyes.*

The bottle dancer was followed by a fashion show. "Go wild, go Jamaica!" the emcee urged. "You'll find all these exciting fashions at our shop, Jamaica Jamaica, conveniently located just three miles down the road in the heart of Negril. We provide free air-conditioned shuttle service leaving Sin and Sand twice a day. Please see me after the show to make your reservation."

The shuttle service might be free, but I had no

doubt a shopping expedition to Jamaica Jamaica could max out a credit card in not time flat.

"What do you say we take a stroll along the beach?" Speedo whispered in my ear during intermission.

Walk on the beach at night? Was the man insane?

It was rumored that if you ventured out for a walk along Negril Beach at night, it might very possibly be your last walk on this earth. The Jamaica Tourist Board had long ago given up trying to do damage control after each "incident," and wisely opted to avoid future litigation and loss of tourist dollars by posting "advisories" in hotels from one end of Long Bay to the other designed to scare the living hell out of visitors.

Since Speedo appeared to be more or less in his right mind, I could only conclude that he was anxious, verging on desperate, to get our romantic evening underway, and thus willing to risk getting robbed or worse.

Fire Guy was already setting up for the evening's big finale, and Uncle Jimmie's mystery man still hadn't made an appearance, at least as far as I could tell. I had two choices: Stay and watch Fire Guy light up the night with his flaming torch, or plead a terrible upset stomach and head up to the tiki bar by the pool to talk to Uncle Jimmie again.

I opted for Montezuma's revenge and was trying to shake off Speedo, who trailed after me as I made a wide detour around the increasingly wild gathering, when a deep voice said, "Good evening, Miss Matilda."

Speedo took one look at the man leaning against a palm tree and slunk away. I can't say I blamed him.

The mystery man had to be close to six and a half feet tall, with the powerful body any coach in the NBA would sell his firstborn son to have playing power forward on his team. I couldn't see him clearly in the shadows, but a long black ponytail and the gleam of a gold nose stud signaled a man who might not take kindly to being messed with.

I guess I must have looked pretty apprehensive myself, because he suddenly smiled and said, "Ginger was a good friend of mine. No need to be afraid. I be Snag."

"Snag?"

He laughed. "I be Snag when it suits me."

"And when it doesn't?" I asked.

"Aston Ewing. At your service."

I liked the man already. "Uncle Jimmie said I should meet you, but I don't know why."

"You came to Jamaica to find out what happened to your aunt. Maybe I can help you. Why don't we take a walk, get to know one another."

I grimaced. "You want to walk on the beach?"

"You be safe with Snag."

"What about Aston Ewing?"

"Him too."

I laughed. There couldn't be a thug, rapist, or homicidal maniac in his right mind who would tangle with either one of them. I followed him out of the little palm grove towards the distant sound of the surf.

My confidence was put to the test almost immediately when two shadows slunk out of the grove to our left. Snag set me gently behind him and stood quietly as they moved to intercept us.

"You folks enjoying your stay in Jamaica?" said one.

"They don't have nothing to say," said the other. "I'd say that wasn't very friendly, wouldn't . . . *Holy Jesus!* We didn't know it was you, Snag."

"Bobby. Owl. You got somewhere else to be, I guess."

Apparently they did, because one second there were four of us there on the beach and the next just two.

"So you're Matilda, Ginger's girl," he said as though nothing untoward had just occurred.

"I'm not her daughter. She was my aunt."

"She call you her girl, I call you her girl."

"Okay." I liked the sound of that: Ginger's girl.

We walked on. I could hear wild cheering from the luau. Fire Guy was doing his thing.

"The man's crazy," Snag said. "Someday that trick gonna go wrong and he be singing soprano in the church choir."

"You knew my aunt. Do you know what happened the night she died, how it happened?"

"Ginger a fine woman," was all he said.

My casual inquiries about her death at Sin and Sand had netted me exactly zilch. No one suspected anything: the rope had frayed, she'd fallen.

"I guess parasailing can be pretty dangerous," I went on. "I read somewhere that polypropylene line can deteriorate from exposure to ultraviolet light. But I talked with the men over at the dock this morning, and they said they use a polyester/nylon braid, which is really strong. I'm surprised it could have just snapped like that." I waited a beat. "Don't you think that's strange?"

"You planning on suing?" Snag asked. "Samuel and Paul, who run the parasailing outfit, they my cousins."

"Of course not. Accidents happen. Aunt Ginger signed a release; she understood parasailing is dangerous. I just wondered if you thought it was strange, that's all. Maybe the line was defective," I suggested when he didn't reply.

"They be her friends too," Snag said.

I gave up. Either he didn't know anything or he had no intention of telling me if he did.

The luau was in full swing when we got back. Speedo started toward me, backed off when he saw Snag walking beside me, and veered away toward a woman who was smearing what appeared to be honey on her nipples and inviting other revelers, irrespective of gender, to lick it off.

We walked in silence along the path that wound through the tropical gardens toward the bright lights of the hotel. I still had no any idea why Snag had come to see me.

He stopped at the bottom of a flight of stairs that led up to the pool area. "You be all right, Ginger Girl," he said. "Thought you would."

"Thank you. You be all right too, Snag," I teased.

"Ginger give me something for you. I send a car for you in the morning."

Don't ask questions, I ordered myself, just say yes. "Yes. Okay."

He started to walk away, then stopped. "You stay off that beach at night, you hear?"

"I will."

" 'Cept, 'course, you with Snag."

"Of course. What about Aston Ewing?"

He laughed. "Him too."

TWENTY-FIVE

Cabbyman—that's how he'd introduced himself, I swear—might have been steering with his knee. I couldn't really tell from where I huddled in the backseat. But one thing I did know for sure: I was about to die, and it wasn't going to be pretty.

Seemingly indifferent to the prospect of making head-on contact with an eighteen-wheeler at seventy miles an hour, Cabbyman took a deep drag on the joint in his left hand and fiddled with the radio with his right to ratchet up the sound. God must have been his copilot, because Cabbyman certainly wasn't the one doing the driving.

"Sir, sir!" I yelled over the pounding music, trying to get his attention. Too terrified even to close my eyes, I clung white-knuckled to the strap and prayed the end would be quick. Forget orgasmic, I'd be happy with quick.

"Gonna cock it up, cock it up, cock it up!" the singer wailed.

It seemed someone was about to get lucky.

"Ah sey!" my driver cheered.

"To your left! To your left!" I screamed.

"Mi kyaan lock mi hose off."

Apparently *coitus interruptus* was no longer an option.

"A right!"

"Slow down, slow down!" I begged.

"Keep it in it, keep it in it!" the singer chanted.

"Yeh, mon! Keep it in it!" my driver urged.

"Brakes! Brakes!"

"Ah-gon-eeeeeee!" the singer screamed in ecstasy.

"Ah-gon-eeeeeee!" my driver echoed.

Obviously someone was having an orgasm, and I could only pray it was the singer and not my driver. A madman stoned out of his gourd ejaculating at seventy miles an hour might not see the church van ahead and . . .

"No, don't pass, don't . . . MOTHER OF GOD!"

I'd been twenty-six when Cabbyman pulled up outside Sin and Sand at nine, jumped out, and bowed me into the backseat of the taxi. By the time we roared through Negril Village, I was thirty-eight. The drive on narrow twisting roads hemmed in by stone walls up into the hills above the town added another ten years, and by the time we screeched to a stop in front of the big Mediterranean-style house, I was fifty-two and had the Virgin Mary's unlisted number on speed-dial.

I also had a mild buzz from second-hand smoke, a fact Snag could not have failed to notice as I swayed along beside him as he ushered me through the cool interior of his elegant house and out onto a shady patio with a fantastic view of Negril.

"A ride with Cabbyman is always an adventure," he

said as he held a chair for me at a beautifully laid table, complete with a crisp white tablecloth and a vase of delicate purple-and-yellow orchids.

It was fascinating, really, how easily he could be sophisticated Aston Ewing one minute, speaking perfectly correct English, and Snag the next, easing into the lilting, colorful local dialect. By day, Aston was every bit as impressive as Snag was by night. On the beach he'd been a dark potent presence, at once menacing and reassuring. There on the patio, dressed in tan slacks and a red, brown and black batik cotton shirt, he appeared cool, enigmatic and undeniably elegant.

A shy girl of about fifteen in a blue dress brought out a carafe of coffee, a bowl of fruit, some toast, and orange marmalade.

"The school bus will be by any minute, Sara," he said. "You better be getting ready."

"Your daughter?" I asked.

"Sister."

"She's very pretty."

So, I thought, was he, very much so. His long black hair, loose to his shoulders this morning, suited a finely sculptured face and dark almond-shaped eyes. You could read the history of Jamaica in that face—European plantation owners, ebony-skinned African slaves, Chinese coolies, Spanish sailors.

Pirates, rumrunners, smugglers.

International art thieves.

Last night as I'd lain in the king-size bed at Sin and Sand staring up at my reflection in the mirrored ceiling, it came to me who and what Aston Ewing, aka Snag, had to be, and what his association with Aunt Ginger had been.

"You remind me of Ginger," he said.

I laughed and shook my head. "Aunt Ginger was a phoenix, a bird of paradise. I'm a common wren."

"There's nothing common about you, Matilda."

Sara came running across the patio, kissed her brother on the cheek, and dashed off to catch her bus. We could hear it chugging off down the hill.

"I have something for you," Snag said. He disappeared into the house and returned with an envelope addressed to me in Aunt Ginger's spiky handwriting.

"She left this for you. If you didn't find your way to Jamaica sooner or later, I was to have someone deliver it to you by hand in Miami. She didn't dare send it through the mail."

He sat quietly drinking coffee as I stared at the envelope, screwing up my courage. I picked up the butter knife, wiped it carefully on a napkin, slid it under the flap, and extracted a letter and a tape cassette.

"Matilda, dear, if you're reading this, you already know, or suspect, the truth. . . ."

Minutes later, I folded the letter neatly and put it back into the envelope along with the cassette. Snag handed me a clean napkin so I could wipe away the tears that had begun to fall as Aunt Ginger's words confirmed what I already suspected, what I hoped for with all my heart.

She was still alive.

"You already knew?" he asked.

"No, not for sure. I knew something didn't quite gel, but I couldn't put it together. Then I opened the cremation urn and it was empty, so I had to come to Jamaica to see if I could find out what really happened."

A black cat strolled across the patio and leaped into Snag's lap. "She has a lot of faith in you. She knew you'd figure it out," he said, running his big fingers through the long silky fur.

"Where is she? Please tell me, Snag. If someone put out a contract on her because of the pillow box and she had to fake her own death, she might still be in danger."

"I'd tell you if I knew," he said. "Last time she called she was in Boston. She couldn't find the box in your place, and she was about to fly down to Miami to see if you were holding it for her at the St. Claire."

"Someone broke into the shop twice without tripping the alarm," I said. "That should have sent up a red flag. And then there was the woman with the stun gun."

"Stun gun?"

I started to tell him about Baskerville and Joseph Alvarez and Richie the Ratfink and the strange woman who came to my rescue, and then somehow I was telling him the whole story from the very beginning, and he was laughing and I was laughing, and for a few minutes I could forget that Aunt Ginger was out there in the world somewhere, on the run, alone. I didn't have any way of finding her. She'd have to come to me. She wouldn't be safe until the pillow box of Win Win Poo turned up. And then there was Will, who, if he knew she was alive, would be as intent on tracking her down as I would now have to be in order to see that he never did.

"According to her letter, Aunt Ginger sent the box to me in Boston, but I never got it. It's out there somewhere," I said. I gave him an appraising look. "I don't suppose you know anything about that?"

He laughed. "If I find out where that box is, you can be sure I'll be keeping it to myself. I'll put all that lovely money in my Cayman Island account, retire, buy a nice big yacht, and see the world."

"You don't seem to be doing too badly as it is," I observed with a smile.

"A treasure like the pillow box of Win Win Poo only comes around once in a lifetime for most people in my line of business," he replied. "There are those who covet it to make themselves richer than they ever dreamed. Others will do whatever it takes just to possess it, like that collector in Singapore. A thing that beautiful and that valuable can bring out the best and the worst in people."

I wondered which it brought out in Aunt Ginger. I didn't want to think about that now, but eventually I knew I'd have to face up to it.

"You need to take care now," Snag said. "Rumor has it there are some really bad people looking for that box."

"I will."

"Of course, he'll be looking out for you too," he added.

I stopped in the middle of pouring another cup of coffee and set the carafe back on the table. "Who's looking out for me?"

"Willy."

"Willy, as in Will *Maitland*?"

"He's the only one I know."

"You know Will Maitland."

"We used to hang out together when we were

young Turks. He'd come in from Ocho Rios; we'd do the clubs, try our luck with the ladies."

"You are aware, I assume," I said slowly, stressing each word, "that *Willy* is now *Special Agent* Will Maitland? Of Interpol? Property Crime? Art Theft?"

"Willy did well for himself."

"But he's . . . and you're . . ."

"By way of being colleagues," he supplied. "We both chase after the same things. Sometimes I cover his back. Sometimes he covers mine." He laughed softly. "We keep score; makes it more interesting."

Oh great, a pissing match. What is it with men, anyhow?

I leaped up and started pacing back and forth across the patio. "Does he know I'm here?" I demanded. "Does he know about Aunt Ginger, that she's still alive? Does he know I know about Aunt Ginger?

"I don't believe this!" I told the good people of Negril, who were going innocently about their business down the hill. "I do not believe this!"

"You're going give yourself a stroke," Snag said. "What are you so upset about?"

"He's been playing games with me. I don't have a clue what he knows and what he doesn't know. You won't tell him about Aunt Ginger, will you?" I implored. "He'll—"

"Ginger and I go back a long ways. I'm not going to turn her over to Willy."

"Does he know I'm here in Negril?"

"He called from Kingston last night, wanted to know if I'd heard anything about a 'blasted Tilly' playing at being a detective here." He laughed. "I guess that's you. He doesn't know where you are, and he's not liking that one bit."

I shook my head. "He knows I'm not where he left me. He told my friends when he gets his hands on me he's going to haul me in as a material witness and throw away the key. He'll do it too," I added glumly.

Snag chuckled. "He get his hands on you yet, Ginger Girl?"

I answered him with my best glare.

"You won't tell him I've been here if he calls again, will you?"

"No."

"And I definitely don't want him looking out for me."

"Nothing I can do about that. It's his way."

"All he's interested in is that damn box; that's why he's 'looking out' for me."

"Hmmm," was all Snag had to say about that.

He dumped the cat off his lap. "Cabbyman is probably sober enough to take you back now."

He walked me out and handed me a card with a telephone number on it. "Call if you need me."

I went up on tiptoe and kissed him on the cheek.

"What's that for?" he said, obviously pleased.

"For caring about her."

Cabbyman was sprawled out fast asleep on the hood of the taxi. Snag poked him awake. "You be careful with the lady, see she get back safe, or you be answering to me," he said, apparently reverting to his Snag persona to emphasize his point.

"Best way to get through a ride with Cabbyman," he advised me, "is take a couple of hits yourself if he lights up."

It proved to be excellent advice. Cabbyman did, and I grinned like an idiot all the way back to Sin and Sand.

Twenty-six

Mrs. Feldman felt just awful about it. It had seemed such a happy idea at the time, and it made such a pretty picture. She would of course reimburse me.

I stared at the fish tank. It had been an all-out massacre. Nary a scale remained of my neon tetras, mollies, and gold-dust guppies, and my ill-tempered angelfish had gone belly up from a surfeit of sushi.

"These things happen," I soothed her. "I wouldn't think of taking your money. I can't tell you how much I appreciate your looking after things and taking in the mail. By the way, are you absolutely sure a package didn't come for me two or three weeks ago?"

"No, I don't think so, dear. Of course, my memory isn't what it used to be. I think I might have overwatered the plants," she confessed. "That tall spiky thing was fine up until last Thursday; I can't imagine what happened."

"Not to worry," I said brightly as I steered her toward the door.

"I'm so sorry about the broken window, dear."

"The window?"

"The one by the fire escape. I can't think how it came to be broken."

I could. Aunt Ginger, looking for the pillow box of Win Win Poo.

"I expect it was those boys who play ball in the back alley. My nephew Roscoe is coming over on Saturday to replace it. In the meantime, I've taped some cardboard over it."

She trotted back to *Judge Judy* clutching the jar of lime-ginger marmalade I'd bought in the Montego Bay airport.

"Welcome home, Tilly," I said.

I slept in my own bed for the first time in over six weeks, sank blissfully into apple-scented bubbles in my own bathtub, and savored my morning coffee from my favorite mug. The garbage truck arrived promptly at 9:15 as it did every Tuesday and Friday. The bells chimed the hour from the steeple of St. Cecilia's as they did every hour.

I was home, if only for a few days, hoping to find out what had happened to the package Aunt Ginger sent from Jamaica, and Boston felt exactly right.

Well, maybe just a bit not right, but right enough.

Actually, not right at all.

I tried plunging back into my routine: went to the gym, pounded out some columns to keep ahead of my schedule, browsed the bookstores in Harvard Square, checked out Filene's Basement for bargains. I ate clam chowder at Legal Sea Foods and ribs at Redbones. I curled up on the couch and watched *Law and Order: Criminal Intent*, *CSI* and, with considerably more interest now, *CSI: Miami*. I checked out the obituaries in the *Globe.* I stared at the telephone and felt guilty for not calling Scarlett and Blossom.

I called Scarlett and Blossom.

Scarlett picked up. "It's about time!"

"I'm sorry, sweetie, I've been tied up." I decided to put a positive spin on it. "I'll be back in a few days," I said cheerfully.

"Tilly, maybe that's not such a good idea."

I didn't want to know why, really I didn't.

I took a deep breath. "Why isn't it a good idea?"

"Will Maitland," she said, as if those two words were sufficient to explain the matter.

"So he's annoyed," I said breezily.

"Tilly."

"He'll get over it. Who says I can't take some time off if I want to?"

"Tilly!"

"I don't have to answer to Special Agent Will Maitland."

"TILLY!"

"Er, yes, Scarlett?"

"He's got a warrant for your arrest. He flew back to Jamaica this morning to try to find you. He traced the call you made to us from that place where your aunt used to stay. Is that where you are, Tilly, in Jamaica?"

"Gotta go, Scarlett."

"Is he back?"

"Last night. He found out you booked a flight to Boston from Jamaica. He's flying up there in the morning. Is that where you are, Tilly, in Boston?"

"'Bye, Scarlett."

* * *

"News?"

"He's in Seattle, I think. Is that where you are, Tilly, with your brother in Seattle?"

"Later, sweetie."

"What's up?"

"He called from Ottumwa, Iowa. Is that where you are, Tilly, in Ottumwa, Iowa?"

"Talk to you soon, Scarlett."

"Any sightings, Blossom?"

"The phone is *tapped,* you moron!" she shouted. "Stop calling, for God's sake!"

TWENTY-SEVEN

A plan, I needed a plan. And advice, I needed advice. And a safe place to think where I wasn't only one airport ahead of one very ticked-off Interpol agent. A friendly face and a shoulder to cry on wouldn't hurt either, but they were going to have to wait.

Some people climb to the top of a mountain to find a quiet place to think; others walk a windswept beach. The New York Public Library is a popular spot, and I've heard good things about empty churches.

Me, I go to Starbucks. You can't get a decent soy latte on top of a mountain, and as far as I know they haven't started installing wireless Internet connections in the family pew just yet. I fetched up at a Starbucks in Cathedral City, California, three days after fleeing the Fairfield Inn in Ottumwa, Iowa. It wouldn't have been my first choice, but the only flight I could get out of Kansas City before the blizzard struck was headed for Palm Springs. The Weather Channel reported the

Kansas City airport was still closed, so I probably had a few days' grace before Will Maitland could take up the chase.

If circumstances had been different—say, I was still Good Old Tilly Snapp and living in the real world—my heart might have gone pitter-pat to think that Will Maitland was chasing after me from one end of the country to the other. What could be more romantic than a man in hot pursuit of the woman he loves?

Tilly Snapp, Sex Detective, however had no time for such nonsense. She knew the cold hard facts: A man in hot pursuit of a woman whom he intends to incarcerate for an indefinite period of time for obstruction of justice and generally being an all-around pain in the butt is unlikely to take her into his manly arms and pledge his undying love when he catches up to her, no matter what the optimists who pen romance novels might tell you.

A plan. I needed a plan. And advice. I needed advice.

But before I could formulate The Plan, I needed to sit back and take a hard look at my situation.

Here is what I knew:

I, Matilda Snapp, was a fugitive from justice. My friends were worried sick about me. My dog hated me. My fish were fish food and my plants were compost. Arthur Kelso hadn't been able to find a loophole in Aunt Ginger's will, my Citibank card was nearly maxed out, and the safe deposit box at Bank of America in Boston where I'd stashed Aunt Ginger's incriminating letter costs $25 a year.

I also knew:

That Aunt Ginger was still alive and lying low, and

it would be up to me to find the pillow box if she was ever going to be safe again from the people who tried to kill her—and from Will Maitland.

Furthermore:

I knew from Aunt Ginger's letter why she'd been in Singapore on May 16, 2004, masquerading as Lorraine Louise Hungwell, and what her role was in the disappearance of the pillow box from the collection of one Mr. Robert Lu, the man who called Erratica on opening day and refused to leave his number.

And finally, I knew who put the hit out on Aunt Ginger and why.

What I didn't have a clue about:

Where the pillow box of Win Win Poo was and what I was going to do with the damn thing when I found it.

I am not even remotely at my best at four in the morning, but I came awake like a shot when the phone rang. I fumbled for the receiver, sent it crashing off the bedside table, and fell out of bed trying to reach down to pick it up. I may have uttered a word or two that Grammie Jones would not approve of.

"Most ladies be glad to hear from Snag he call this time of night. 'Course, you ain't most ladies."

"I fell out of bed," I explained.

"I be there, I make sure that don't happen, Ginger Girl."

Yikes!

"Thanks for calling back. I'm sorry to bother you."

"You're no bother," he said.

I hauled the blanket off the bed and wrapped it around me. "I've got sort of a problem, Snag."

"I'd say you have a big problem, Ginger Girl. Willy came up to the house when he found out you'd checked out of Sin and Sand. He wanted to know if I'd seen you. I told him you dropped by one morning for breakfast. I swear he started spitting fire. Today he called me from Alaska, yelling that he was stuck in snow up to his ass and he has plans for putting yours in jail."

"Not Alaska. Ottumwa."

"Where's that?"

"Nowhere you want to be, believe me. And he wouldn't be stuck in snow up to his ass if he'd just stop chasing me all over creation like a lunatic."

Snag laughed. "You sure put a bee up that boy's butt."

Now there was a happy notion. "Good. I hope it stays there."

"You'd better hope he doesn't catch up with you. I've never seen him so mad."

I switched on the lamp and made myself comfortable cross-legged on the bed. "I can't keep running like this, Snag. I'm starting to feel like Harrison Ford in *The Fugitive.*"

"Don't be jumping off no dams, now," he joked.

"As I see it, I have two problems," I told him. "I need to shake him off and I need a way to keep in touch with my friends in Miami. He's got the damn phone there tapped."

"No problem. Call the airlines, Amtrak, Greyhound, and make a dozen reservations all over the country. Be sure to buy the refundable tickets. You're in California, right?"

"How do you know that?" I asked suspiciously.

"Area code of the number you left. You're close to the border, so drive down to Mexico. Fly back on a foreign carrier, then cancel the other reservations.

He'll be checking reservations inside the country and flying out, not coming back."

"You learned this in a book, right?" I said dryly.

I could hear a woman's voice in the background. "You've got company. I'll let you go. Thanks for—"

"She don't mind waiting for Snag. She know it be worth it."

I bet it would too.

"A wiretap won't work if you get a disposable cell phone with prepaid minutes on it," he went on. "They're hard to trace."

"Is that legal?" I said.

He laughed. "You telling me you're worried about *legal* right now?"

He had a point. "Where would I get one?"

"You can't buy one without an ID. You could try a big discount store where they're too busy to ask for one, but it would be safer to get a fake ID. I've got a friend in LA who can work up a California license for you in an hour."

"Is it expensive?"

"I'll take care of it."

"I couldn't—"

"You're Ginger's girl," was all he said, and that was the end of that. It looked as if I would be making the acquaintance of Bingo in North Hollywood.

"Willy's going to track you down eventually, you know."

"Not before I find the box," I boasted. "Um, Snag, if he gets in touch with you again, are you going to tell him I called?"

"Hell no. I'm having too much fun watching you two play cat and mouse all over the damn globe."

"Just as long as *you're* having fun," I grumbled.

TWENTY-EIGHT

"So that's what I think we should do," she concluded.

"Totally out of the question."

"No way."

Good Old Tilly Snapp had expected she'd have a fight on her hands. "Let's keep an open mind here, ladies. Will Maitland is not the enemy. He wants the same thing we do: justice for Aunt Ginger. The pillow box of Win Win Poo is the key. We should team up with him, not try to thwart him at every turn."

"Whoa, now wait just a minute," Tilly Snapp, Sex Detective said. "What's with this 'justice for Aunt Ginger' stuff? The man wants the damn box so he can put another notch on his Interpol Property Crime/Stolen Works of Art belt. If he can prove she stole it or was involved even peripherally, that's two notches."

"You sure do think about that man's belt an awful lot," sneered The Fugitive.

"It's just a figure of speech," retorted Tilly Snapp, Sex Detective.

The Fugitive's eyes opened wide in mock surprise. "Oh, is that what it is? Silly me."

"May I remind you, Ms. Cynical Sex Detective," said Good Old Tilly Snapp, "that Special Agent Maitland is also pursuing this case in his capacity as a member of Interpol's Criminal Division? He's after a murderer, possibly more than one."

"And after us," The Fugitive reminded them. "He's like a bulldog; the stupid man just won't let go. I really thought he had us in Ottumwa."

"You *hoped* he'd have us in Ottumwa, and often," smirked Tilly Snapp, Sex Detective. "Face it, you like him chasing us all over creation. I bet you wouldn't mind one bit if he caught us."

"That's not true!"

"I'm afraid it is," Good Old Tilly Snapp said gently. "If we hadn't insisted you change your mind and go to Canada instead of Mexico, he would have nailed us in Tijuana."

"Oh, I do like the sound of that," said Detective Snapp. "That would make a great book title. No, wait! I see a trilogy. *Nailed in Ottumwa,* followed by *Nailed in Tijuana,* with a rousing finale, *Nailed in South Beach.* I see a movie option. I see Drew Barrymore, I see Brad Pitt—"

"That will do, Detective Snapp," Good Old Tilly Snapp admonished.

The Fugitive pouted. "How was I to know the man already had the Border Patrol on the lookout for us?"

Good Old Tilly Snapp poured another glass of wine and topped off the other two. "That's a no-brainer, Fugitive. He may have been up to his ass in snow in Ottumwa, but all he had to do was call the airlines to find out we made the last flight out of Kansas City to Palm Springs. It couldn't have been too big a leap of the imagination to think we might make a run for the border."

"Well, it all worked out, didn't it?" the Fugitive pointed out. "We went to Canada instead, and now we're in Miami, and he hasn't a clue we've come back, and even if he suspects, he won't be able to trace us here to the inn because we used the fake California ID. I'm not turning myself in, and that's that," she declared.

"Chase me 'til I let you catch me, huh?" jeered Tilly Snapp, Sex Detective.

Stung, The Fugitive struck back. "You're not one to talk. You got us into the sex thing in the first place.

" 'Will, you are the first man I've had in three years,' " she mimicked. " 'Will, you are the first man I've wanted in three years. Take me, take me, take me! Oh! Oh! Oh! Yes! Yes! *Yes!*' "

"I don't recall hearing you objecting at the time," Tilly Snapp, Sex Detective shot back.

"Ha! I wasn't there at the time. So there!"

"Ladies, please," Good Old Tilly Snapp said, hoping to head off a flaming row. "There will be time enough down the road to figure out who was responsible for getting tangled up with Will Maitland—"

"Oh, we already know that," the Fugitive declared. "You."

"Me?"

Tilly Snapp, Sex Detective, nodded her agreement. "Yes, you, Miss Goody Two-Shoes. All that rationalization after Alex died. '*I* shall not be as lesser women—

I shall not settle. I will have love—*love*, I tell you!—or I will have nothing at all. Begone, base desire!' "

Good Old Tilly Snapp narrowed her eyes. "So what's your point?"

"You try to bottle up all that 'base desire' for three years and eventually you're going to blow. Special Agent Will Maitland wanders into your line of sight with all his studly charms and a package a girl would sell her immortal soul for, and you'll settle all right, settle for whatever he's willing to offer. If what you told Scarlett and Blossom is true, you settled all right. Oh, say four times in three hours, wasn't it? Probably not a world record, but nothing to sneeze at either."

"Maybe that's a tad harsh," The Fugitive interjected. "I think she's falling in love with him."

"I am going to find the pillow box of Win Win Poo and the people who put out the hit on Aunt Ginger," Good Old Tilly Snapp snarled, "and then I am getting the hell out of South Beach."

"Uh-huh."

"Right."

"I am!" Good Old Tilly Snapp protested. "You just wait and see!"

"When pigs fly," Tilly Snapp, Sex Detective, said. "Anyhow, I have no intention of working with Special Agent Will Maitland—package or no package. You're outvoted two to one, Good Old Tilly Snapp. We go on as planned."

"Rats, bats, and jelly beans," she grouched.

"First thing, we need to make contact with Scarlett and Blossom," Tilly Snapp, Sex Detective, said.

"And we need a disguise," said The Fugitive

"What we *need*," I grumbled as I finished off the bottle, "is a good psychiatrist."

* * *

Hell will hold no surprises for me. I've already been.

Good Old Tilly Snapp had to go, and if she had to go, I figured, she might as well "go Beach." She'd also have to go cold turkey and all by her lonesome—no hand to hold, no one to whisper, "There, there, sweetie, it's almost over," every few minutes, no one to buy her a pistachio ice cream cone with chocolate sprinkles when the ordeal was over as a reward for being a brave little girl.

The problem was, I didn't dare "go Beach" *in* South Beach, where I might be spotted by Richie the Ratfink or Mr. Clean, or heaven forbid, the scary Joseph Alvarez or Will Maitland, if he'd finally decided to give up the chase and wait me out at the St. Claire. So I drove down to Coconut Grove in my canary yellow Beetle rental car to "go Co," which I figured was close enough.

In only three interminable, excruciating hours, at a mere cost of $262.78, plus tips, with my ego battered, possibly beyond repair, and my dignity in shreds, the Tilly Snapp who had looked back at me from the mirror every morning for twenty-six years was no more.

Buzz and Nikkolai at The Kindest Cut would be regaling their upscale clientele for years with the sidesplitting tale of the madwoman who had to be restrained from plunging a pair of cutting shears into her heart when she was finally coaxed into opening her eyes to behold her new look.

Okay, I may be exaggerating just a tad, but I can honestly say I'd rather barrel through Negril, Jamaica, at sixty miles an hour with Cabbyman high as a kite than relive that harrowing morning in Coconut Grove.

I staggered into a Starbucks, ordered an iced soy chai latte, and tried to pull myself together.

"Excuse me," I said to the woman sitting at the next table. "What color would you say my hair is? Is it, like, purple?"

She leaned forward. "More of a plummy black, I think," she said after a moment's consideration. "It's a good color for you."

I blinked. "It is?"

"It gives your eyes just a hint of a violet hue, sort of like Elizabeth Taylor. And I really like the cut."

"You do?" I said, shocked. "It doesn't look like a nest of plummy black snakes?"

She frowned. "Now that you mention it, it does sort of, but it's very interesting."

"Oh God," I moaned.

"I've been thinking of making a change. Where did you have it done?"

I waved a vague hand toward the chichi salon across the street. "Tell them the lunatic sent you."

The warning must have gone out that a fashion disaster wearing Lands' End was prowling the boutiques of Coconut Grove. Saleswomen became deaf, dumb, and blind the minute I walked in the door. Customers cowered in dressing rooms. Security guards went on red alert.

Unlike Blossom, I do not possess the fashion gene and I was not born to shop. I hate to shop, with a vengeance. I dither, invariably set my sights on the one item they don't have in my size, and make the mistake of looking at the price tag first, a surefire way to slink home empty-handed.

By two o'clock that afternoon, the sum total of my

purchases amounted to one floppy straw beach hat, a pair of Guess wrap sunglasses with blue lenses, and two pairs of shorts from Banana Republic. At this pace I'd be "Beach" sometime in 2009. Something had to be done.

I retreated to Starbucks to reconnoiter, considered my options, and came up with a plan. Some lucky salesperson would be dining out for months on the story of the day a woman marched into her store and confided that she was on the run from the mob and needed a completely new identity if she wasn't going to end up floating in Biscayne Bay with a bullet in her brain.

That fortunate saleswoman turned out to be one Krystelle O'Banion, "Customer Satisfaction Representative," who knew a good sales commission when she saw it and threw herself into the task at hand with a studied politeness that could not quite mask the smirking condescension lurking just below the surface.

I figured I could live with that if it meant I could get this ordeal over with before I had a nervous breakdown.

As I headed for the yellow Beetle loaded down with bags and boxes, I spotted my reflection in a store window. I stopped dead in my tracks, so foreign was the woman staring back at me. She smiled at me smugly and purred, "I'm here, I'm hot, and baby, I am *happenin'*."

TWENTY-NINE

Some of the buffest bodies in Miami can be found catching the rays and strutting their stuff along the stretch of South Beach near Twelfth Street and the Cardozo Hotel. That those bodies belong to gay men makes the area particularly attractive to heterosexual women hoping to escape the sleazeballs, Peeping Toms and pick-up artists who trawl the beach from morning to night. Stake out your spot, slip off your top if you're so inclined, and you can spend your day at the beach hassle-free.

Scarlett, Blossom, and I discovered this secret early on, which is why at ten o'clock on the morning after I went "Beach" in Coconut Grove, I lay sprawled out on a huge white beach towel, patterned with grinning dolphins, about two hundred feet from our usual spot near the yellow Art Deco lifeguard stand decorated with smiley faces.

My little plot of beach real estate positively screamed "tourist": striped beach umbrella, the floppy straw hat, wraparound sunglasses, soft insulated lunch pack and matching thermos featuring Betty Boop, sunscreen and lip balm (both SPF 30), Danielle Steel's latest, *People*, and *The South Beach Diet*.

My bathing suit—what little there was of it—consisted of something called a "stationary triangle halter top" and a "deep-waist skirtini" in a pretty print of coral, turquoise and gold flowers that skidded to a halt just millimeters north of indecent exposure.

There was no guarantee Scarlett and Blossom would make it a beach day, but since it was Sunday with the temperature already a toasty eighty-five degrees, it seemed likely they'd make an appearance sooner or later. I settled down to wait, keeping an eye out for them and whoever might be tagging along behind them keeping an eye out for me.

I might have gone to ground in Tierra del Fuego for all anyone knew, but as Scarlett and Blossom were my closest friends, Richie the Ratfink, Joseph Alvarez, and Mr. Clean would assume, correctly, that eventually I'd try to contact them again. As would Will Maitland, who must surely be back in Miami by now with that bee still buzzing up his butt, to use Snag's wonderfully evocative turn of phrase.

By the end of the first hour I'd read *People* from cover to cover—including a puff piece on Lincoln Steele's latest blockbuster—and was suffering a severe case of celebrity overload. I stared at the ocean, a stunning deep blue when viewed through blue lenses, eavesdropped on a lovers' spat on the blanket next to me, and munched trail mix.

I trekked down to the water's edge twice to cool off, but didn't swim because I didn't dare take off my hat and sunglasses. It was on my third expedition, a few minutes short of noon, that I spotted Scarlett and

Blossom trudging across the hot sand from Lummus Park toward our usual spot.

I tucked my hands behind my back and wandered aimlessly through ankle-deep wavelets in casual beachgoer fashion, watching them set up, scanning the beach for the men who were sure to be close behind. Sure enough, I spotted Richie under a tree up by the volleyball courts and a newcomer with a red moustache settling down on a blue blanket not ten feet away. If Joseph Alvarez, Mr. Clean, or Will were around anywhere, I couldn't see them. I sauntered back to my own towel, took my magic, untraceable cell phone in hand, and waited for my chance.

Blossom and Scarlett headed straight for the water, plunged in, and paddled around for a good fifteen minutes. I waited patiently while they dried off and slathered themselves and each other with suntan lotion, then punched in Scarlett's cell phone number.

"Hello?"

"It's me," I said. "No, don't look around! Repeat after me: 'You must have the wrong number.' "

"I beg your pardon? Oh. Um. Sure. You must have the wrong number."

"Now hang up."

"No, no problem at all," she said, getting into the spirit of the thing.

She stretched out on her stomach beside Blossom, and a moment later Blossom's head came up, swiveled casually to the left and right, then settled back down onto the towel.

I punched in Scarlett's number again.

"Hello?"

"In the water, directly in front of the lifeguard stand, half an hour. Now say I've misdialed again."

"I'm sorry, you've misdialed again."

"Look for the purple hair."

"Purple . . . ?"

"Hang up, Scarlett!"

I watched Blanket Boy carefully to see if he'd noticed anything amiss, but he was busy ogling a particularly buxom woman of middle years who had thrown both caution and good sense to the wind and lay splayed out on her towel with her bare boobs creeping sludgelike toward her armpits.

Exactly half an hour later, Scarlett and Blossom wandered down to the water near the lifeguard stand. I anchored my hat with a sneaker so it wouldn't blow away, asked a nice old queen next to me if he could keep an eye on my stuff, tightened the cord that secured my sunglasses, and strode down the beach straight into the water without looking left or right. I struck out in the general direction of a group of teenagers, who were yelling and splashing and generally making a nuisance of themselves. Treading water, I saw Blossom paddle off to my right and Scarlett to my left. I flipped over onto my back and floated, staring up at fluffy blue clouds in a deep blue sky.

"Tilly?" Blossom said from close by.

"Don't look at me," I cautioned her. "Richie's got binoculars."

"You've got purple hair," Scarlett accused.

"It's not purple," I replied huffily. "It's plummy."

"You look like an eggplant."

"Can we discuss my hair some other time? We've got more important stuff going on here."

"Uh-oh," Scarlett said. "Kerwin's coming in."

I figured Kerwin must be Blanket Boy. "I'm staying at the Miami River Inn," I said quickly, "near the First

Street Bridge in Little Havana. Meet me there tonight at nine. There's a parking lot at the side, on Southwest Second Street, I think. I'll be there to open the gate. Can you do it without being followed?"

"Ain't a tail in Miami we can't shake by now," Blossom boasted.

"Don't be late. And please be careful."

"Tilly Snapp, woman of mystery," Blossom laughed.

"This isn't a joke anymore, Blossom," I said. "I'm in danger, and so are you two."

Something in my voice must have convinced her I was serious. "We'll be careful," she promised.

"He's coming," Scarlett said.

I heard them splashing away in different directions, and stayed where I was for another few minutes floating and humming nonchalantly until I figured the coast would be clear. I waded to shore and headed up the beach to my spot. I could see Scarlett and Blossom playing cards and Kerwin sacked out on his blue blanket fast asleep. Richie no longer lurked beneath his palm tree, so I figured he must be on his lunch break. Mr. Clean was nowhere to be seen, probably back at Zephyr slurping down his sixth double cappuccino of the day, and there was still no sign of Will. Feeling smug and clever, I toweled off, stretched out, set the big straw hat over my face, and dozed off to the soothing harmony of murmuring voices, lapping waves, and whispering grains of sand.

"You're dreaming about me again."

"I am not dreaming about you. You just happen to be in the dream I'm dreaming. So are all these other people on the beach."

"Yes, but I'm the only one who's not wearing any clothes."

"Your point?"

He shrugged. "I would think the sexual imagery is pretty obvious."

I rolled my eyes. It certainly was.

"You could be a dream symbol or a metaphor," I pointed out. "I could have a deeply repressed desire to smoke cigars."

"Uh-huh."

"Hey, stop that!" I said.

One brow went up. "Stop what?"

"You know what," I growled. "What you're doing with . . . um, that twitching."

"Twitching?" He looked down. "Oh, you mean this?"

"Yes, that," I growled. "Stop it this minute."

"I don't see how that should bother you," he said with a laugh. "I'm only a metaphor, remember?"

"Go away, now," I ordered. "I don't want you here."

"That's entirely up to you," he pointed out. "As long as you're dreaming me I have to stick around."

"That," I replied with a sniff, "is easily remedied. I can just wake up."

"Have it your way. But you might want to take a look up on the promenade before you do," he said, his expression too smug by half.

I looked. He had a point. I could deal with Will Maitland, naked, grinning, twitching studly god, or I could deal with Will Maitland, fully clothed, steely-eyed, relentless Interpol special agent.

"How did you know I was here?" I demanded.

The Will of my dreams dropped down on the towel

beside me and helped himself to a handful of trail mix. "I don't know yet that you are; I haven't been able to spot you. Of course, I'm not looking for a woman with purple hair."

"Plum," I said stiffly. "I couldn't decide between Hot Mahogany and Red Copper Spritz. Nikkolai suggested the Chilled Plum, so I went with that."

"Hmmm."

"And just what's that supposed to mean?" I demanded.

He coiled a plummy spiral around a long finger. "You've gone 'Beach,' Tilly."

"It's only a temporary look," I assured him.

He let the spiral spring back and trailed a lazy finger down between the ineffectual little triangles of the stationary halter top. "Nice."

"When I get back to Boston, I'll . . ."

The finger meandered south, detoured in a circle around my belly button, and gave it a little pat.

"I'll, um . . ."

"No, I don't think you will," he murmured as the finger trailed along the northern border of the deep waist skirtini.

"It's all your fault," I managed, wondering if I should have gotten the Brazilian bikini wax after all.

"You're the one who's running, Tilly."

I scooted back on the towel and glared at him. "I wouldn't be running if you weren't chasing."

He shrugged. "It's my job. By the way," he said, "how did you get hold of a fake ID?"

"I have my sources," I informed him.

"Snag. You made quite an impression on him. It takes a lot to impress Snag."

I stared at the far horizon and smiled a cryptic little smile. "I think you could say it was mutual."

I could tell he didn't like that. He cupped my chin and turned my face towards him. "Stay away from him, Tilly," he warned in a low voice. "Snag isn't someone you want to get mixed up with."

Wow, did I see a flash of green in those dark eyes? I cocked a single brow—this was a dream, after all—and widened my violet-blue eyes. "I don't?"

"No, you don't. If Snag sees something he wants, he'll do whatever it takes to get his hands on it."

I switched to the other brow. "Would he now?"

"Did he get his hands on you yet, Tilly?" he said quietly.

"No."

He stood up abruptly. "See that it stays that way. Now, are you going to wake up so I can go get a shower and get the sand out of my butt?"

"You might want to get that bee out of there while you're at it," I suggested.

"Another dream symbol?"

I grinned up at him and shook my head. "Sometimes a bee is just a bee."

THIRTY

I kept well back in the deep shadow of the palms at the edge of the Miami River Inn's parking lot, watching the white car as it cruised slowly along South River Drive, made the turn onto Southwest Second Street, and parked at the curb beside the high iron gate. Since I'd been expecting Scarlett and Blossom to be driving Aunt Ginger's Grand Cherokee, I backed away slowly, poised to make a run for it if necessary. The passenger-side window slid down, but I couldn't see into the dark interior. I stood frozen to the spot.

"Tilly?"

Scarlett. Thank God.

I trotted across the parking lot and dragged the big gate open. Almost before I knew it, they were out of the car, hugging me close, laughing, scolding, throwing questions at me. Was I okay? Where had I been? Why was my hair purple?

"This way," I said, leading them along the path that led to the historic inn's front door. We crossed the small lobby, lit only by an old brass lamp, and climbed the stairs to the third floor.

"Wow," said Blossom, surveying the hardwood floors, beautiful old bedspread, and antiques that filled my room. "I never imagined a place like this in Miami. This is so cool."

"A room with a view!" Scarlett exclaimed, peering out the window at the Miami River and beyond it the sparkling towers of Brickell Avenue and Downtown. "Not bad for a girl on the run."

Without so much as a sniffle of warning, I burst into tears. "I'm so glad to see you," I blubbered. "It's been so crazy, and you aren't going to b-believe what the letter said and I know I swore off pot but Cabbyman was steering with his knee and she put the angelfish in the other tank, God only knows why, and I almost got nailed in Tijuana—well, not *nailed* nailed, not with real nails but not the other nailed either—and this guy set his penis on fire and—"

"Wine, Scarlett," Blossom barked.

"I'm already on it."

"My hair's purple," I wailed.

Scarlett thrust a plastic cup into my hand. "Drink."

I took a sip of wine, hiccuped a couple of times, and slurped up the rest.

"We missed you too, sweetie," Scarlett said.

"Does Baskerville hate me?" I sniffled.

"I don't recall his saying so in so many words," Blossom replied.

"Gingersnap?"

"She disappeared for a few days. We thought maybe he ate her, but she turned up in the washing machine."

"Virgil and Alonzo? How are they doing? Did they make up?"

"Virgil moved back in. They're talking about getting married."

I managed a watery smile. "We could do a garden wedding."

Blossom refilled my glass. "So what's with the guy setting his penis on fire?"

"Maybe we should begin at the beginning," Scarlett suggested.

Blossom curled up in a huge wing chair. "You're on, Tilly."

I gave them all of it. Well, almost all.

I told them about Sin and Sand, Uncle Jimmie, Speedo the Wonder Stud, the luau, the bottle dancer, Fire Guy, Aston Ewing and his alter ego Snag, and the two thugs on the beach. I took them along on the wild ride with Cabbyman and walked them through Snag's elegant home. I moved on to Boston and the great sushi massacre; the mad dash to Seattle, Ottumwa, Cathedral City; to Bingo the ID guy in North Hollywood; the Mexican border, Tijuana, Vancouver. I brought them back to Miami and down to Coconut Grove, Nikkolai, Chilled Plum, Krystelle O'Banion.

By the time I finished, we'd eaten most of the Brie, emptied the first bottle of wine, and uncorked the second.

"She left something out," Blossom said to Scarlett.

Scarlett narrowed her eyes at me. "The most important something."

"Okay, okay, I was getting to that. Aunt Ginger left a letter for me with Snag. She told him that eventually I'd suspect what really happened to her and go to Sin and Sand to learn the truth."

"But you already knew what happened," Blossom pointed out. "You knew it wasn't an accident, that she was murdered."

"Yes, of course I knew." I busied myself spreading the last smidgen of Brie on a cracker, realizing I'd almost given myself away.

"She's holding back," Scarlett said to Blossom.

"I can see that. Come on, Tilly, out with it. All of it."

They weren't going to get all of it, but I told them what I could. "Aunt Ginger asked me to keep some things confidential, but I will tell you that she knew someone was out to kill her. Someone who knew she had the pillow box of Win Win Poo. And I think she may have suspected who that someone was."

"She did? She actually had the box?" Scarlett said.

I nodded.

"So she did steal it, after all."

"Not exactly."

"Not exactly? What does that mean?" Blossom demanded.

I told them.

Blossom was the first to recover. "You have got to be kidding."

I shook my head.

"Hold on, hold on," Scarlett said. "Let's be sure we understand this. You are telling us that the pillow box of Win Win Poo wasn't stolen?"

"Uh-huh."

"This collector in Singapore—the Mr. Lu who's been calling and asking us about pillow boxes—and your aunt Ginger were running a scam on an insurance company?"

"Uh-huh."

Blossom paced back and forth, thinking it through. "So Robert Lu reports the box stolen and collects on the insurance. I bet it was insured for at least twice its market value—legitimate market, that is. Meanwhile Ginger smuggles it back to the U.S., finds a buyer on the black market, and sells it. Or maybe she had the buyer lined up first. Either way, they rake in a fortune. No harm, no foul. Everyone lives happily ever after. Well, maybe not the insurance company, but they can write off the loss on their taxes. Wow, is that cool or what?"

"Um, Blossom," Scarlett said gently, "aren't you forgetting one thing?"

Blossom stopped, frowned, and spun around. "Oh, God. Oh, Tilly. Your aunt Ginger. I am so sorry. I wasn't thinking."

"That's okay, sweetie. I guess if you look at it from an objective point of view, it really was a pretty good scam."

"Maybe Robert Lu put the contract out on Ginger," Scarlett surmised. "Then he wouldn't have to split the money with her."

"Maybe." I already knew it wasn't Robert Lu, but that wasn't something I was willing to share with them.

"Anyhow, if it was someone she knew—" Blossom said.

"He has to know about you—" Scarlett continued.

"Which means," said Blossom, "that if he thinks you know where the box is—"

"He's going to come after you to get it just like he did with Ginger," Scarlett finished up.

I poured another half glass. "That about sums it up."

"But this is terrible!" Scarlett said, appalled.

"There's a big difference," I said, wanting to ease her fear. "Aunt Ginger had the box and they knew it; they probably thought they'd just be able to search her room after they killed her and walk off with it. I don't have the box, so they're not going to put a hit out on me."

Not yet.

"Does Will know about the letter?"

"No, and if you tell him I will never forgive you. I don't ever want him to find out about the scam. I don't understand why Aunt Ginger would do such a thing—she's—she was—somewhat unorthodox in her business dealings, but greed just wasn't in her nature. She was one of the most generous people I've ever known, and this whole scheme just reeks of greed. So there's got to be another explanation."

And I'll know what it is when I find her, or she finds me.

"Did it ever occur to you, Tilly," Blossom scolded, "that one of the reasons he's trying so hard to find you is that he's worried about you?"

"It crossed my mind," I muttered.

"I think you should turn yourself in," Scarlett declared. "The only place you'll be absolutely safe is in protective custody."

"I'd be protected, all right." I snorted. "For the rest of my life. Let's see: So far I'm facing charges of obstruction of justice, perjury, conspiracy, illegal flight, aiding and abetting, forgery, and illegal use of a Class II substance. And that's just the penny-ante stuff. Let's not forget being an accessory after the fact to first-degree murder, fraud, grand larceny, and smuggling."

Blossom giggled. "You forgot littering."

"And loitering," Scarlett pointed out.

"Failure to observe the leash laws."

"Cruelty to animals," I chimed in. "For abandoning Baskerville."

"Unpaid parking tickets!"

"Jaywalking!"

By now Blossom was rolling on the floor, laughing like a loon. "Wearing Lands' End," she choked out.

Scarlett plopped down beside her. "Thinking impure thoughts!"

I tumbled off the bed. "Choosing Chilled Plum instead of Funky Cherry!"

For long minutes we just lay there gasping and giggling, happily embracing absurdity, celebrating friendship.

Some friend you are, Tilly Snapp. My conscience was working in overdrive.

Go ahead, tell yourself you didn't actually lie to them. You merely omitted one small fact in Aunt Ginger's letter. Okay, okay, the huge fact in Aunt Ginger's letter. She's alive.

Don't be so hard on yourself. Maybe things will work out somehow and one day she can miraculously reappear. If they don't and she can't, you will take that knowledge to your grave. You owe her that much.

As for the other thing, about not knowing who put the hit out on Aunt Ginger—the subject just didn't happen to come up in the course of the conversation. All right, it did, but you absolutely did not tell a lie. You equivocated, which is a whole different thing.

It's not going to do any good to tell them Halsey Wickerby and Carlotta Flores are probably the ones who put the contract out on Aunt Ginger. You won't know for sure until you go to Kingston and find out the name of the man who was murdered in the brothel.

Stop with the guilt. You couldn't tell them everything. Your first duty is to keep Aunt Ginger's secret, and you want to protect them too. The less they know right now, the safer they are. They'd do the same for you.

Yes, you could tell Will that you have an idea about who put out the hit, but then he'd have to know about the letter and the Singapore scam, maybe even the fact that she's alive.

That is not going to happen, not as long as there's a breath left in your body.

Believe me, he wouldn't be thanking you any time soon for making him look like an ass. Actually, you'd be in jail, so he wouldn't be speaking to you at all for, oh, the next forty or fifty years. If then.

You know what you have to do, even if you're not exactly sure how to go about it. You'll just have to wing it. And you're going to have to fly solo, at least for now.

Yes, you can *do it. And do you know why?*

Because you know who you are.

You're Tilly Snapp, Sex Detective.

And you're about to go out and kick some butt.

THIRTY-ONE

I had to start somewhere. It might as well be in the belly of the beast as anywhere else.

"I'm sorry, Ms. Snapp," the secretary said. "Mr. Wickerby is out of town today. I see he has an opening at ten on Thursday. Would that be convenient for you?"

"There's no rush," I assured her. "It's nothing urgent. I just need to tie up a few loose ends regarding my aunt's estate before I go back to Boston. Monday or Tuesday of next week would be fine, maybe around noon?"

"Let me see. Yes, I'll just pencil you in for noon on Monday. If you'll leave your number, I'll check with Mr. Wickerby when he calls in and get back to you to confirm."

"My cell phone's been on the fritz for a few days. It would probably be better if I call you."

Here it was my first day on the case, and already I was paranoid. Snag had said cell phone calls were hard to trace; he didn't say they were impossible to trace. I'd stick to public phones as much as possible.

"By the way, would you happen to have the telephone number of my aunt's accountant handy? I seem to have misplaced her card."

I laid Carlotta Flores's card on the table and waited for the secretary to come back on the line.

"Here it is, Ms. Snapp. Do you want all the information?"

"That would be helpful, thank you."

"It's actually Flores-Perpinan, but I believe she prefers simply to go by the name of Flores."

We urged each other to have a nice day and disconnected.

For a long moment I sat staring down at the card. Not Flores. Flores-Perpinan.

I shot off the bed and started pacing around the room, my mind humming with excitement.

"Perp sing!" There it was, the one piece of the puzzle that pulled it all together. Aunt Ginger had seen someone named Perpinan in Singapore, and that someone had seen her. Since it couldn't have been Carlotta, it had to be the man in the brothel.

"Alberto P. is here in Jamaica," she'd said in her letter. "I wonder if he could be her brother." She must have been referring to Carlotta, so she'd made the connection between Alberto Perpinan, his sister, and, of course, Halsey Wickerby. I didn't know how she'd found out Alberto was in Jamaica, but she obviously knew she was in serious danger from him, serious enough to decide she'd better see to her own death before he did.

I perched on the edge of the bed and wondered

how she must have felt when she learned that Carlotta and Wickerby, two people she'd known for years and was on friendly terms with, would have her killed in cold blood. It was a wonder she'd dared to come back to Miami to look for the box in Erratica.

Of course! The woman with the stun gun. What a dunce I was! I'd been so stunned by my encounter with Joseph Alvarez that I hadn't recognized her, or possibly she'd been in disguise. But it made perfect sense now why she didn't leave her name at the hospital. Missy Mae was right after all. Aunt Ginger had been my guardian angel that night.

Tilly Snapp, Sex Detective. Who'd have thought it?

I needed to get to Kingston, and fast. Will had to know about the Perpinan-Flores-Wickerby connection, although he didn't have enough information to link it to the pillow box because he didn't know Aunt Ginger had been in Singapore. And he didn't know she was alive. But I wasn't about to underestimate him; at any minute he might figure out the whole darn puzzle.

I called Air Jamaica, finished my packing, and punched in Scarlett's cell phone number. I was ridiculously relieved when I got her voice mail; it was going to be a lot easier to say what I had to say to a machine.

"It's me. I know you're going to be really mad at me, but I have to go out of town again for a few days, and I can't tell you where I'll be. I know it won't do any good to tell you not to worry about me, because you will anyway, but I promise I'll be careful. I love you guys, I really do. I couldn't ask for better friends."

I hung up and tried not to cry.

* * *

"Red Copper Spritz? What was wrong with the Chilled Plum?"

"My boyfriend hates it," I lied. "He says my hair looks like a nest of purple snakes."

Nikkolai took instant umbrage. "Purple snakes!"

"It's not your fault, Nikkolai," I assured him. "Baskerville wears bow ties and black socks with his tennis sneakers, so you can see where he's coming from."

"A bumpkin," Nikkolai sniffed.

"I know," I said sadly, "but what's to be done? You can take the boy out of the backwoods, but you can't take the backwoods out of the boy. Anyhow, I thought maybe I'd try the Red Copper Spritz this time. And do you think you could get rid of the snakes? I don't mean cut them off, just relax them or something."

He ran his fingers over my hair, frowned at my reflection in the mirror, and consulted his muse. "Hmmm. Yes, I will do it. This Baskerville will not recognize you when I have finished with you."

I couldn't ask for more.

In the movies it usually goes something like this:

The getaway van is weaving back and forth through four lanes of traffic at a good eighty miles an hour; the driver's eyes flick back and forth between the side and rearview mirrors. "I think they made us, Charlie," he snarls. "Black Mazda RX-8, '03, Florida plates, coming up on our right four back. Driver's Hispanic about forty-five, passenger white female, maybe twenty-six, mole on her left cheek. Gotta be the Feds."

One can only marvel that the van doesn't slam straight into the huge cement truck ahead, which is meandering along at a sedate forty, burst into flames, and vaporize the horrified passenger and the driver, who has apparently ignored the first rule of driving: "Keep your eyes on the road."

But hey, this is Hollywood: There has to be a big shootout at the end, so the van swerves into the breakdown lane, fishtails past the truck, veers back onto the pavement, and the chase goes on.

I only mention this because I try never to think about what's going on behind me when I'm driving at high speed. Oh, I might keep an eye on a semi that's been tailgating me for the past ten miles, trying to decide whether to pass or simply flatten me like a pancake just to save himself the trouble of changing lanes, but generally I like to know what catastrophe lies ahead.

So under normal circumstances I might not have given a moment's thought to the white car that swung in behind me on the ramp leading up onto I-95 in Coconut Grove and was still right behind me when I turned onto I-395 heading for the airport. But it was a white car, and that could mean only one thing.

"They made me," I snarled to myself. "White Chevy Malibu, Florida plates, on my tail. Driver's a white female, thick glasses, about twenty-eight, passenger white female, maybe twenty-nine, big hair. Gotta be Ginger's Angels."

There wasn't time to wonder how Scarlett and Blossom had tracked me down after I checked out of the inn. Between them, these two women appeared to be on intimate terms with every neuron, dendrite, axon, and synapse in my brain. And once they were on my trail, they wouldn't have any trouble keeping me in sight. I was driving a canary yellow Volkswagen Beetle, for pity's sake. I made a quick mental note to go for a nondescript Kia next time.

Since we didn't cover fishtailing down the breakdown lane at eighty miles an hour in my high school driver's ed class, I had to think quickly, or more accurately, out-think them quickly. They would anticipate I was heading either to the main terminal or the section of the airport where rental cars were picked up and returned. The exit for the terminal was about two miles ahead; cars were already jockeying into the two right lanes. Anyone trapped in the far right lane would have to take the exit, whether they wanted to or not.

I made my move a half mile before the exit: I swerved into the breakdown lane, slammed on the brakes, and skidded to a stop. Scarlett and Blossom shot right on by and were carried away in the flood of cars exiting onto the airport's main road. By the time they could negotiate the heavy traffic that inched its way past the enormous terminal and check out every car rental lot, I could drop off the Beetle, take the courtesy van back to the terminal, and be safely through security where they wouldn't be able to intercept me. Feeling smug and only marginally guilty, I managed to edge my way across the two exit lanes and sped on toward the next exit whistling a smug little tune.

Guilt caught up with me at Gate 12 on Concourse E.

Scarlett answered her cell phone on the first ring. I didn't even have to say hello. "That was a dirty rotten trick, Tilly Snapp."

"Let me speak to her," I could hear Blossom saying in the background. "Have you lost your mind?" she demanded a moment later. "What harebrained scheme have you hatched up now? We were scared half to death when we found you'd left the inn. And driving like a lunatic—in a goddamn yellow Beetle. A Beetle, for heaven's sake."

"Okay, I'll agree the Beetle was a mistake," I said. "And I'm sorry, really sorry I bailed out on you like that, but—"

"You're going back to Jamaica, aren't you? Why are you going back to Jamaica, Tilly?"

"How do you know I'm going to Jamaica? Maybe I'm going back to Ottumwa. Maybe I met the man of my dreams at the QwikStop and we're going to buy a little farm and raise goats and make babies and vote Republican."

"That's not funny," came Scarlett's voice. "Tilly, what's going on? Just tell us what's going on. Why can't you trust us?"

The gate attendant announced the flight was now ready to board. I joined the long line inching toward the gate. "I do, I do trust you, Scarlett. Okay, I can tell you this." I lowered my voice. "I think I know who put the hit out on Aunt Ginger; I just have to get one more piece of information and I'll know for sure."

"And that piece of information is in Jamaica?"

"Yes. At Sin and Sand," I said to throw them off the scent.

"You're not going to try to go after this guy yourself, are you?" Scarlett said, horrified. "Oh, God, Tilly, please don't—"

"You'll have to shut off your cell phone if you want to board, ma'am," the gate attendant said.

"Okay, sorry. No, Scarlett, I promise I won't. Yes, I promise! I have to go now—"

"Ask her how she likes the Red Copper Spritz," I heard Blossom say. "How do you like the Red Copper

Spritz, Tilly? Nikkolai said it came out really well."

"I like it. Maybe next time I'll try the Lively Auburn. I'll be back in a few days. Bye. Love you."

My life as Tilly Snapp, Sex Detective, wasn't coming cheap. Flying hither and yon at last-minute fares, hotels, rental cars, meals, "going Beach," Nikkolai, aspirin—lots of aspirin—it was adding up, way up.

I wasn't heading for bankruptcy court or a cardboard box on Boston Common, but I was going to have to dip into the high-interest CD account that I set up with the money Alex's insurance company finally coughed up. It had been a down-and-dirty, no-holds-barred battle between Arthur Kelso and Liberty Mutual as to whether being struck by lightning on the sixth hole of the Greenways Country Club constituted an Act of God, which was not covered, or negligence on the part of the club for not sounding the bad weather warning signal in a timely manner to warn golfers to get the hell off the course, which was.

Fortunately Arthur Kelso is a very good lawyer, and I came away with a comfortable safety net, and Arthur Kelso came away with the down payment for a new vacation home on Martha's Vineyard.

Naturally, Good Old Tilly Snapp hadn't touched one single penny of that money in three years, being the fiscally responsible sort, but in only six weeks Tilly Snapp, Sex Detective, was already eyeing it like a wolf going after a baby bunny.

What the hell, I thought, as I checked into the Hilton in Kingston and handed over my American Express Card. You only live once.

"Here's your key card, Mrs. Snapp-Allenby," the desk clerk chirped. "Room 887. Just take the elevator on your left to the eighth floor. Oh, and I believe you have a message on your room phone. All you have to do is press '8875' to retrieve it."

"I have a message?"

"Yes."

"A message," I said slowly. "For me."

"Actually, the call came through to the front desk here about twenty minutes ago, but I had it transferred to your room."

"For Matilda Snapp. Twenty minutes ago."

"He asked for Matilda Snapp-Allenby, but I checked our guest register, and there wasn't another Matilda Snapp." She smiled brightly. "If there's anything we can do to make your visit to Jamaica more enjoyable, please don't hesitate to ask."

"Thank you," I muttered under my breath, "You've done quite enough as it is."

I stared at the telephone, trying to figure the odds. Best case scenario: The message was from Snag. Worst case scenario: Will had tracked me down. They were fifty-fifty; not all that promising.

I took another swig of courage from the small bottle of Chablis I grabbed from the room's minibar and dialed 8875.

"Hey, Ginger Girl. What mischief are you getting yourself into now?"

Thank you, God, I thought.

"Lucius tells me he can hardly keep up with you. He wasn't too happy when you got by him in Tijuana and took off for Canada, but he didn't have much trouble picking you up at the Miami River Inn. I can hear you from here—you don't need looking after—but as I said, Ginger wants me to look out for you, so

I'm looking out for you. 'Sides," he added, slipping into Snag-speak, "you be my girl too now."

It was a good thing I was in love with Will Maitland, because Aston Ewing sure knew how to sneak into a woman's heart.

"Kingston's a mean town, Ginger Girl, so whatever you've got to do there, do it quickly and get yourself on a plane back to Miami. You stay in the hotel after dark, hear? And don't try to shake off Lucius; I wouldn't like that. It wouldn't surprise me if Willy tracks you down there, so you better keep an eye out for him. Maybe it's time you let him catch you. Heh-heh-heh."

I had to admit there was some comfort in knowing Snag was watching over me. Not that his motives were entirely altruistic, of course. He was after the pillow box of Win Win Poo just like everyone else, and he was under the impression I would eventually lead him to it. He and Ginger might have been friends and occasionally done business together, but she certainly never had any intention of letting Snag get anywhere near her treasure. I wondered if he even knew about the Singapore scam.

Lucius turned out to be none other than Mr. Clean, the cappuccino addict from Zephyr. I spotted him in the lobby when I went down to the coffee shop to get a sandwich to take up to the room for dinner. He must have been wearing a hat on the plane, because I certainly would have noticed that gleaming pate. I waved; he smiled.

All I needed to find in Kingston was a name, one name. How hard could that be?

Nearly impossible, apparently, as I discovered the next day. Every paper-pusher in the Jamaica Constabulary Force knew that someone would know the name of the man who'd been found with his throat slit in the brothel in Trenchtown in September; the file would be somewhere, only not here in this office. I should try down the hall, in the record room in the basement, up on the fourth floor, over in the new annex. Eventually, I was pointed in the direction of the Kingston morgue, where, I was told, the victim's body lay unclaimed. The file would be there.

I think the less said about my experience at the Kingston morgue, the better. Lucius actually had to pull a gun—from where on his person, I cannot imagine—to extract me from the mob of "dead-hustlers" who descended like a flock of vultures the minute I stepped out of the taxi, hawking coffins, hearses, mortuary cosmetic services, grave sites, headstones, and even mourners at deep discounts. Matters didn't improve inside when, after two miserable hours of waiting in a cement cell that masqueraded as a waiting room, I learned that not only had the body been claimed some weeks earlier by the victim's sister, but—surprise, surprise—the file was nowhere to be found.

The following day found me in St. Catherine near Spanish Town, pawing through piles of unfiled death certificates in the Registrar General's Department. Shortly before closing time, I found it.

Flores-Perpinan, Alberto; d.o.b. 7 March 1960, Cali, Colombia; d. 23 September 2004, Kingston, Jamaica. Cause of death: Homicide, knife wound to the throat.

THIRTY-TWO

"Thanks again, Lucius," I said as we pushed through the revolving door into the blessed cool of the Hilton lobby. "I have what I came for. You're off the hook."

"Ain't off the hook 'til Snag take me off the hook," he said with a grin. "Besides, I got a thing going with that Darcy at Zephyr. Wouldn't want her wasting all that talent on someone who don't appreciate her."

"I'm surprised you don't have a hole in your stomach with all the coffee you've been drinking these past weeks. I hope she appreciates your devotion."

He laughed. "She appreciate some other things more."

"I'm sure she does. I'm just going to go get an iced tea in the coffee shop. Can I get you anything?"

"Red Stripe be nice."

"Sure thing."

When I walked back into the lobby, he was gone. I figured he'd gone to the men's room, and I didn't want to leave the beer on the table, so I perched on the arm of a sofa beside a burbling fountain to wait. I smiled over at the desk clerk who had checked me in. She didn't smile back; in fact, I was pretty sure she pretended she didn't see me at all. I looked around, feeling vaguely uneasy. That was when I saw the two police officers, one at the far end of the counter, the other at the entrance to the gift shop. No wonder Lucius decided to take a stroll.

I took the beer up to my room and put it in the refrigerator, puttered around, called my brother Matthew in New York to tell him I had to cancel for Thanksgiving, and checked my e-mail. I changed into my new triangle-halter-top-skirtini and went down to the huge pool to swim a few laps and laze in the last rays of the setting sun.

Feeling relaxed and righteous after a day's work well done, I took a long hot shower and wrapped myself in the luxurious white terry robe provided "for the comfort of our guests." I towel-dried my hair and grinned at myself in the mirror. The woman who grinned back almost managed to cock a brow and purred, "You are here, you are hot, and, baby, you are *happenin'*."

I switched off the bathroom light and padded over to the window. Kingston, all shimmery and pulsing with life down there, didn't look like a mean town from the eighth floor of the Hilton.

The phone rang. I nearly jumped out of my skin. I told myself to calm down; it was probably Snag again.

"Hey, Ginger Girl. You okay?"

"I'm fine. Why?"

"Lucius called, said you were in trouble."

"Trouble? I'm not in any—"

"Yes, you are," Will Maitland said from the darkness behind me.

I kept my cool, just. "Actually I may be in just a bit of trouble."

"Willy there?"

"It appears he is."

"Then I'd say you're in a lot of trouble, Ginger Girl. Tell Willy Snag wants to talk to him."

I held up the phone without turning around. "Snag wishes to have a word with you, *Willy*."

I heard the slight give of the mattress on the queen-size bed by the wall as he got up. A hand reached over my shoulder to take the receiver, and before I could make a break for the bathroom, a strong arm draped itself around my neck and anchored me to his side. Just what I thought I would achieve if I did manage to lock myself in there I really can't say, as I wasn't thinking all that clearly at the moment.

I could hear Snag's deep rumble, but couldn't make out the words. Will's side of the conversation, mostly monosyllabic, wasn't particularly enlightening, so I spent the next few minutes preparing for the confrontation to come. Sure, he had the full weight of the American judicial system on his side, not to mention the fact that he was a lot bigger than I was, but the odds of weaseling my way out of this mess were only ninety-nine to one against, so I figured I still had a chance.

Will passed me the phone.

"The best way to handle the situation is to go along," Snag said. "Be cooperative, but if he starts asking questions, say you want a lawyer. He's got a thing for you; it wouldn't hurt if you were extra nice, if you know what I mean."

"You are a sick, sick person," I informed him.

"Whatever works. Willy's a good man, Ginger Girl; trust him to do right by you."

"You think so?"

"You got old Snag's word on it."

I had to smile. "Well, then, it must be true. Thanks for the advice, Snag. Oh, I almost forgot: Bingo sends his regards from LA. I'll send you a Christmas card from Leavenworth."

"Where's that, girl?"

"Nowhere you want to be, believe me."

It started badly and went downhill from there.

"You have the right to remain silent and refuse to answer questions. Do you understand?"

"Could you repeat the question?" I said.

"You have the right to remain silent and refuse to answer questions. Do you understand?"

"I refuse to answer the question 'Do you understand?' on the grounds that I have the right to remain silent and refuse to answer questions."

"Anything you do or say may be used against you in a court of law. Do you understand?"

I took time to think it over. "Nothing I do or say may be used against me in a court of law because I do not understand the question 'Do you understand?' and therefore cannot understand that anything I do or say may be used against me in a court of law."

A tiny muscle jittered at the corner of one fathomless pool of bittersweet chocolate. "You have the right to consult an attorney before speaking to the police and to have an attorney present during questioning now or in the future. Do you understand?"

That was a deep one. "Give me a minute here.

Hmmm. Okay, I've got it: I cannot answer the question 'Do you understand?' until I consult an attorney before answering the question 'Do you understand?' "

Someone was losing his temper. "If you cannot afford an attorney," he ground out, "one will be appointed for you before any questioning, if you wish. Do you understand?"

"Could you run that by me again?"

"No."

I shrugged. "Okay, but if I get it wrong, it's your own fault." I concentrated hard. "I cannot answer the question 'Do you understand?' because I do not know if I understand that if I cannot afford an attorney one will be appointed for me before you ask the question 'Do you understand?' "

I thought I heard the gnashing of teeth. "If you decide to answer questions now without an attorney present, you will still have the right to stop answering at any time until you talk to an attorney. Do you understand?"

"That's very considerate of you," I said. "However, I cannot answer the question 'Do you understand?' because I have no grounds upon which to decide whether to answer questions now without an attorney present and will still have the right to stop answering at any time until I talk to an attorney regarding the question 'Do you understand?' "

"Knowing and understanding your rights as I have explained them to you," he snarled, "are you willing to answer my questions without an attorney present?"

"I'm sorry, were you speaking to me?"

Evidently Special Agent Maitland took his duties as an officer of the court a great deal more seriously than I did as a future defendant, which was how I came to be handcuffed to the towel rail in the pitch-black bathroom of Room 887 in the Hilton Hotel in Kingston, Jamaica.

"Police brutality!" I shouted. "Cruel and unsanitary punishment!"

I thought about demanding to see a lawyer, but Jamaican lawyers wear those creepy white wigs that always remind me of John Cleese dancing around naked in *A Fish Called Wanda.* It's hard to take the British-style judicial system seriously after seeing something like that.

"Hey, what about my phone call? I demand my phone call! And food, I need food! I am not an animal, I am a human being!"

This wasn't getting me anywhere. I didn't even know if he was out there. For all I knew he could be down in the bar knocking back shots of Absolut and looking to get lucky.

I plopped down on the side of the tub and thought about Will Maitland getting lucky with someone other than me. I found the idea vaguely unsettling; I might even go so far as to say disagreeable. Okay, okay, it was loathsome and intolerable and made me want to tear my hair out by the roots.

"You'd better come to terms with it here and now," I advised myself. "Even if you do manage to crawl out from under the raft of federal charges, he's never going to speak to you again. At best, he thinks you're difficult, insolent, and irrational; at worst, a pain in the ass and not worth the trouble."

"A person can change," I argued. "She can fall down a rabbit hole and decide to climb a mountain just because it's there, hear the music in the call of the wild, go over the mountain to see what she can see."

"She's still not going to settle," I pointed out.

"True," I admitted. "She can't; it's not in her nature."

"So it will be just you, the vibrator, and *Sex and the City* reruns until the day they carry you out in a pine box?"

I sighed. "It looks that way."

"Snag says he's got a thing for you. Why don't you try being extra nice to Agent Maitland like he suggests?"

"That would be underhanded, immoral, and unethical."

"Talking to yourself again?" Will said from the doorway.

I blinked against the sudden brightness. "You need a warrant to eavesdrop on a person's conversations," I informed him. "I don't see a warrant in your hand, Agent Maitland."

"Not when she's talking to herself, which you seem to do a lot."

"How long were you standing there?" I demanded, mortified.

"Don't worry. You mumble when you talk to yourself. Hungry?"

"Will I have to eat in the bathroom?"

"Are you going to behave yourself?"

"I suppose so."

"Then we'll go out."

He turned on the TV and settled down to watch a soccer match while I got dressed. It must have been a hundred degrees in Kingston that afternoon and I doubted it had cooled down all that much after the sun went down, so I slipped into a loose sundress of sheer yellow lawn and wrestled my hair into a topknot to keep it off my neck. A quick flick of the mascara brush, a bit of blusher, and a touch of bronze lip gloss, and I was ready for a big night out with the man who would be carting me off to jail in the morning.

"What happened to the purple hair?" he said as we stepped out of the lobby into a blast of heat and humidity that nearly knocked me off my two-inch strappy sandals.

I stopped. "How do you know about the purple hair? And it wasn't purple; it was plummy."

"Nikkolai," he said.

"And just how did you happen to be talking to Nikkolai?" I demanded.

"Blossom and Scarlett went after you when you checked out of the inn, and I followed them."

That's how he'd traced me to Kingston, I realized. All he had to do was follow Blossom and Scarlett, who were following me.

"That was a pretty impressive move you pulled on I-395," he said. "I couldn't get over in time."

"I thought so," I said smugly.

We walked on. "Where are we going?" I asked.

"The Hot Pot. I like it."

"The Hot Pot?"

"The Red Copper Spritz."

"Oh, well, thanks," I said, feeling all fluttery inside. "I'm reinventing myself. I'm going 'Beach.' "

"What the hell does that mean?" he said as he guided me around the corner toward a glowing neon sign with red flames licking up around a glowing pot.

"I'm on the run—was on the run—and I needed a disguise, so I decided, when in Wonderland, do as the Wonderlanders do."

The Hot Pot appeared to be patronized mainly by locals, a cheerful noisy crowd that somehow managed to converse despite the reggae music blasting out from the open door of the kitchen. I loved it.

I left the ordering to Will, since he grew up in Jamaica and was pretty much a local himself. We drank ice-cold coconut water with Appleton rum and ate ackee with salt fish and red beans and rice and fried plantains.

We talked and laughed and told our life stories and smiled at one another in the warm candlelight, and walked back to the hotel through the soft Kingston night holding hands.

And I was Tilly and he was Will.

"I wish I could, but I'm escorting a prisoner back to Miami tomorrow."

The prisoner, who only fifteen minutes earlier had been Tilly, looked up from her laptop and glowered at the special-agent-who-had-been-Will, who lay stretched out on the bed in his stocking feet talking to his mother in Ocho Rios.

"Yes, I'll be there for Christmas."

The prisoner turned her attention back to the screen of her laptop and resolutely tried not to eavesdrop on the conversation.

> Hi. Just to let you know I'm safe. I'm at the Hilton in Kingston and tomorrow I'll be in jail in Miami because the bureaucrat with the bee up his butt caught up with me.
>
> I'm going to need a lawyer, so will you call Arthur Kelso of Kelso Kelso & Kelso on School Street in Boston and ask him to get you the name of a good criminal defense attor-

```
ney in Miami? Tell Baskerville
I should be up for parole in
twenty or thirty years and ask
him to wait for me.
Love from your friend,
Tilly Snapp, Sex Detective
```

"No, I'm not bringing Danielle this year."

Who was this Danielle and why did I hate her already?

"Yes, I know you thought so. I'll explain when I see you."

My ears perked up. Could it be Danielle was history? God, I hoped so.

I'm not even going to pretend that sleeping in the same hotel room with Will didn't raise a serious concern in my mind as to how I was going to survive the night without going into sexual meltdown. The best plan I could come up with to safeguard against such an embarrassing possibility was to hustle into an oversized T-shirt while he was showering and dive under the covers.

With any luck I'd be asleep by the time he emerged. With any luck he'd pretend I wasn't even in the room. With any luck he'd be wearing something, anything, briefs, a towel. With any luck he wouldn't kiss me goodnight.

I wasn't asleep.

He didn't pretend I wasn't in the room.

He wasn't wearing anything.

And yes, he did kiss me goodnight.

Meltdown.

* * *

"Snag said I should be extra nice to you."

"Snag's a wise man."

I snuggled closer. "Will."

"Mmmm?"

"Do you . . . um, do you have a thing for me?"

"Thing?"

"You know, a thing."

"Yes, Tilly, I certainly do have a thing. Want to see it?"

"That's not what I mean and you know it," I huffed, trying to wriggle out of his arms.

He pulled me back against him, laughing as I tried to make a convincing show of putting up a struggle.

One thing led to another, and a long time later, as the huge disk of the sun rose up out of the sea and washed Kingston in rosy glow, I thought I heard him whisper against my hair, "Yes, I have a thing for you."

Thirty-Three

There's a lot to be said for being in federal custody when it comes to international air travel. Let law-abiding, God-fearing citizens cram into shuttle vans or pay exorbitant taxi fees to get out to the airport. Let them inch along the zigzagging check-in and security lines roped in like cattle being herded from one pen to another. Let them be interrogated, poked and prodded, relieved of both their shoes and their dignity, and finally be spit out into departure lounges where they are condemned to listen to endless repeats of CNN headlines until they are finally funneled, sooner or later, onto their planes and sent on their way. If that's the way they want to travel, I wish them well.

We felons, on the other hand, speed to the airport in the back of police cruisers at no expense whatsoever, bypass check-in entirely, and are whisked through security with a nod and a smile and a have-a-nice-day. We're the first to board and always get the window seat. If we happen to be in the custody of a drop-dead gorgeous Interpol agent, we can be sure the female flight attendants will drop by often to see that we are comfortable and have everything we need to enjoy our flight.

The fact that we are handcuffed to the gorgeous federal agent—albeit discreetly with a plastic strap rather than clanking metal cuffs—in no way diminishes the pleasure of the flying experience. It's not for everyone, of course, but I will say it started my journey through the federal detention system off on a positive note, and I would certainly consider doing it again, provided I got the drop-dead gorgeous Interpol agent.

I'm lying through my teeth, of course. It had to be right up there in the top ten most humiliating experiences of my life, which include getting my period at a junior high picnic while wearing white shorts, and walking right through a sparkling-clean sliding glass door at the garden party my wealthy future in-laws hosted to celebrate my engagement to their son.

Will didn't speak a word the entire trip, which was just fine with me, because I was spitting mad and would have bitten his head off if he'd so much as asked me to pass the sugar.

Gone was the intimate, fun couple of the previous night. Tilly and Will had left the building, and Fugitive Tilly Snapp and Special Agent Will Maitland were back on stage. It was by far the weirdest relationship I'd ever had with a man and, I can tell you, not one I'd recommend.

"You have got to be kidding," I gasped when he informed me just before we left for the airport that not only would he have to confiscate my passport and wallet while we were en route, but that Interpol regulations required that I be handcuffed to the agent escorting me.

First I yelled bloody murder. Then I made a number of uncomplimentary references to his parentage, personality, and personal attributes. Then I cried.

I can't say whether, under normal circumstances, Will Maitland would have given me, Good Old Tilly Snapp, a second glance, or I would have opened myself to the possibility that such a stunning man might actually like me and desire me, but our circumstances were anything but normal. Fate, in the person of Lorraine Louise Snapp, had determined what our relationship was to be long before we met, and I was only going to cause myself pain if I didn't find a way to deal with it. We each had a role to play in tying up the loose ends of Aunt Ginger's life; that had to be the nature of our relationship whether or not I wanted it to be.

I didn't have a clue what he wanted or if he even thought about it, but I can tell you that he was in full special-agent mode as he marched me through Miami immigration and customs and across the huge arrival hall to a room exactly like the one Agent Dixon had deposited me in; the only difference was that the laminate on the table was a dusky blue and President Bush looked as though he might be worrying about the deficit or Social Security reform now.

While I sulked at one end of the long table, Will sat at the other leafing through a sheaf of papers, jotting down notations here and there, and making a very convincing show of ignoring me altogether.

I responded in kind by opening my laptop and concentrating on getting my life in order: transferring money from my CD account into personal checking, paying my credit card bills, mortgage, and car insurance. Life went on even when you were about to become a guest of the Federal Bureau of Prisons.

A cheerful ping alerted me that I had mail.

> Tilly, maybe you should tell him what you told us. Most of it, anyhow. He's not the enemy.
>
> We'll call Kelso in the morning. Wickerby called to say he couldn't reach you on your cell phone. We told him your Monday appointment might be a problem because you'd be in jail; I think he actually dropped the phone. Carlotta Flores called too. They both seem really concerned about you. Alonzo actually went and bought the ring!!! Virgil cried and we all drank champagne. The wedding is set for New Year's Eve, so you'd better be out of jail by then! We still can't find the urn and Gingersnap is gone again. Don't worry: she always turns up. Missy Mae found her in a kitchen cupboard last Tuesday. Please ask Will to let us know where you'll be so we can come visit. We'll tell them we're your sisters. Well, we are!

Richie the Ratfink says hello and Baskerville says he isn't sure he can wait that long.
Love, love,
S & B
PS: It's not nice to keep things from your friends, Tilly Snapp. We think we might have figured out your big secret.

"God, I hope not," I said.

"Tell me what?" Will said when he read it a few minutes later.

My sulk was fast becoming a snit. "I believe I've been properly Mirandized. I don't have to answer questions without a lawyer present."

"Don't start, Tilly. I'm just doing my job."

"You'll have to excuse me; I'm new at this. I think I'm getting the hang of the suspect thing, but I've never been someone's 'job' before."

"Why," he said, "do you have to make everything twice as difficult as it has to be? Somehow I've become the bad guy in this movie. There are people out there who murdered your aunt in cold blood, and I'm the bad guy. You go running off to Jamaica and I go after you to try to keep you out of trouble, and I'm the bad guy. You cozy up to Aston Ewing, who is one very dangerous man if you cross him—"

"And your friend," I pointed out.

"And I'm the bad guy," he continued without missing a beat. "Grimes takes out a warrant for your arrest for substituting that computer and lying to investigating officers, and I'm the bad guy. You take off, I have no choice but to get another warrant to bring you in as a material witness and chase you to hell and back, and that makes me the bad guy too.

"I warned you, Tilly. I warned you right from the start not to interfere in this case, but you went right ahead and did it anyhow." He gestured to the room. "So here we are, seven weeks later, and you're on your way to jail. You *made* yourself part of my job."

Of course he was absolutely right. From his perspective he'd done everything right and I'd done everything wrong.

"Hmmm," I said. "So if you really are the good guy, then I guess that means I have to switch sides and go over and join the bad guys' team."

"Not necessarily. Maybe if you told me what you told your friends, we could keep you on the team."

I shrugged. "Sure, why not? I'd hate to be kicked off the team."

"Why do I get the feeling I'm about to get bamboozled?" he said.

"No bam, no boozle. This is exactly what I told Scarlett and Blossom:

"I went to Negril to see if I could find out more about Aunt Ginger's last days there. I met Snag through the bartender at Sin and Sand—I'm sure you know him, Uncle Jimmie?—and Snag gave me a letter Aunt Ginger left with him for me in case anything happened to her, which of course it did. She said she thought someone might be out to kill her."

"I don't suppose she happened to mention the pillow box of Win Win Poo?" he inquired.

"Well, she did mention it, now that I come to think of it."

"Now that you think of it."

"There's no need to get sarcastic. I don't have to tell you this stuff, you know. I'm trying to cooperate here. She said she thought the warning she received must have something to do with the box."

"And what's the 'big secret' that your friends think they've figured out now?"

I frowned. "Beats me. I'll have to ask them. That's it. So now you know what I told Scarlett and Blossom. Oh, there was other stuff—the guy who sets his penis on fire every night and Speedo the Wonder Stud and Cabbyman—but that's not pertinent here."

"Speedo the Wonder Stud?"

I plastered a leer on my face and pitched my voice low. "Chip Stearns, Cincinnati, Pisces, real estate, divorced. And you, little lady?"

"Ah."

"He was sort of pathetic," I added.

"I don't suppose you'd care to show me the letter," Will said.

"I'm afraid not. There's some personal stuff in it I wouldn't feel comfortable sharing. Besides, I think I left it somewhere, maybe back in Boston."

In a safe-deposit box where no one will ever see it.

He looked at me for a long thoughtful moment, got up, and left the room. He came back twenty minutes later.

"Why are we sitting here?" I demanded. "What are we waiting for?"

"Grimes."

"FBI Grimes?"

"Uh-huh."

"Why? Why are we waiting for him?"

Will sat back in his chair and tapped his pen on the

table. "We have a problem with jurisdiction. There are two warrants out for you: one for obstruction of justice, the other as a material witness. A federal judge has to determine which takes precedence. That determines who takes it from here. We're waiting to hear back from Judge Teitelbaum."

I shrugged. "What difference does it make? Either way I'm going to jail."

One brow went up. "It doesn't matter who takes you in? My feelings are hurt."

"As a matter of fact, no. Wait, I have an idea! Why don't you just cut me in half? Then you both get your little gold-foil star for the day."

The killer smile caught me off guard, and I had to take a minute to start breathing again.

"You're really pissed off, aren't you?" he said.

"Who, me?"

"I told you, Tilly, you brought this on yourself."

"It must be nice to be God," I remarked.

"I gave you a chance to tell me the truth about the letter and the box," he went on. "You decided to play games with me and you lost."

"I would have lost anyhow," I shot back, "because it wouldn't have made one jot of difference if I had crossed every *t* and dotted every *i*. I'd still be a criminal and you'd still be a bureaucrat with a bee up his butt."

Both brows went up, a bad sign. "I see. You do have a way with words, Tilly. But you're wrong on one point. I would have been able to make a better case with Judge Teitelbaum that the suspect was cooperating fully with the investigating officer, and that the material witness warrant would yield better results than obstruction of justice. You blew it."

A girl can only take so much. I leaned forward and

rested my elbows on the table. "Frankly, my dear," I said à la Clark Gable in *Gone with the Wind*, "I don't give a damn."

I gave a huge damn, but it was a relief to be led off an hour later by Detective George Grimes, who didn't appear to hold a grudge about the computer and gave me the short version of the Miranda warning. I dutifully answered the question, "Do you understand?" with a firm "yes" to show him what a cooperative person I could be. He seemed to appreciate that.

He explained that although I'd been Mirandized, I wasn't technically under arrest. He would escort me to the Federal Detention Center on Northeast Fourth Street, where I would be held as a material witness until a determination could be made as to what to do with me. I would be free to consult with a lawyer, who could apply to the court to have the warrants rescinded for due cause.

All in all, I figured I came out ahead: no personal baggage getting in the way of bureaucracy and a spare but pleasant interview room on the sixth floor instead of a cell in the basement.

Thomas Spinney appeared shortly before five, by which time I was stretched out on the table counting the little holes in the tiled ceiling, having given up all hope that anybody would ever remember I was there. Tall, slim, blue-eyed, and silver-haired, he looked as though he'd been bought off the shelf at Lawyers 'R Us. It turned out that he'd known Aunt Ginger socially. He didn't say how, when, where, and for how long, and I didn't inquire, but I had the feeling he might have been one of her "very good" friends at one time.

I told my story—I think it was version three, or

maybe it was four. He listened, jotted, listened some more, asked questions, jotted, and asked some more. Then he sat back, pursed his lips, furrowed his brow, and thought lawyerly thoughts. Finally he explained what he thought we should do.

Then it was my turn to ask the questions, which he answered with commendable patience, and when we were agreed that that was what we should do, he went in search of Agent Grimes to inform him that he would be seeking a court order to have me released into his—Thomas Spinney's—custody.

Off he went to the Federal Building next door to apply for the order. I had another good cry over Will and the unfairness of it all, and finally went to sleep on the table. Sometime around eight, Agent Grimes popped in to say that unfortunately the order couldn't be processed until morning. Since we'd developed a nice rapport, he gave me the option of sleeping on the table or climbing into a nice comfy bunk bed in a cell with three other miscreants in the holding cells in the basement. I opted for the table, and spent a reasonably comfortable night dreaming about anything but Will Maitland.

It turned out that being released into Thomas Spinney's custody did not require that I actually *be* physically in his custody. In point of law, he was my court-appointed guardian, although his role sounded more like that of a probation officer. I had to report to him three times a day, advise him of my every tremor and tic, and promise on my mother's grave not to set foot outside the Miami city limits. I was not considered a flight risk, as they'd confiscated my wallet and passport.

I staged a triumphant return to the St. Claire at noon the next day. I cried; Scarlett and Blossom hugged and scolded me; Virgil showed off his engagement ring; and Missy Mae celebrated with a rather long prayer of thanksgiving.

Gingersnap made an appearance, clawed her way up onto my shoulder, and fell asleep. Baskerville, on the other hand, was not in a forgiving frame of mind. Every time I tried to catch his big brown eye, he'd turn up his nose and find something riveting to look at across the street, high in a tree, or up on the ceiling.

I waved off the inevitable questions and spent the rest of the day doing laundry and settling back in. More than once, I heard the distant echo of "I'm home" from somewhere deep in my subconscious, but managed to drown it out by tuning Janis Joplin up to full volume.

Scarlett, Blossom, and I walked over to the Eleventh Street Diner for dinner. I adamantly refused to discuss recent events. They pushed and bullied and connived, but I stood firm, even going so far as to stick my fingers in my ears and chant, "I'm not hearing you, I'm not hearing you," over and over until they finally gave it up.

Sometime in the night I smelled doggie breath and felt a cold wet nose sniffing in my ear, and I knew all was forgiven.

Thirty-Four

It turned out that Scarlett and Blossom hadn't figured out the fact that Halsey Wickerby and Carlotta Flores-Perpinan put out the contract on Aunt Ginger, but they were moving right along in that direction. I'm not sure just how they do what they do, but they have this weird chemistry between them; when they put their brains together, a megabrain is born.

"Scarlett and I were thinking that maybe it was someone close to Ginger who learned about the scam, knew she smuggled the box back to the U.S., and went after her before she could sell it," Blossom said over breakfast the next morning. "It doesn't necessarily have to be someone in the underworld. What do you think, Tilly?"

I leaned down to slip Baskerville a piece of bacon. "I suppose."

"I knew it!" Scarlett exclaimed.

"Knew what?"

"We were right, Blossom. She knows something."

"I can't imagine what you're talking about," I said

She stabbed an accusing finger at me. "Don't you try to play innocent with us, Tilly Snapp."

"I'm not playing innocent. I really don't know what you're talking about."

"You gave Baskerville a piece of bacon," Blossom said, as though that explained matters.

I bristled. "Your point?"

"Body language, Tilly. You never let Baskerville eat bacon, but when I suggested that someone close to Ginger put out the hit on her, not only did you do something totally out of character, but you tried to hide the fact that we're onto something by leaning down so we couldn't see your face."

I really can't understand why these two women haven't been awarded a Nobel Prize for mind reading yet.

"Who was it?" Scarlett said.

Blossom folded her arms across her chest. "Come on, Tilly, out with it."

I sighed. "Okay, but before I do, I want you to understand that I didn't tell you because I'm worried about your safety, not because I don't trust you."

They looked at me expectantly.

"Halsey Wickerby and Carlotta Flores."

"Oh my God!" Scarlett said.

For once even Blossom MacMorrough was speechless.

"Carlotta Flores's full name is Flores-Perpinan. She doesn't use the 'Perpinan.'"

"The 'Perp' in Singapore!" Blossom exclaimed. "But she wasn't in Singapore, was she?"

"No, but the man who was murdered in Kingston was her brother, Alberto Flores-Perpinan."

"That's why you went to Kingston, to find out who the victim was!" Scarlett said. "Tilly, you're amazing!"

"So Alberto Flores-Perpinan must have seen Ginger in Singapore, and suspected she stole the box," Blossom reasoned. "He told his sister, and she and Wickerby decided to cash in. He found out she was at Sin and Sand, and figured she had the box with her there."

"My God," Scarlett said, "that's just horrible. They'd kill a woman they'd known for years, who was their friend and trusted them, for the box?"

"I hope they rot in hell," Blossom said. "So Alberto Flores-Perpinan was going to kill Ginger. Who killed him?"

"I wondered at first if Wickerby and Flores had him killed so they didn't have to split the money three ways, but that wouldn't make any sense because he died a week before Aunt Ginger's 'accident.' I'm beginning to think his death didn't have anything to do with it. He was murdered in a brothel; there could be any number of reasons."

Baskerville nudged my knee and gazed up at me with big hopeful brown eyes. If there was one piece of deliciously forbidden bacon up there, there might be more.

"I don't think they knew about the scam. It doesn't matter anyhow. All they needed to know was that she had the box. They must have thought they really lucked out when Aunt Ginger 'died.' "

"This is absolutely amazing," Scarlett said.

"There's more," I said.

"I need ice cream," Scarlett said. "I don't care if it is eight o'clock in the morning." She grabbed a pint of

Häagen-Dazs pistachio out of the freezer and started spooning it up straight from the carton. "Okay, I'm ready now."

"Aunt Ginger knew Alberto Flores-Perpinan," I said, "because he was a player on the black market. Rumor had it that he bought valuable art and antiquities on behalf of certain South American 'businessmen'—read 'drug lords.'

"I noticed on the death certificate in Kingston that Alberto was born in Cali, Colombia," I continued. "As you know, big-time drug cartels are based there. Now, the day the FBI conducted their search here, there were agents from the Money Laundering unit as well as Art Theft. I also know Will told Richie that PST—that's the Public Safety and Terrorism Sub-Directorate under Homeland Security—had been looking at Aunt Ginger's case and Perpinan's death, but decided it didn't pertain to whatever it was they were investigating."

Blossom shook her head. "Tilly Snapp, what in the name of God has come over you? You've been playing it safe since you were sixteen and suddenly you're mixed up with money launderers and drug lords and terrorists and the FBI and Interpol and God knows what else."

I bit into my bagel and chewed thoughtfully. "I think it must be in my nature."

Scarlett nearly knocked over her orange juice. "Your *nature?*"

"It's the only explanation I can come up with," I said. "This me has been lurking deep down in my nature all these years, waiting for its chance. I just didn't know it."

"Ladies and gentlemen, step right up and see the icicles forming in hell today," Blossom announced.

"Excuse me," I said, somewhat miffed. "I have this friend who has spent the last five years of her life driving a train around in circles all day showing tourists where Ernest Hemingway relieved himself in the bushes. Suddenly *she's* mixed up with money launderers and drug lords and terrorists and the FBI and Interpol and God knows what else. Oh, and then there's the woman I know who is on intimate terms with every mainframe in the Boston metropolitan area and making a mint while she's at it. And what is *she* up to this fine morning? Why, surprise, surprise! She's mixed up with money launderers and drug lords and terrorists and the FBI and Interpol and God knows what else.

"Coincidence?" I asked the ceiling fan. "I think not.

"Now," I said into the dumbfounded silence, "let's say Alberto Flores-Perpinan has links to one of the Colombian drug cartels. One of the ways they launder drug money is to buy and sell valuable works of art. They buy it here—usually on the black market, but not always—smuggle it into South America, and sell it through the black market there for twice its value. Voilà! The drug money can't be traced.

"And let's say," I continued, "that Alberto tells his sister and Wickerby that Ginger has the pillow box of Win Win Poo and he knows exactly where it is: in the hotel safe at Sin and Sand right where Ginger put it for safekeeping."

"Oh, let me, let me!" Blossom burst in. "They can't get at it in the safe, but what if Ginger were to meet with an unfortunate accident and her attorney, the executor of her will, shows up at Sin and Sand to gather his poor client's possessions in order to return them to her grieving family?"

"Yes, yes, yes!" Scarlett shouted, pounding on the table. "Ginger will meet with her accident and Wickerby will retrieve the box from the hotel safe! But Alberto gets his throat cut in the brothel, so Wickerby and Carlotta have the box, the contacts to sell it, and only the two of them to split their take!"

"Except there's just one little problem," Blossom sang out triumphantly. "Ginger takes the box out of the safe when she becomes suspicious and hides it somewhere. But how did she make the connection? I mean, how did she come to suspect that Wickerby and Carlotta put the contract out on her and were involved in money laundering?"

I finally gave in to Baskerville's ceaseless importuning and dropped another piece of bacon into his drooling maw.

"She said in her letter that last Christmas Carlotta dropped by Erratica, supposedly to buy a present for her brother Alberto. She took particular interest in a folio of infamous erotic prints ascribed to Giulio Romano that had somehow escaped the bonfires of the Spanish Inquisition. It's known as '*sedici modi*, the sixteen positions, a series of formidable fornications' and is worth around seventy-five thousand dollars."

"Formidable fornications! That is so cool," Blossom said. "Why don't I ever get Christmas presents like that?"

"Because you don't know anyone who can afford to buy them. Anyhow, Carlotta told Aunt Ginger she couldn't afford to buy the folio for her brother, but he might be interested in buying it for himself. As a favor to Carlotta, Aunt Ginger sold the folio to him at a considerable discount. She never met him face to face; it was Carlotta who paid for it on his behalf and took it away. Aunt Ginger had no way of knowing that—"

"Carlotta's brother was Alberto Flores-Perpinan!" Scarlett interrupted. "Hyphenated names are common in Spanish-speaking families. He dropped the hyphenated 'Flores' and went by the name 'Perpinan,' and she dropped the hyphenated 'Perpinan' and went by the name 'Flores.' When Ginger somehow discovers that Carlotta's full name is Flores-Perpinan, she makes the connection between them."

Scarlett and Blossom gave one another an exuberant high-five and collapsed back into their chairs grinning like idiots.

I smiled an indulgent smile. "The end."

Of course it wasn't, not really.

Thirty-five

You have a ghost who's giving you trouble? Who do you call?

Ghostbusters, naturally.

You absolutely, positively have to get it there overnight? Who do you call?

Easy. FedEx.

You need to learn how to set a foolproof trap to bring down a gang of dirty, lying, murderous thugs? Who do you go to for advice?

You go straight to the experts, the men and women of law enforcement, whose training, qualifications, and experience will guide you through the intricacies of planning and executing the takedown.

God knows, by this time I had these people coming out of the woodwork, and the joke was, I couldn't go to a single one of them. If anyone found out that I was going after Halsey Wickerby and Carlotta Flores-Perpinan, eventually they'd discover Aunt Ginger's insurance fraud as well.

All was not lost however. This was Wonderland, and in Wonderland, you have another option.

You go to the movies.

"This is a message for Jimmy Crane.

"Hi, Jimmy. This is Tilly Snapp. I feel sort of funny about this, but you said if I ever needed anything to let you know, and I could really use your advice about something, so if you're in town and you have a few minutes, maybe you could give me a call on my cell phone: 305-555-9009. Don't call Erratica because, well, just don't. I can't explain; it's sort of complicated. Really complicated actually. I promise I won't take up more than a few minutes of your time. I'd really appreciate your help. 'Bye."

"You're going out on a date with Lincoln Steele?"

"No, Blossom, I'm not going out on a date with Lincoln Steele. I'm having a business meeting with Lincoln Steele."

"Right. That's why he's taking you out to dinner. To talk about *business.*"

"No, Blossom, he's not taking me out to dinner. We're going to have supper in."

"*In?* Like in his *house?*" Scarlett said. "Don't he and Artemis live together? I hear she's insanely jealous."

"No, not in his house, of course not. On, um, on . . ."

"Oh, for God's sake, Tilly," Blossom practically shouted, "will you just tell us? You're driving us crazy."

"His boat," I blurted out.

"I'll get the car," Scarlett said to Blossom.

"I'll call and make the appointment," Blossom said.

I made a grab for them as they bustled into action. "Car? Appointment?"

"You don't think we're going to let you have an intimate dinner on a private yacht with one of the sexiest men on the planet, who just happens to be a superstar worth a gazillion bucks, looking like something the cat dragged in, do you?"

"Hot Mahogany?" Nikkolai said. "What was wrong with the Red Copper Spritz?"

"It doesn't go with her outfit," Scarlett explained.

"Hold on," said Blossom. "What about the Copper Blast? No, too much orange. I kind of like the Funky Cherry."

Scarlett looked at the color chart. "Too much red. I think we should stick with the Hot Mahogany."

"Okay," said Blossom. "Hot Mahogany it is."

"Don't I have any say in this?" I grouched.

"No." She shooed me toward the black marble sinks at the back of the salon. "Off you go. We're going down the street to check out that jewelry boutique. Back in a while."

"Stop being a baby," Scarlett said. "You're getting your teeth whitened, not having a root canal."

"Mmmmph."

"Don't give me that look, Tilly Snapp. I'm not the one cruising around South Beach picking up movie stars."

"Glllggg."

"It's your own fault. People who drink as much coffee and Coke as you do ought to get their teeth whitened on a regular basis."

Blossom poked her head into the treatment room.

"I'm going over to Starbucks. Can I get you anything, Tilly?"

"I am not wearing that and you can't make me."

"He'll love it," Blossom said.

"He won't be seeing it."

"You never know."

"It's just a pair of panties," Scarlett said reasonably.

"No, it's not. It's five pieces of string pretending to be a pair of panties, and it costs $68. I am not buying it. That is my final word on the subject."

Blossom handed over my Visa card. "She'll take it."

THIRTY-SIX

"What's so funny?" Linc said with a smile.

"This," I said, waving a hand around at the main cabin of the *Man of Steele*, Linc's forty-eight-foot sports yacht. "You. Me. Me being here."

I suppose I might have been a bit tipsy after three glasses of wine, but I couldn't help laughing at the absurdity of finding myself, Good Old Tilly Snapp, hanging out with a man so recognizable that billboards didn't have to proclaim his name or even the title of his next film. Just a close-up of his blue, blue eyes and the promise "Coming this summer!" were enough to guarantee weeks of sellout crowds when it finally opened.

At least I didn't feel like something the cat dragged in this time. Scarlett and Blossom waved their magic wands and sent their Cinderella off on her "date" in true style. I wore flowing white silk trousers and a satin halter top that shimmered silver and blue and a rich dark green. My hair was a beautiful Hot Mahogany; my teeth practically glowed in the dark; and my eyes and lips sported color by Sisley.

Linc settled back on the butter-soft black leather banquette, propped his feet on the glass coffee table, lit up a slim Cuban cigar, and cocked a sandy brow. "So, Tilly, I am always at the service of a maiden in distress. How may I ride to the rescue?"

God, the man was charming.

"I need some advice. But, could I ask you a personal question first?"

"That depends on how personal."

"Not *personal* personal," I assured him.

"Shoot."

"That brow thing you do. You know, cock a brow to look quizzical. Do you have to practice that in the mirror or did it come with the package? No, no, wait! I didn't mean that kind of package. I mean, have you always been able to do that?"

"And here I thought I'd been asked every question in the book," he said with a grin. "Practice, lots of it."

"I can't do it," I confessed. "There must be a brow-cocking gene, or at least a predisposition to be able to do it with practice."

"She hates it."

"She? Oh, Artemis, right. She seems very fond of you, very, um . . ."

"Possessive?" he supplied with a grin. "You could say that."

"She must care for you a lot," I said, feeling more than a little awkward discussing the love life of the most famous couple in America at the moment.

"Hell no. We don't even like each other very much."

"Oh. So it's a practical arrangement?"

He cocked his head and gave me a long look. "Tilly, don't tell me you're a reporter. It would break my heart."

"No. No! I write a newspaper column, but it's about language, words, not celebrities. And I just inherited Erratica from my aunt who fell out of a parasailing harness—which is what I came to ask you about—and now I'm a sex detective, but I never intended—"

"Whoa, girl! Slow down. Let's back up a step here. Sex detective?"

"That's what my friend Blossom calls me. It's sort of a sideline."

"I see."

"I'm looking for a box of sex toys, but I wouldn't want you to get the wrong idea."

"Of course not," he said solemnly.

The conversation wasn't going exactly as planned, and I kept looking at the door worrying that Artemis was going to come barreling through it any minute, claws out, teeth bared, and tear me to pieces.

I cleared my throat. "So, the reason I'm here. You do a lot of action stuff, right? Chases, shootouts, that kind of thing.

"Say in a scene you're the good guy—well, I guess you're always the good guy, aren't you?—and you want to set a trap to bait the bad guys and take them down. They're thieves, and worse, they've put out a hit on someone you love just to get their hands on a valuable antique. How would you go about it?"

"How many are there? Are they armed?"

"I'm not sure how many, maybe three or four; at least one of them might be armed."

"Am I alone or do I have backup?"

"You have to go in alone. Your backup probably

aren't going to be much help if it gets violent, but they'll be there to cheer you on."

"Will they be wearing short skirts and waving pom-poms?"

"Be serious."

Linc leaned forward, elbows on knees, and got serious.

"Wow," I said ten minutes later. "You really know your stuff."

"For what they pay me, I'd better. Remember, it's the element of surprise—the unexpected twist that throws the bad guys off guard and gives me one last chance to pull it off. I have to have miscalculated some one element; otherwise there's no tension. But that unexpected thing—a dog barks or a nun walks by—that's when I seize the moment and the tide starts to turn in my favor."

"Hmmm," I said, thinking about Baskerville and dismissing the thought out of hand.

"Are you going to tell me about it?" he said. "I get the feeling you're not an aspiring screenwriter."

"It's a long story."

"Oh, hell," he groaned. "She's supposed to be visiting her mother in Boca Raton."

I heard it too: the sound of voices at the end of the long dock. The thought of Artemis coming at me with those trademark bloodred nails and gouging my eyes out made me want to rush up on deck and dive overboard.

Linc stubbed out his cigar with a deep sigh. "Better get this over with."

At the end of the dock, it looked as if trouble was closing in on us from all sides.

I don't know which was worse: Artemis stalking towards us from the left with murder in her eye, the photographer homing in directly in front of us, or Will Maitland leaning against the railing to our right, hands thrust into the front pockets of faded jeans, wearing his most impressive cop face.

"Ain't gonna be pretty," I said out of the side of my mouth. "Wanna make a run for it?"

Linc slipped smoothly into character. "Who's the dude, cupcake? Want I should take him out for you?"

"Nah, I got it," I drawled. "Guy's Interpol, but I got him wrapped around my little finger. You better take care of the babe. Looks like big trouble there."

"You better believe it. Interpol, huh?"

I nodded.

"Aren't you just full of surprises, Tilly Snapp."

"Good luck," I said to Linc as I walked towards Will.

From the look Artemis's face, he was going to need it.

From the look on Will's, so was I.

Thirty-Seven

Will drove me back to the St. Claire in stony silence. I practically leaped out of the car before it even stopped, and stormed into the hotel. Half an hour later when I emerged with Baskerville, Cinderella no more, he was still sitting there. I swept past him with my nose in the air and headed for the boardwalk.

"I'm a grown woman," I told Baskerville as we marched down Collins with Will sauntering along half a block behind. "I am not in the habit of having to explain myself or my actions to anyone, especially him. I can do as I like, go where I like, associate with whomever I like. If I want to while away the evening on a luxurious yacht with my very good friend Lincoln Steele, superstar and object of unbridled desire of half the women on the planet, it's nobody's business but my own."

Actually, that wasn't quite true. It would very much be Judge Teitelbaum's business if she discovered I was out walking my dog through the streets of South Beach at three o'clock in the morning, six hours past my mandated curfew. I'd be back in the Federal Detention Center before I could blink, sharing a cell with Big Mama.

"You know what I think?" I said to Baskerville, who seemed more interested in investigating a large pile of something black and squishy than listening to my latest rant. "I think he's jealous, that's what I think."

"You hope he's jealous," my catty self whispered in my ear.

She had a point. I wanted Will to be jealous of me because I was jealous of Will. Jealous of this Danielle, who might be his pet parakeet for all I knew. Jealous of the first woman he'd ever slept with, and the next, and the next, and the next. Jealous of the beautiful women I would never be—the supermodels, the goddesses of Victoria's Secret, the *Playboy* centerfolds, the Dallas Cowboy cheerleaders, the movie stars. Jealous of the girls he'd flirted with in junior high, his date for the high school prom, the cute freckled little darling who sat next to him in the first grade. I hated, loathed, and detested every woman he'd ever set eyes on and every woman who'd ever set eyes on him.

"Um, you might want to consider getting some help with the jealousy thing," my catty self said nervously. "You're freaking me out here."

"Sorry."

"Tilly."

I looked around, surprised to find I'd arrived back at the gate that led into the garden. "Huh?"

"You've been talking to yourself all the way home," Will said. "You might want to consider getting some help with that."

I unsnapped Baskerville's leash. He made a beeline for his water dish by the gas grill and lapped greedily.

He was thirsty and I was tired and irritable. The last thing I needed was to get into it with Will again. "What do you want?"

He didn't ask if he could come in, just sauntered over to the table and pulled out a chair. "I want to talk to you, and for just once I want you to listen."

"What if I don't want to listen?" I retorted. I held up a hand before he could speak. "Oh, right, I know—*You'll arrest me!* Let's see what charges we can come up with today. I'm out past curfew—that's a big one. I forgot to bring the pooper scooper—"

"Sit down, Tilly," he said firmly.

I sat.

"You're driving me crazy."

Well, well, well. So my studly god was jealous of Lincoln Steele after all.

"I don't understand why you won't back off and let me do my job."

Okay, he was insanely jealous of Lincoln Steele, but he was fiendishly clever at hiding it. Whatever could I have been thinking? Will Maitland, bedmate and quickly becoming the love of my life, would naturally take a backseat to Will Maitland, pain-in-the-ass secret agent.

"Everywhere I turn, there you are," he said. "Or if you're not there, I have to use up valuable time and resources to go chasing after you."

"No one asked you to chase after me tonight," I informed him sweetly. I was rewarded with a flash of green in those fathomless pools of bittersweet chocolate, Irish coffee, aged brandy. "Does it ever occur to you that maybe, just maybe, I don't want you chasing after me? Frankly, I don't see why you bother."

I was fishing, I know, but a girl might like to hear

something along the lines of, "Because I worry about you and I couldn't go on living if anything happened to you."

"To keep them from going after you."

That gave me pause. "Someone's after me?"

"Jesus Christ!" he exploded. "You're marching at the head of a goddamn parade and you don't even know it."

"Oh. You're not just talking about Richie the Ratfink and Alvarez and Blanket Boy and Lucius, then? There are others?"

"Of course there are others. Every Tom, Dick, and Harry in black market antiquities knows your aunt stole the pillow box."

"She did not steal it."

"She got hold of it somehow, because it's a sure bet she had it with her in Jamaica. You know it too, or you wouldn't have been poking around in Negril and Kingston."

"I was not poking," I informed him. "I was investigating."

"Well, you damn well better stop investigating. These are not people you want to bump up against, believe me. If they get even a hint that you know where the box is, it's going to be open season on you. And your friends here and your grandmother, your brothers, your sister, even your goddamn dog. They'll use them to get to you if they have to. How the hell am I going to get through to you, Tilly? What's it going to take?"

"I'm sorry," I said quietly.

It was time. I would tell Will as much as I could in good conscience, just as I'd done with Scarlett and Blossom. Then I'd do one last thing on my own and let him take it from there.

"Would you like some coffee?"

By the time I came down with the carafe, two mugs, and a plate of lemon drop cookies, the sun was just rising. Across the street at Zephyr, Darcy was setting up. Baskerville was dead to the world, on his back in a pool of sunlight with all four paws sticking straight up in the air, and, in a startling new development in their relationship, Gingersnap lay draped over his belly taking the first of a dozen of her kitten-naps of the new day.

Will lounged at the table looking tired and rumpled and adorable as hell. He took a cookie and dipped it into his coffee. "I want all of it, Tilly. No games."

"No games," I agreed. "So I'm going to start by telling you straight off that there are three things I absolutely cannot and will not tell you. You will have to trust me that you'll be able to solve your case without them."

"You know these things from the letter?" he said.

"I figured them out because of the letter."

"Where is it?"

I shook my head. "That's one of the three things."

"I'll need it in evidence," he said. "I may not be able to get a conviction without it."

I set down my mug and folded my hands in my lap. "No. It's a matter of honor and conscience. If you're going to insist and make trouble about it, then I don't have anything to tell you."

"Tilly?"

I looked up to see Scarlett peering down at us from an upstairs window. I shook my head in warning and she disappeared.

Will refilled his cup and settled back. All he said was, "Go."

Over the next half hour I took him through it step by step, from my decision to reopen Erratica right through to opening day.

When my throat got too dry to go on, I excused myself and went upstairs to grab two bottles of water from the fridge. Blossom and Scarlett were making breakfast.

Blossom dropped her toast on the floor, jelly side down. "You're telling him everything?"

"Not Singapore." I looked at them in silent appeal, and they nodded. I knew they'd never tell. These two wonderful women would go to the wall for me.

Back in the garden, Baskerville now lay hunkered down beside Will, and Gingersnap was purring madly under his caressing hand. I remembered what it was like to be caressed by that hand and wished I was in his lap and Gingersnap was the one eating a lemon drop cookie and confessing her sins.

"Where was I?"

"The party after opening day."

I told him about Sin and Sand, and how Uncle Jimmie had told me to go to the luau.

"Jesus, Tilly, you went out onto the beach in Negril at night?" he groaned.

I smiled brightly. "Snag was with me."

He scowled. We moved on.

This was where it got a little tricky. "So now we come to Aunt Ginger's letter," I said. "I hope we understand one another."

He nodded, but I could see he didn't like it.

"Before I tell you what she wrote," I began, "I should tell you that Snag never read it. I expect he can be pretty ruthless, but he's got his own code of honor and he's loyal to his friends. If Aunt Ginger asked him not to read it, he didn't read it. In any event it was still sealed when he handed it to me.

"So," I continued, "she knew someone was going to try to kill her and wanted me to know in case anything happened to her. That someone was a man by the name of Alberto Perpinan. He has a sister, Carlotta Flores."

I waited to see what Will's reaction would be. He didn't blink an eye.

"Carlotta Flores-Perpinan," I said.

Nothing.

"Aunt Ginger's accountant."

I wanted him to say something, anything, but he just sat there at his ease, legs stretched out over Baskerville, hands behind his head, and a look of only mild interest on that gorgeous face.

"You know, if I'm boring you, just say so," I said sweetly.

"You're not boring me."

I nodded graciously. "Thank you. Then I shall continue. Now we come to the box. Yes, Aunt Ginger had the pillow box of Win Win Poo with her. She knew Perpinan was a shady character, and when she learned he was in Jamaica, she took the box out of the safe at Sin and Sand and mailed it to me in Boston for safekeeping. I went to Boston to look for it, but apparently it never arrived.

"It couldn't have been Perpinan who cut the towline," I went on, "because he was already dead. You say there are a lot of people after the box; it could have been anyone. And I swear on my mother's grave, Will, that I do not know where it is."

"Hmmm."

"He speaks," I remarked to no one in particular.

"Let's go back to Perpinan and Flores," he said. "Do you think your aunt made the connection between them?"

"Yes, apparently she did. But that wasn't clear in the letter, which is why I went to Kingston to find his death certificate."

"And did your aunt know why Wickerby and Flores planned to kill her?"

"She had the box; they wanted it."

"Why do you think she had the box?"

"She said so."

"Where did she get it?"

I shook my head. "That's the second thing I will not tell you. Don't even think of asking again."

He nodded. "Okay, why do you think they wanted the box, other than the fact that it's worth a fortune?"

I leaned on the table, clasped my hands, and delivered the coup de théâtre.

"I believe Carlotta Flores-Perpinan and Halsey Wickerby launder money for a Colombian drug cartel."

Will smiled. "You're right. They do. We've been monitoring their actions for a while now."

There is no person on the face of the earth more irritating than the one who attends your every word, nods encouragement as you lead him step-by-step toward a stunning revelation, and then smugly announces he knew what you were going to say all along.

"You know."

He shrugged. "It's my job to know. We've had them under surveillance for over a year."

"I see," I said slowly. "You've known all this time."

He nodded.

I climbed to my feet. "The first time you interviewed me?"

"Yes."

I paced away, turned, paced back. "At Zephyr? In Key Largo?"

Apparently that did not require a verbal reply.

I walked over to the gas grill, tapped my fingers on the metal hood, and stalked back to the table.

"Hobie Beach? The afternoon we . . . you dropped by?"

His eyes said yes, and maybe something more, which I chose to ignore.

"Kingston."

"Of course."

I tucked my hands behind my back and strolled over to the fence. Zephyr was coming alive. Three tourists were perusing the menu; Darcy stood poised to take their order. I sauntered back to the table and sat down, folded my arms across my chest, and looked him straight in the eye.

"My aunt," I said slowly, "was eccentric; she was unpredictable; and she was often reckless. She was a luminous soul who loved beautiful men and beautiful places and beautiful things. She may on occasion have bought and sold on the black market, but like your friend Snag, she had her own code of honor. Believe me when I tell you that she would never, even to save her own life, have laundered money for the filthy people who are in the business of destroying lives for the sake of profit.

"If you believe she was capable of that—and I don't care what evidence you think you have that proves she was—there is no way I'm going to be able to convince you otherwise. She's gone and she can't defend herself. But I can. Write this case up any way you like, but I promise you that if the slightest suspicion she was involved with those people gets out, I will use my column and my contacts in the press to clear her name and blacken yours.

"You may hold the sword," I declared, "but I wield the pen. We'll see which is the stronger."

I didn't look back as I stormed through the gate and strode away.

THIRTY-EIGHT

"The least you could have done was wait to hear what the man had to say," my conscience scolded. "But noooooo, you have to play judge, jury, and executioner."

"He implied—"

"No, he did not. You inferred. He said he knew Carlotta Flores-Perpinan and Halsey Wickerby laundered money. He did not say he knew or even suspected that Aunt Ginger conspired with them to launder money."

"The box—"

"Ah, yes, the box," Conscience mused. "You tell him she had it—which apparently he already knew—and when he asks where she got it—a perfectly reasonable question under the circumstances—you tell him to mind his own business. Which, if you will recall, is precisely that: to recover the pillow box of Win Win Poo and restore it to its rightful owner."

"Hah!" I said. "It doesn't have a rightful owner. So there!"

"Ah, now we are six again, are we?"

"He made me look like a fool," I muttered.

"No, you made you look like a fool. You put on your Tilly Snapp, Sex Detective, hat and tried to strut your stuff when you aren't even wet behind the ears yet. He's been playing the game for ten years or more. You're way out of your league."

I scooped out another handful of sand and tossed it aside. Up here on the dune you had to dig pretty deep to reach the wet sand. "Maybe," I allowed.

"There's no maybe about it—"

"Could I get a word in edgewise here?" my common sense snapped.

"Thank God!" I said. "I was wondering when you were going to show up."

"Better late than never," she said brightly. "My turn. I'll agree with Conscience that it might have behooved you to do a reality check back there, but whatever Will Maitland suspects or believes doesn't count for a hoot or a holler, as Uncle Elwood used to say so pithily, because he doesn't know what we know and he never will."

"Uncle Elwood always did have a way with words," I agreed.

"We did our civic duty," Common Sense went on. "We gave him what he needed to know. What he does with it is up to him."

Conscience picked up a gum wrapper and stuck it in her pocket to dispose of later. "I'm a little worried about the letter situation," she said. "He might not be able to get a conviction without it. What if Carlotta and Wickerby get off because we wouldn't submit the letter and tape as evidence? You might be able to testify about what it said, Tilly, but wouldn't that be considered hearsay?"

We thought about that for a while.

"I'll ask Scarlett," I decided. "She'll know. She and Blossom will figure it out. They always do."

"Look, we had to make a choice, right?" Common Sense reasoned. "Aunt Ginger or Will Maitland. We made it. We did the right thing. Let's not start second-guessing ourselves now."

Conscience pumped her fist. "Right on! We rock."

"Um, remember me?" ventured my heart, who'd been quietly sculpting a sweet little sand castle.

"Here we go," groaned Common Sense. "She's coming after me."

"She's going to get all mushy," Conscience grouched. "She'll just confuse things."

"Excuse me, is this spot taken?"

I looked up and around, surprised to see how crowded my piece of dune real estate had become. It was still early and cool enough for older people to venture out of doors. As it was a long hike across the wide beach to the water's edge, they settled onto the dunes like flocks of migrating gray geese.

The woman who settled down beside me, with that relieved sigh the elderly make when they can finally take the weight off their tired old bones, made you understand why the word "frumpy" was invented. She was drab from the top of her wiry iron-gray head to the bottom of her beige Kmart sneakers. Apparently floral cotton housedresses were still in vogue somewhere in the universe, as were those white plastic marshmallowy purses. Dollar-store sunglasses and a wooden cane completed the ensemble.

I scooted over to give her room and stretched out on my back with my arm thrown over my face against the sun's glare.

"If you're not careful," my heart informed me, "you're going to end up like that, and I'm going to just wither away and die."

"Always the drama queen, Heart," Common Sense sneered.

"Leave her alone," I said. "She can't help it; she's a heart, for God's sake."

"I can take care of myself, thank you," Heart huffed. "I've been doing it for years and I don't need you to defend me."

"Who's side are you on, anyhow?" I grumbled into the crook of my arm.

"I am always on your side, Matilda, dear."

I turned my head and found a pair of lively hazel eyes smiling down at me.

I smiled back.

"It's about time you turned up, Aunt Ginger."

Thirty-Nine

If you asked my aunt Ginger what she considered the best thing about being dead, she'd point out that if you're already dead, nobody can kill you.

Right, you'd say, I can see the advantage in that. But you'd feel obliged to point out that she would have to stay dead—unless, that is, she didn't have any strong objections to spending the next ten to twenty years in jail for conspiracy to commit insurance fraud and illicit traffic in stolen cultural property.

Not necessarily, she'd reply. You could probably cut a pretty good deal if, for instance, you could provide incontrovertible proof that led to the downfall of one particularly pernicious cog in the great wheel of an international criminal organization.

You would have to agree that that would be a noble undertaking. But how, you would want to know, could someone pull it off? Habeas corpus, you'd remind her; you have to have the body.

Friends in high places, she'd say with a fond smile.

And a fair amount of financial incentive where necessary, to help things along.

Okay, you'd say. What about this? Say you got the proof and cut the deal. Your family and friends think you're dead and one day you suddenly show up alive and kicking and scare the living hell out of them; and then they have to readjust their thinking and return all your stuff. They could be pretty ticked off.

Not if you'd thought it over and discovered that being dead provided a lot of other unexpected advantages you hadn't originally considered, she'd reply; like taking on a whole new identity and making a new life with a very good friend in a small island nation ninety miles from the equator on the other side of the world. She might just decide she didn't want all that stuff.

Not a half-bad idea, you'd have to admit. Just as long as everything went exactly according to plan.

"It never arrived."

"But it did!" Aunt Ginger protested. "I sent it FedEx International Priority and tracked it online. I marked it 'Do not open 'til Xmas.' Then when I searched your condo—pity about the fish, dear—and I couldn't find it, I thought perhaps you'd brought the package to Miami, but I couldn't find it in the shop either. Oh dear, maybe they got hold of it somehow."

I shook my head. "No, Wickerby was there the day the FBI served the warrant, and he knows they didn't find it."

"But where can it be?"

"I don't have a clue. But they think I have it or know where it is. They've had two men following me for weeks—Richie the Ratfink and a really scary guy named Joseph Alvarez."

"Which one attacked you that night?" Aunt Ginger asked.

"Alvarez, but he really wasn't attacking me. He just sort of fell on me when Baskerville said hello."

"Well, I couldn't tell, so I zapped both of them."

"Thanks, by the way. I wish you'd stayed at the hospital."

"I didn't dare, dear."

I wondered if Aunt Ginger had any idea how devastated I'd been when I thought she'd been murdered, how I'd cried when I read the letter, how worried I'd been ever since. Had she considered that she might be putting me in jeopardy? Would she have turned herself in to face the consequences and exonerate me if it had come to that?

I guess when you reach a certain age, you become aware that the people you've looked up to or idolized all your life are far more complicated than they appeared in your child eyes. They are full of imperfections and contradictions and secrets, and rather than love them less because they are imperfect, you will love them even more because you are old enough to know that you too are imperfect; you too are full of contradictions and secrets.

Aunt Ginger had been my bird of paradise, my phoenix, and she always would be in my child heart. I still loved her and always would, but sooner or later I'd have to get clear with her.

Now was not the time. I wasn't about to cast shadows over our happy reunion. There would be time enough somewhere down the road.

She poked around in her purse, and extracted a small, jade green velvet pouch. "From a mysterious land beyond the misty sea," she intoned, just as she always had when she flew in on the east wind.

I held the exquisitely carved jade Buddha with his laughing face and bulging belly in my hand, and felt a tear track its way down my cheek.

FORTY

I thought Nikkolai was actually going to burst into tears the next day when I hurried into The Kindest Cut shortly before noon, again without an appointment, and told him Baskerville had threatened to take back the ring if I didn't get rid of the Hot Mahogany immediately. He wanted my hair black again, and furthermore, he wanted the snakes back. Could he possibly fit me in?

Yes, I said contritely, I knew tomorrow was Thanksgiving and he was fully booked, but Baskerville and I were driving up to his parents' house in Orlando first thing in the morning, and it was going to be a disaster if I showed up looking like a streetwalker. Well, not like a streetwalker, I amended, when Nikkolai reared back in horror, more like a character on *Sesame Street.* I would be so very, very grateful if somehow he could help me. I could just sit over there in the lounge area and wait as long as necessary.

"You're a prince among men," I told him when he

finally realized I wasn't going to go away and said it would be at least an hour and a half.

I went across the street to get a cappuccino at Starbucks, and spotted two men watching me. The one at a table by the front window, drinking a latte with a clear view of The Kindest Cut, was Joseph Alvarez, and the other was Kerwin the Blanket Boy, who was engrossed in the *Sports Illustrated* swimsuit edition at an outside table. When I emerged, Richie was two doors down from the salon, ostensibly window-shopping. I waved.

Aunt Ginger breezed in about fifteen minutes later, no longer elderly and frumpy, but angrily middle-aged and overdone. Too tan, too gay. She wore white skin-tight toreador pants, an oversized T-shirt in screaming pink, and huge tortoise-shell sunglasses. A bouncy blond ponytail poked out the back of a pink baseball hat.

She told the receptionist in a whiskey-flavored, two-pack-a-day voice that she knew she didn't have an appointment, but she just had to get her roots touched up or she'd have a nervous breakdown, and she wasn't going to take no for an answer. She'd just sit over there in the lounge area until someone could fit her in.

She settled down in the huge rattan fan chair next to me and began to browse through the latest issue of *Cosmo*.

"Did you call your neighbor?" she murmured, not looking up.

"She's in the hospital getting a hip replacement, but her sister said she doesn't recall a FedEx delivery after I left."

"Well, it's got to be somewhere. I've got a buyer waiting. Thank God I didn't ask for payment in advance."

Through the plant-filled window, I checked on the watchers. Nothing had changed, and they appeared resigned to a long wait.

To all appearances, over the next half hour, we were just two gossipy women leafing through magazines, chatting about fashions and hair and the latest Hollywood divorce scandal, waiting to get their hair done. In truth, we were two conspirators hatching a plan to put Halsey Wickerby and Carlotta Flores-Perpinan away for life.

By the time I got home, I was back to my old Medusa self and Scarlett had already left for Maine to spend the holiday with her family. Missy Mae, Virgil, and Alonzo were holed up in the kitchen, bickering over recipes for cornbread stuffing and pecan pie and knocking back shots of Southern Comfort. Blossom was just about to leave for her mother and stepfather's home in Key Largo.

She caught up with me in Aunt Ginger's bathroom, where I was staring at myself in the mirror, feeling a bit wistful about not giving the Copper Blast a try. The time would come soon enough when I'd be back in Boston, Good Old Tilly Snapp with the black Medusa locks. I should live it up while I could.

"What in the name of God did you think you were doing yesterday, Tilly Snapp?" she demanded. "You never even gave the man a chance to open his mouth."

"He had plenty of opportunity to open his mouth," I retorted. "He just let me ramble on and on like a blithering idiot and then shot me down. 'We've been monitoring their actions for a while now,' " I mimicked. "And by the way, just how did you know that?"

"We were listening from the upstairs window, of course. When you stormed off, we invited him upstairs for breakfast and filled him in. Don't panic. We didn't mention Singapore or the scam. We were more concerned with embarassing personal details, like how well-meaning you are despite your fits of mild insanity."

I cased the closet for something to wear the next day when I took Grammie Jones out for Thanksgiving dinner. "Nothing any of us could say would hit him like a bolt from the blue," I grouched. "He already knew most of it." Including my leanings towards bizarre behavior on occassion.

I settled on a beige linen shift, hauled the ironing board out of the hall closet, and set it up in the living room.

"He's worried about you, Tilly."

"He's worried about his case," I snapped.

Blossom snorted. "He really cares about you; we could tell. It's not just the case that has him hanging around. He could put other agents on you; he doesn't have to do it himself, you know."

"Blossom, don't you see?" I sighed. "He wants the box, and now that he knows it exists, he wants the letter. That's why he's hanging around. He could probably get a conviction some other way, but Aunt Ginger's letter would really nail them."

I tested the iron to see if it was hot enough. "And you know I can't give it to him. I won't give it to him. He can hang around until the cows come home, but he's not going to get that letter and the tape. He'll find some other way.

"Anyhow," I went on, "in a week or two this will all be over. He'll be off doing his Indiana Jones thing in Swaziland or wherever and I'll be back in Boston."

Blossom wandered over to the window. "So," she said after a long pause, "you found a way around Ginger's codicils, I guess. You're going to sell. Well, that's great. Yeah, that's really great, Tilly."

It wouldn't be great, not for Blossom and Scarlett, who had come to love Erratica and the St. Claire and Virgil and Alonzo and Missy Mae and Gingersnap. And South Beach.

I walked over and put my arms around her.

"No, sweetie. I'm not going to sell. I'm turning it over to you and Scarlett."

FORTY-ONE

I wasn't sure what the well-dressed person of interest in an ongoing criminal investigation should wear when she makes an office visit to the agent in charge, so I spent the Thanksgiving weekend researching the subject by watching *Law and Order* and *NYPD Blue* reruns on cable. In the end, I went with crisp natural linen slacks, a wide brown belt, and a cream silk camp shirt, accessorized by Blossom's very own hand with gold hoops at my ears and two long strands of amber beads. The ensemble was, I thought, modest but not prim, casual but not sloppy, practical but not starkly professional. I will admit I bought some new lip gloss—Bronzaroo—and volumizing mascara, whatever that might mean, but otherwise I looked pretty much like Good Old Tilly Snapp again.

I called ahead and spoke with a secretary who said Agent Maitland would be in a meeting until eleven but should be free the rest of the day. He was usually in the office Mondays, Wednesdays, and Thursdays. Tuesdays and Fridays were his field days. I didn't need to make an appointment. I told her I just needed to drop something off, but that I wanted to be sure he got it. She suggested I come at 11:30; that way I would catch him before he went to lunch.

If Will was surprised to find me standing at the counter in the waiting room when he came out of his meeting, he certainly hid it well. He ushered me down a long gray-carpeted hallway to an office, evidently shared by two agents as there were two desks. He indicated the chair I was to take and settled back to take my measure with cool special-agent eyes.

I had practiced exactly what I intended to say as I drove into Downtown Miami:

In the interest of justice, I had reconsidered my decision not to hand over Aunt Ginger's letter. If doing so would ensure the conviction of Carlotta Flores-Perpinan and Halsey Wickerby, then in all good conscience I could not withhold such a crucial piece of evidence. I hoped that handing over the letter and tape would in some measure make up for any previous interference in the conduct of the investigation or appearance of unwillingness to cooperate. I would of course be available to testify should it become necessary. As for the missing pillow box of Win Win Poo, I was sorry I couldn't be of more help and wished him every success in recovering it and returning it to its rightful owner.

I started out well enough. "I'm sorry to drop in on you without an appointment like this," I said with a winning smile. "You must be awfully busy."

I waited a beat. He should have said something to the effect that it wasn't a problem and he was always available to clients—I had decided he'd call me a client—if they felt they had valuable information to share with him. How could he help me?

When he didn't say anything at all, I forged ahead. "So I've been thinking about what you said about Aunt Ginger's letter, and I guess I've been a little inflexible on the subject."

At this point things started going downhill.

"Well, a lot inflexible, actually—but now I've been thinking about it. Um, I've given it some thought, as I said, and you said it's important, so I thought about it."

A brow went up. Obviously I hadn't expressed myself as clearly as I would have liked.

"What I'm trying to say is, justice has to be served, right?"

He didn't appear to have an opinion one way or the other, although you would think someone in his line of work would have something to say on the subject.

"Anyhow," I said, tamping down my irritation, "I've come here today to tell you that I've changed my mind. You can have the letter, but I want it back when you're done with it, because it means a lot to me, and you won't need it anymore after they're convicted."

"May I ask," he said, "what brought on this sudden change of heart?"

"I just told you. I want to see justice done."

"Hmmm. I'm wondering what happened to honor and conscience. I believe those were your reasons for adamantly refusing to hand it over less than a week ago."

"I thought about it," I said testily.

"Yes, you've mentioned that several times."

"I'm just trying to put things in their proper perspective," I explained, trying to look earnest and cooperative. "I want to do what Aunt Ginger would want done. She'd want me to hand over this letter, and that's what I'm doing."

Will leaned back, clasped his hands behind his head—I now recognized this as his listening position—and said, "You do realize, Tilly, that Wickerby's lawyer will do whatever it takes to discredit your aunt. He's going to drag her name through the mud. Even if he's convicted, you'll never be able to resurrect her reputation."

Aunt Ginger had said as much, but that it couldn't be helped. I promised her that by the time I got finished with Wickerby—and if necessary Will Maitland—she'd look like Mother Teresa.

I took the padded envelope out of my bag and handed it to him. He didn't open it at once, but sat for a few moments tapping his fingers on the desk and frowning at me. Finally he sat back, lifted the flap, and slid the envelope's contents onto the desk—the letter Aunt Ginger and I had written that would put Wickerby and Carlotta behind bars for the rest of their miserable little lives, and the cassette tape that I'd dashed up to Boston to retrieve from the safe-deposit box.

He set the tape aside and opened the letter.

"As you can see, it's obvious she wasn't involved in the money laundering," I pointed out when he'd finished.

"It certainly seems that way. What's on the cassette?"

"It's a tape-recorded message from Carlotta confirming her brother's interest in buying the folio of Giulio Romano for seventy-five thousand dollars—the folio that two months later turned up on the black market in Colombia. Francisco Coronado, of the Coronado cartel, was accepting bids starting at one hundred thousand."

"Interesting."

The man was really starting to get on my nerves. I had just handed him irrefutable evidence that exonerated my Aunt Ginger; would convict Halsey Wickerby and Carlotta Flores-Perpinan on charges of conspiracy to commit murder and money laundering, among many other things; and deliver a serious blow, if only temporarily, to the financial operations of the Coronado cartel. And all he could say was, "Interesting"?

"You won't mind if we authenticate the signature, and check the letter and the cassette for prints, of course."

"Of course," I said sweetly. "Please, do whatever you feel is necessary to get a conviction."

"Hmmm."

"Is there a problem?" I inquired, all innocence.

He slipped the letter and the cassette into the envelope. "I can't help feeling I'm being bamboozled."

"Oh, I wouldn't ever do that again," I assured him.

"Of course you wouldn't."

"I'm a changed woman."

He nodded. "Of course you are."

Maybe it was time to go while the going was good.

I stood up. "I should go. I've taken up enough of your time already. I'm so glad I decided to do this," I said brightly as he walked me to the door. "I feel so much better now."

"Your cooperation will be noted."

God, he smelled good. Cinnamon today, with a hint of allspice.

"I'm sorry about the other day, in the garden. I said some awful things to you. I think—no, I know—you're a good person and you've been looking out for me."

"Apology accepted."

"Maybe you're not just a boring bureaucrat with a

bee up your butt," I added, and wondered why the hell I couldn't just shut up and leave well enough alone.

"Thank you," he said gravely.

"You're just doing your job, right?"

"You understand me so well, Tilly."

I guess I was fishing, hoping maybe he'd say something personal like, "You aren't just a client to me, Tilly. You've become more, much more. Perhaps if we'd met in another time, another place, we . . ."

That's what Special Agent Lincoln Steele would say if he were playing an Interpol agent who'd fallen for the person of interest in an ongoing investigation.

And then I'd say, my eyes luminous with unshed tears, my voice breaking, "I know, I know."

"You must go now, Tilly," he'd say.

"Yes, yes."

He'd smile down at me sadly. "I'm no good at being noble," he'd say, à la Bogie as he valiantly gives up Ingrid Bergman in *Casablanca*, "but it doesn't take much to see that the problems of two little people don't amount to a hill of beans in this crazy world."

The last words I would ever hear from those god-yes lips would abide in my heart forever.

"We'll always have South Beach."

Slow fade to black.

Will Maitland scowled down at me from those special-agent eyes, and the last words I heard from those god-yes lips would jangle in my brain all the way down to the lobby.

"Don't leave town."

One of these days I'm going to get one of those BlackBerry thingies—or maybe they're BlueBerries. I'll be able to organize my life once and for all and look like I'm an important person with important things to do.

In the meantime, I'll stay with my current system: the Post-it notes that dot the walls, doors, mirrors, and appliances of my condo and the steering wheel, dashboard, and sun visor of my car. Lest you think the system inefficient and primitive, I will have you know that they're color-coded, although I can never quite remember which color means what.

My penchant for Post-it notes drives the superorganized Scarlett absolutely crazy. I can always tell when she comes across one, because I hear her muttering. The day she discovered a Post-it note on the little Post-it notepad reminding myself to buy Post-it notes was the final straw. "This is the *twenty-first century!*" she yelled and stomped off.

As for using my cell phone on a regular basis, the thing I cannot make my friends understand is that although I love, admire, esteem, and value them, I don't have all that much to report in the course of, say, a trip to the produce department of my local Stop & Shop. Nor am I capable of appreciating a blow-by-blow description of who's singing what and who's being booted off *American Idol* when I'm caught in the passing lane on Interstate 93 at seventy miles an hour with a maniac riding my bumper yelling into a cell phone in *his* hand.

Anyhow, the lime green note on my steering wheel reminded me that I was due at Thomas Spinney's office at 2:00 to discuss my current legal situation. Day-Glo orange on the dashboard—"Bask 4:00!!!"—ordered me not to forget to pick up Baskerville and drag him to the vet to get his teeth cleaned; even the most devoted dog lover can only take so much. I frowned at a sky blue stickie evidently meant to remind that "F?12-5." I couldn't make heads or tails of it, decided if it was sky blue it couldn't be all that important, and crumpled it up and tossed it into the backseat.

I had a lot of thinking to do, so naturally I headed for Starbucks. Fortified with a mocha latte, I settled down at an outdoor table under a green umbrella and happily let the world pass me by. Thoughts came, thoughts went, some more coherent and pertinent to my current situation than others. Now and again a solution to a particular problem would present itself, often as not change its mind, and march away. My heart kept interfering with my common sense, and my conscience did nothing but nag, nag, nag.

Blossom and Scarlett looked unusually grave. Alonzo, Virgil, and Missy Mae were curious and perhaps a little apprehensive. Baskerville gazed up at me with his usual endearingly dopey what-game-are-we-going-to-play-now? look, while Gingersnap expressed her indifference to the proceedings by stretching out on the back of the red velvet couch and pretending to be asleep.

"I've got a problem," I continued. "In a way it's a problem for all of us, but since I'm the one who has to make the final call, I want to explain what I've decided to do about the St. Claire and why. For whatever reason, Aunt Ginger wanted to leave this property to me, and she did it in such a way that I can never sell it. My lawyer in Boston says the will is airtight; the codicils stand."

And I can't get Aunt Ginger to change her mind.

"I never expected to find myself in this situation," I went on. "Owning a historic building in Miami Beach, renovating it, running a business. I don't know anything about any of those things. Aunt Ginger obviously didn't take that into account when she added those codicils."

"Why don't you listen when I tell you things, girl?" Missy Mae interrupted. "I already told you why. Ginger seen something in you you don't see in yourself. She wanted you to get out of that hole you dug up there in Boston and have some fun in life. You disrespect her if you run away."

For someone who never got past the sixth grade, Missy Mae could really hit the nail on the head with a few well-chosen words.

"You're right, Missy Mae," I said. "I know that now. But you have to understand that there's a lot more to my problems here in South Beach than just the St. Claire and Erratica. I've gotten myself into a serious legal situation because of the pillow box of Win Win Poo."

And I've fallen in love with Will Maitland.

"What's in that box, everybody so excited about it?" Missy Mae demanded. "Pillows ain't worth all this running around and the FBI turning the place upside down."

Every head turned toward her, including Baskerville's. Even Gingersnap opened one yellow eye.

"Why don't we discuss it some other time, Missy Mae," Scarlett suggested. "I'd be happy to explain if you'll come to the office tomorrow. I can show you some pictures, and then you'll understand."

"Excellent idea," I said. "So, to get down to it, here's what I've decided to do.

"I'm thinking about going back to Boston."

"I was afraid of this," Virgil said.

I held up a hand. "I haven't made a firm decision yet, so there's no use talking about it. But no matter what I decide about my own future, I want you to know that on Friday I have an appointment with Wickerby to draw up papers to lease the St. Claire to all of you for the sum of one dollar a year. No, please let me finish. Anyone who wants to live here can do so for as long as he or she wants. You may want to form some sort of cooperative to make sure everything runs smoothly.

"As for Erratica," I hurried on, "I intend to turn the management of the business over to Scarlett and Blossom, on the condition that profits be put back into completing the renovations and the upkeep of the St. Claire.

"Okay, I know you have questions," I said. "Fire away."

Forty-two

"I don't like it, Matilda," the bag lady said.

I popped a tangerine segment into my mouth and swallowed.

"I know, Aunt Ginger, and I'm sorry, but I've got to get the legal stuff cleared up before Will and the FBI move on them. Because when they do, they'll cart away every scrap of paper that pertains to the St. Claire, Erratica, and you. And me," I added. "The same goes with Carlotta's files. I don't want to be in legal limbo for years because we can't get access to our own information."

Aunt Ginger shook her head. "Halsey Wickerby and Carlotta Flores. To look at them, you'd think they were dull as dishwater. But I suppose that's exactly what works in their favor; they just don't fit the part. I'm not sure I would have caught on if a contact of mine hadn't mentioned that four very valuable items I'd brokered had been stolen from my buyers in less than six months and turned up on the black market in South America. Those particular items weren't on my books, of course, but other things I sold out of Erratica started disappearing too, one or two buyers down the line.

"I suspected someone I knew had to be involved. And when I realized that Carlotta and Alberto Perpinan were related, I knew for sure."

I tossed a bit of peel to an expectant gull. "Somehow they learned, or at least suspected, that you'd picked up on them. And they sent Alberto after you because they thought you had the box, which you did of course. I guess dying was a reasonable option under the circumstances. You couldn't very well go to the police."

Aunt Ginger laughed. "It was more in the way of a necessity. Seriously, Matilda," she went on, "I wonder if it's wise for you to meet with them on Friday."

"I don't see why," I said. "I'll tell them I'm going back to Boston and want to tie up a few loose ends. I'll say I'm glad to leave: I'm sick and tired of hearing about the box and as far as I'm concerned you probably buried it somewhere in Jamaica before your unfortunate accident and it will never be found and good riddance. To the box, not you, Aunt Ginger," I thought to add.

"You'll be careful, dear?"

"I promise." I stood up, stretched, and signaled to Richie that I was about to leave. "Saturday, same time, same place," I said. "By the way, Aunt Ginger, you make a great bag lady."

"And you, dear," she said with an impish smile, "are going to make a wonderful sex detective."

I expect there are any number of women out there who include Lincoln Steele in their prayers every night, but I may be the only one who's ever prayed *to* him.

"Okay, Linc, stay with me here," I entreated as I stepped out of the elevator onto the sixteenth floor of the Bliss Building in downtown Miami. I turned left, right, left again, following the arrow that would take me to Wickerby & Son, Attorneys at Law, in Suite 1647.

You always begin with motivation. What is it the character wants? What's his objective? Always state it in terms of action.

Her first objective is to prove Halsey Wickerby and Carlotta Flores-Perpinan ordered the assassination of her aunt. The larger objective is to expose them as members of an international criminal conspiracy to smuggle illegal drugs into the United States and foster a culture of drugs and dependency.

Once you've defined the objective, decide what your character would do in order to achieve it.

The thing I remember most about that next hour was how utterly normal everything seemed. So normal that it verged on creepy. You might say it was Norman Rockwell–creepy.

She would try to rattle them with the information that she had received a letter from her aunt written shortly before her death. She would attempt to sow discord and turn them against one another.

"Hey, hold on just a minute here," my common sense said. "What's with the rattling and sowing? I thought we were here to get the financial and legal stuff sorted out before the good guys, who know what the hell they're doing, move on them."

"Yes, but if you recall, I did ask Linc how to take the bad guys down. I'm not even going to try, but I thought rattling and sowing would be a good way to start. You know, throw them off balance."

"Listen up, dunderhead," Common Sense snarled.

"You are not Lincoln Steele and you are not starring in a summer blockbuster."

"Okay, okay," I agreed. "I'm not Linc, and this isn't a soundstage on the back lot at Paramount. But a little rattling and sowing can't hurt. Besides, it will be fun."

"It could too hurt—a lot. It might get us killed, and that won't be any fun at all," she retorted.

"Spoilsport," I grumbled.

Next, determine your character's strengths and weaknesses.

Um, she knows a lot of big words and—

"May I help you?" inquired the receptionist.

"Yes, I have an appointment with Mr. Wickerby. Tilly Snapp? Five-thirty?"

"He's running a bit late this afternoon, Ms. Snapp. Please have a seat and help yourself to coffee. I'll let him know you're here."

There are four things your character must never do.

One: Never go in without backup.

Would she need backup if she was only doing a bit of rattling and sowing?

"No," I decided.

"Yes!" my survival instinct yelled.

Two: Never go in without a Plan B.

Plan B? She barely had a Plan A.

Survival Instinct surged to her feet. "That's it. We're out of here."

Three: Never forget to leave the car running in case she needs to make a quick getaway.

That could be a problem. Not only hadn't she left the car running, it was parked three blocks away.

Common Sense tore at her hair. "God, does she never learn?"

Four: And she never . . .

I frowned down into the Styrofoam cup.

And she never, never . . .

"This way, please, Ms. Snapp."

"Oh well, it couldn't have been all that important if it was number four on the list," I decided.

"Stop her!" my common sense yelled.

"Too late," sighed my survival instinct. "Frankly, if you ask me, the woman's too dumb to live."

"Lights, camera, aaannnd action!" declared the action heroine, and went in to rattle and sow.

Common Sense muttered, "At least get the paperwork out of the way first."

Wickerby was the concerned, paternal lawyer, Carlotta the efficient certified public accountant, and I the confused-but-eager-to-understand client. He wore what a conservative middle-aged lawyer might be expected to wear; dark suit, white shirt, blue-and-burgundy striped bow tie. Her navy blue suit and low-heeled pumps were appropriate to her profession, as were the neat little bun at the nape of her neck and the tiny pearl earrings. I went with my person-of-interest linen trousers again, but swapped the clingy silk camp shirt for a long-sleeved peacock blue knit shirt and tiny silver hoops.

Wickerby led off with a careful inquiry into my recent encounter with the FBI and—of all things!—Interpol. I explained that the trouble was merely a continuation of the FBI's interest in the pillow box of Win Win Poo and my late aunt's possible connection with its disappearance from the Singapore collection.

"But, my dear, whatever possessed you to go chasing off to Jamaica like that? Did you think perhaps your aunt had the box in her possession at the time of her unfortunate accident?"

I admitted with a good deal of embarrassment that I

did think so at the time. It turned out to be a wild-goose chase, of course, but an overzealous Interpol agent decided I was interfering in his investigation and took out a warrant for my arrest as a material witness.

Mr. Wickerby pushed his bifocals back up his nose and exclaimed, "What nonsense! He had no just cause." Carlotta agreed. I closed out the subject by telling him about Thomas Spinney—"Good man, good man"—and that he would be in court the following Monday to get both warrants rescinded.

I segued rather nicely, I thought, with, "So I've come here today because, frankly, Mr. Wickerby, I'm sick and tired of the whole pillow box nonsense, and I don't like South Beach. It's just not me. I want to get back to my own life in Boston."

"Very understandable," he said.

"I know I can't sell the St. Claire or Erratica, but what I'm thinking is that I could rent out the building and maybe hire Scarlett and Blossom to run the business for me. I don't have a clue how to go about it, so that's why I asked to meet with you and Ms. Flores. Oh, and we haven't carried out Aunt Ginger's wishes to scatter her ashes at sea, so I need to find out how I go about doing that, if I need a permit or something."

It's hard to believe that while I sat there in that pleasant office, sipping coffee, making small talk, smiling and nodding, the two most despicable people I could ever hope to meet were sitting right there with me doing exactly the same thing. If I hadn't known who and what they were, I never would have seen past that perfect facade. I could only hope they couldn't see behind mine either.

Shortly before seven, we agreed we'd covered just about everything. Mr. Wickerby said he'd have the documents ready for me to sign by next Wednesday at the latest, and Carlotta would make an appointment to meet with Scarlett and Blossom.

"Oh, I almost forgot," I said as I slipped my notebook into my bag. "It's the strangest thing. My neighbor in Boston has been forwarding my mail to me, and she was dusting a bureau in her hallway a few days ago and found a letter addressed to me that had somehow slipped down behind it. You'll never guess who it was from! Aunt Ginger! Isn't that strange? To get a letter from someone two months after they died?

"She mailed it the morning before the accident," I chattered on as I stood up and hitched the long strap of my bag over my shoulder. "I can't tell you how happy it makes me to know she was thinking of me that day. I guess that's another reason I went to Negril, to get some closure. I met some of her friends there too; they told me all these great stories about her. I don't know, maybe there's some truth to all those rumors about her after all.

"You know," I went on as I started for the door, "buying and selling stuff on the black market and getting mixed up with smugglers and drug dealers and people like that. She kind of hinted that she was in Jamaica to make a big sale, but I think that if it had been the box, she buried it somewhere to keep it safe and no one's ever going to find it again."

"Ms. Snapp," Mr. Wickerby said behind me. "Sit down."

I don't know what I expected to see when I turned around, maybe Wickerby with a gun pointed at my heart or Carlotta foaming at the mouth.

What I did not expect to see was Joseph Alvarez.

. . . and he never, never sits with his back to the door.

* * *

According to Lincoln Steele's rules for the big climactic moment, the hero has to have miscalculated some one element that puts him in mortal danger. I put my miscalculations at three, possibly four, as ten minutes later I was escorted out of the suite, through the silent corridors, and into the elevator.

My first mistake was to embellish rather more on the letter and its contents than was absolutely necessary. The second, to make an appointment in a huge anonymous building after everyone had left for the day, and the third not to notice the second door leading into the room. Joseph Alvarez had come in through that door while I was rattling away.

But I have to say the biggest miscalculation of all was going to Halsey Wickerby's office alone in the first place.

It was all very civilized really. No one pulled a gun and threatened to blow me away. Wickerby interrogated me about the letter in his usual mild, lawyerly way, although I didn't like the look in his eye when I said I couldn't remember where I'd put it. He told me that was somewhat of a problem and I'd have to try very, very hard to remember. I was permitted to use the ladies' room, accompanied by Carlotta, of course, before we left the suite.

Just because Alvarez, who followed us along the corridor and into the elevator, wasn't prodding me along with the barrel of a gun didn't mean he didn't have a gun. I was fairly certain he was the kind of man who wouldn't think of leaving home each morning without at least one.

"Good night, Sidney," Wickerby said to the security guard behind the desk in the lobby.

"Enjoy your weekend, Mr. Wickerby," Sidney replied cheerfully.

Out through the revolving door we went one by one, then reformed with Carlotta on one side, Wickerby on the other, and Alvarez directly behind me. If that first hour in Wickerby's office was Norman Rockwell–creepy, the stroll down Brickell Avenue was positively Macy's Thanksgiving Day Parade–creepy.

I could see we were headed for the huge parking garage where I'd left the car. There wasn't a chance in hell I was getting into a car with these bastards without a fight. If a dog didn't start barking soon or a nun wander by, the tide wasn't going to turn in my favor, and I knew I would be in deep doo-doo.

I figured I had maybe a minute left to make a move, and since by now I was too scared to be scared, and too stupid to know I should be, I used the only weapon I had at my disposal: anger.

"I think I should tell you right now, Mr. Wickerby, that I am not going into the parking garage with you. In fact," I said, stopping so abruptly that Alvarez bumped into me, "you're a piece of garbage and I'm not going anywhere with you."

"Hey, you leave that girl alone," an old bag lady in a nearby doorway shouted as Alvarez made a grab for me. I danced back out of his reach and saw his hand go to his pocket. I figured I had two choices: run and get shot in the back, or go on the attack.

I must have made a thrilling sight as I barreled towards him, head lowered like a charging bull, and I have to say it would have been a pretty impressive takedown but for the fact that suddenly he wasn't there and

I just went flying through thin air right across the sidewalk straight into a *Miami Herald* vending box.

"That would never have happened to Detective Lincoln Steele," I grumbled a split second before the fade to black.

The feel of warm lips on mine and soft breath fanning little wisps of hair from my cheek went a long way to make waking up in the emergency room to the headache from hell a far more positive experience than it might otherwise have been. If, when I opened my eyes, I discovered that those lips belonged to Will Maitland, I would happily have slammed headfirst into *Miami Herald* vending boxes at least once a day, seven days a week. Twice a day, three, even four times would be even better.

"Tilly?"

"Mmmm."

"Are you awake?"

"Mmmmmmm."

"Can you understand what I'm saying?"

"Mmmmmmmmmm."

"Good. Then. Perhaps. You. Can. Tell. Me. What. The. *Hell* was going on in that slap-shot brain of yours when you decided to take on one of the Coronado cartel's meanest, craziest enforcers with your *head!*"

I decided not to open my eyes—even if I could open my eyes. "It seemed like a good idea at the time," I croaked.

"Didn't you see we had the situation under control?" he demanded.

"I guess I didn't, no."

"There were two agents in the lobby, one just outside the revolving doors, two more at the corner, and three behind you."

"Oh."

"The second he went for you, we had six men there. With guns drawn, Tilly."

"Oh."

I heard him pacing around the room muttering to himself. "You're nuts, Tilly. You know that, don't you?"

"Am not," I retorted, opening one eye to glare up at him.

"What the hell were you doing at Wickerby's office, anyhow?"

Some invisible hand was busily hammering nails into the back of my skull, and I'd just about had it with his badgering. "I was there on personal business, if you must know. I'm thinking of going back to Boston, and I needed to make some arrangements about the St. Claire." It would probably be just as well to leave out the rest of it. "Now if you'll excuse me, I'd like to be left alone to die in peace."

He wasn't done with me yet. "We had a tip."

"Tip?"

"A woman phoned in an anonymous tip that you were in Wickerby's office and in trouble. You wouldn't happen to know who that could have been, would you?"

"Not a clue. Maybe I have a guardian angel."

"When?"

"When what?" I groaned.

"When are you going back to Boston?"

"I said I was thinking about it."

"Well, stop thinking about it."

"I'm going to sleep now, Will. Good night."

"One last thing," I heard him growl from the doorway. "What the hell does Lincoln Steele have to do with this?"

My studly god was jealous.

I tucked that happy thought under my pillow with a happy sigh and drifted off.

Forty-Three

"'. . . held for observation overnight at Jackson Memorial Hospital and released Saturday morning,'" Scarlett read aloud to the avid audience gathered on, under, and around my bed in Aunt Ginger's room.

"'"The FBI sincerely regrets that an innocent bystander was injured during this very important operation," Agent George Grimes told reporters. "We make every effort to ensure the safety of the public at all times, but unfortunately, in this particular instance, she was just in the wrong place at the wrong time." Agent Grimes went on to say that the woman's identity would not be made public. He gave no reason.'"

"So you got your fifteen minutes of fame, chica," Alonzo said.

"No, she don't," said Missy Mae, "on account of they didn't give out her name. How you gonna be famous if nobody knows it's you? Same goes when she got her picture in the paper with that movie star."

I rolled my eyes, a mistake I decided I wouldn't be making again anytime soon when I felt the explosion rip through my skull. The picture to which Missy Mae referred appeared on the front pages of the *National Enquirer*, the *Star*, and *Us* four days after Linc and I had dinner on his yacht.

"Linc's New Love?" the headline screamed.

Apparently Artemis had done some screaming herself, and my evening in the company of "the only man I will ever love" destroyed her cherished dream of sharing the rest of her life with him and bearing his babies.

Will called twice, once to see how I was feeling and once to tell me that it turned out Richie the Ratfink had been working for Wickerby. Poor Richie got caught in the net when the FBI did a sweep of all Wickerby's known associates. After close questioning, the FBI was convinced he hadn't been party to or had any knowledge of Wickerby's ties to the Coronado cartel, and he was released. I liked Richie and hoped he'd check out his employers a little more carefully in the future.

I was still abed on Sunday afternoon because Scarlett and Blossom wouldn't let me get out of it. Blossom caught me sneaking toward the kitchen shortly after nine and marched me back as though I were a schoolchild out playing hooky. My release from the hospital with a clean bill of health, except of course for the concussion, made no impression on the residents of the St. Claire whatsoever. I might as well have been at death's door as far as they were concerned, and they rotated in and out of the room in shifts as though I were about to rattle out my last breath.

That was Sunday. On Monday afternoon I was permitted to keep my appointment with Thomas Spinney, chaperoned by Scarlett and Blossom, who stayed so close that it would have been easier for them to whip up a harness and leading strings to prevent me from wandering more than five feet in any direction.

I wouldn't even let myself speculate on how much that hour was going to cost me. Thomas Spinney was one of Miami's high-profile lawyers and naturally charged high-profile fees. He was also worth every penny, as any number of high-profile clients who had run afoul of the law would attest.

We discussed the warrants—rescinded that morning by Judge Teitelbaum. He had heard about Halsey Wickerby—the stunning revelations were sending shock waves through Miami's legal community—and was sorry to hear the man had been handling Ginger Snapp's, and now my, business affairs. He referred me to one of his partners to see what could be done for me.

I suffered through the rest of the week, eating when ordered, sleeping when ordered, fussed over and scolded until, on Saturday night, I declared my independence by stealing the car keys out of Alonzo's coat pocket, sneaking down the fire escape, and spending a happy hour alone at the kids' arcade in the mall playing pinball. Good Old Tilly Snapp had secretly wanted to learn to play pinball all her life.

Friday morning, just before I left for the dunes to meet Aunt Ginger, I called the Fisher Island Club.

"This is a message for Jimmy Crane. Hi, Jimmy. Tilly again. I just wanted to thank you for your advice. The scene I had in mind would have played out perfectly if I'd remembered that an action heroine never sits with her back to the door. Having a Plan B might have helped too. The good news is I got the bad guys.

The bad news is I made an ass of myself and ended up in the hospital. I'm new at this sex detective thing, so I try to look on it as a valuable learning experience. The cheerleaders couldn't make it, so no pom-poms, alas, but the cavalry did arrive just in time. Now that I think about it, the story would make a terrific film—a screwball comedy like they made in the '30s and '40s. The hero would be a great role for you—a hotshot Interpol agent who can quirk his brow at the drop of a hat, leer charmingly, and make a woman sit up and shout, 'Hallelujah!' Let me know what you think. Oh, and if you ever find yourself in need of a sex detective, you know where to find me."

"It has to be somewhere," Aunt Ginger remarked. Back in the persona of Frumpy Old Woman, she gazed out at the sea as though the pillow box of Win Win Poo might float by at any moment.

I sat up, clasped my knees to my chest, and considered the possibilities. "It's probably on the shelf right next to the Ark of the Covenant."

"Matilda, perhaps you shouldn't be out in the sun so soon after suffering a concussion."

"A mild concussion," I reminded her. "Anyhow, at the end of *Indiana Jones and the Last Crusade,* the Ark of the Covenant gets lost because of some bureaucratic snafu. In the last scene, you see a forklift carrying it away through a cavernous warehouse that's filled to the roof with cardboard boxes exactly like the one the Ark is in."

Aunt Ginger sighed. "I suppose anything's better than the Coronado cartel getting their hands on it."

"Aunt Ginger?"

"Yes, dear."

"There's something I have to ask you. I've been trying to think of a delicate way to put it, but maybe I should just say it straight out."

"Of course."

I took a deep breath. This was hard. I might not like what I heard. But I had to know.

"Why did you do it? I'm not going to sit here and pass judgment on you for the scam and for dealing on the black market. That's between you and your conscience. But why both? You're the most generous person I've ever known, but it just seems so—"

"Greedy?"

I couldn't look at her. "Yes. I mean, you're well off, and you had the St. Claire and the business. If you needed money, you could have sold the St. Claire, moved Erratica somewhere else."

"I wanted you to have them, Matilda. My life has, well, taken an unexpected turn. Just as yours has."

I swiveled around to face her. "What turn?"

"I met Robert."

As day gave way to dusk and the shadows of the big hotels along Ocean Drive stretched out over Lummus Park towards the beach and the sea, she told me about Robert Lu, a wealthy Singaporean surgeon and art collector, who left his lucrative practice and went to work for Médecins Sans Frontières. About the lost children in Southeast Asia, orphaned by AIDS and abandoned, and the cowardice of a world that looks away.

"You fell down the rabbit hole! No, it's not the concussion," I assured her when she cast a worried look at me. "You woke up one morning and you fell down the rabbit hole, like Alice, like I did, and suddenly the world wasn't quite the same world and you weren't quite the same Ginger."

"How clever you are, Matilda. Yes, that's exactly how it was. I can't walk away now that I know what needs to be done for those children. I need to *do* something. And what I know how to do is make a lot of money selling antiques. Legally or illegally. We would have gotten double for the pillow box of Win Win Poo if we could have collected the insurance and sold it too. Such a pity," she sighed.

I'd have to think about the moral implications of Aunt Ginger's actions, but right then I just wanted to hug her, which I did.

"So Tilly Snapp becomes a sex detective and I try to become Mother Teresa," she said with a laugh.

"Welcome to Wonderland, Aunt Ginger."

Forty-Four

I think the less said about the Sunday service at the Blood of Christ Evangelical Mission Church, the better. I'm surprised the elderly in the congregation survived the ecstatic shouting, writhing, and stamping without dropping like flies from strokes, pulmonary embolisms, and catastrophic heart failures.

I must say Grammie Jones emerged from the ordeal in better shape than I did, with a spring in her step and a sparkle in her eye. As usual, McDonald's was packed with the after–Sunday School crowd, but we managed to snag our favorite table by the window, and while she prattled on about this and that, I stared out the window at the parking lot, remembering the first time Will kissed me. "Shut up, Tilly, and just do it," he'd said. I think I must have been a goner right then and there.

". . . and Lucille had just left for her vacation," Grammie was saying, "and it was just sitting there on the desk, so I thought to myself, why not? Why wait?"

"Why not what, Grammie?"

"Open it," she chirped, fingering the strand of beads wrapped around her bony wrist. "Aren't they pretty?"

I watched my hand slide across the table in slow motion, take her gnarled hand gently in mine, and touch one of the golden balls with the tip of my finger.

"I hope you didn't pay too much for it, dear."

Grammie said later she thought I'd found the Lord at last as I threw my head back against the orange plastic seat and laughed and laughed until the tears ran down my face, and I finally just slid off the seat and disappeared beneath the table.

The manager of McDonald's thought I'd lost my mind, and called 911.

FORTY-FIVE

"Why not?" I asked myself. "Why wait?"

Since I couldn't think of one good reason, I picked up the phone and made the call.

"Yes," was all he said.

First things first, I decided when I heard him on the stairs. Obviously, we were of one mind, because he didn't even break stride as he scooped me up and headed straight for the big bed.

Later, much later, as I lay safe and warm in his arms, I said, "Will, do you like surprises?"

"That would depend on who's doing the surprising."

"A person of interest in an ongoing investigation."

"Would the surprise mean I'd end up having to chase her to hell and back?"

"Nope."

"Would it mean I'd have to arrest her?"

I shook my head.

"Watch her knock herself out cold on a sidewalk?"

"Probably not."

"Would she be going away, say to Boston, after she gave me my surprise?"

"No, she wouldn't."

He smiled down at me. "Then, yes, I'd like the person of interest in an ongoing investigation to give me a surprise."

I slipped out of bed and wrapped myself in one of Aunt Ginger's kimonos: black silk embroidered with pink and white lotus flowers. "I'll be right back."

Ignoring the plaintive noises coming from the direction of the kitchen, where Baskerville and Gingersnap had been exiled for the night, I padded down the hall to the living room, lifted the carefully bundled pillow box out of the antique trunk that served as a coffee table, and padded back.

I don't think I'll ever be happier than I was at that moment.

"Your surprise, Special Agent Maitland."

FORTY-SIX

"No!"

"Yup."

"The Blood of Christ Evangelical Mission Church?"

"Uh-huh."

"McDonald's?"

I nodded my complete understanding. "I know."

"Matilda, dear, tell me you didn't leave it there. Tell me the pillow box of Win Win Poo isn't still stashed under your grandmother's bed in the Hope of Resurrection Home in Key Largo."

"No, of course not. Your plane is going to board soon. Why don't we sit down and I'll give you the short version."

The waiting area around Gate 19 was crowded and hectic, so we moved across the way to an empty departure lounge where we could have some privacy.

"It all began in a galaxy far, far away. . . ."

"Matilda," Aunt Ginger warned.

"Okay. It all began with Mrs. Feldman, then."

"Better."

"You sent the package Federal Express to me in Boston marked 'Do not open 'til Christmas.' That gave you a comfortable cushion of time—almost two months—to stage the accident, get out of Jamaica, hunker down somewhere for a while if necessary, and get to Boston to retrieve it."

Aunt Ginger patted my hand. "Knowing you, dear, you wouldn't allow your curiosity to get the better of you. I counted on that."

"What you didn't count on was Dr. Phil," I said.

"Dr. Phil?"

"Mrs. Feldman is in love with Dr. Phil. As far as she's concerned, the earth stops spinning on its axis when Dr. Phil's talk show comes on between five and six."

Aunt Ginger nodded. "Federal Express delivered between five and six."

"Right. Apparently she rushed to the door, signed for it, and shoved it under the couch, and forgot all about it. A few weeks later, her son found it. By that time Will was chasing me all over the country, and Mrs. F. called the St. Claire and learned I wasn't in South Beach. She didn't know where to send it, so she came up with the brilliant idea of shipping it to Grammie Jones to hold for me.

"Usually the manager, Lucille, would have intercepted it," I continued, "but she was off hiking in Nepal and her assistant, Consuela, left it out on the front desk. Grammie scooped it up and thought, why wait until Christmas to open her present *from me.*

"And that's how a strand of seventeenth century solid gold Chinese Climax Beads ended up as a bracelet on Grammie's wrist."

"Amazing," Aunt Ginger said, "absolutely amazing. You've put it somewhere safe?"

I smiled. "Believe me, Aunt Ginger, it couldn't be in safer hands."

"Well, are you going to tell me where it is, dear?"

"Hmmm," I pondered. "Am I going to tell her where it is?"

"Matilda!"

"I gave it to Will."

"You *what*?"

"I gave it to Will. It was a matter of honor and conscience."

"I don't understand, dear."

"When I refused to turn over your original letter to him, and told him it was a matter of honor and conscience to me to protect you—or your reputation, rather, since he believes you're dead—he understood. He didn't like it, but he understood.

"At first I thought you were just another case to him. But he didn't go after the pillow box of Win Win Poo just because it was his job to retrieve it. He went after it because he wanted to find the people who killed you, to give you justice."

"I see."

"And he wanted to find the people who killed you because it mattered so much to me."

"I see."

"Aunt Ginger, he's going to return the pillow box to Robert Lu himself. He doesn't have to; he could delegate it to someone else. It's a matter of honor to him to see it through to the end."

"Honor. Yes, I think I understand what you're saying."

"Last call for Delta flight 66, nonstop to Los Angeles. Please have your boarding passes ready."

We walked hand in hand to the departure gate.

"Robert and I will find another way," she said quietly. And, Matilda, thank you."

I stood at the window watching the big Delta jet join the long line of planes rolling sedately along the taxiway, turning onto the accessway, stopping, moving forward, stopping again, until finally it made the wide turn onto the main runway and paused, waiting.

Strong arms came around me from behind and held me close to a warm, hard body that smelled spicy and limy and alpha-male.

"How did you know I'd be here?"

"Intuition."

"Intuition, right. How did you find out?"

"I got hold of the hospital's security tapes the night she brought you in."

With a mighty roar, the Delta jet rumbled down the runway.

"She'll do the right thing, Will."

It picked up speed, lifted off, and angled up and away into a cloudless sky.

"If she's anything like her niece, I'm sure she will."

I turned in his arms and pressed my lips to his heart.

"Thank you," I said.

I've decided to take up sex detecting for real. Aunt Ginger has hired me to find Harry Hungwell, who seems to have disappeared off the face of the earth. And Lincoln Steele left a cryptic message on my answering machine saying he was in need of a kick-butt sex detective—something about an indiscretion early in his career—and no woman in her right mind would turn down an opportunity like that.

Will was "loaned" by Interpol to the government of

Thailand to help recover religious scrolls stolen from a Buddhist monastery in Chiang Mai, and heaven only knows how long that's going to take.

He stopped in Singapore on his way to Bangkok to return the pillow box of Win Win Poo to Robert Lu and his new bride, the former Lorraine Louise Hungwell, who were most grateful that he took the time to return it in person. I understand they reimbursed the insurance company in full, and was delighted when a few weeks later the company offered to underwrite his efforts to establish group homes throughout Southeast Asia for children orphaned by AIDS.

I feel certain Win Win Poo would have approved.

Will and I intend to live happily ever after when he gets back. I'm not worried that he's on one side of the world and I'm on the other for a while. We'll meet up back at the St. Claire when we can't stand being apart for another day.

So there you have it. Good Old Tilly Snapp has decamped to parts unknown, and I wish her well.

I'm a Sex Detective.

I'm in love with a studly god and a studly god is in love with me.

Anything's possible when you fall down the rabbit hole.